The Calling of the Protectors

The Calling of the Protectors

The Legend of Chief

Louis Paul DeGrado

iUniverse

THE CALLING OF THE PROTECTORS
THE LEGEND OF CHIEF

iUniverse books may be ordered through booksellers or by contacting:

iUniverse
1663 Liberty Drive
Bloomington, IN 47403
www.iuniverse.com
1-800-Authors (1-800-288-4677)

ISBN: 978-1-4917-8811-0 (sc)
ISBN: 978-1-4917-8812-7 (hc)
ISBN: 978-1-4917-8813-4 (e)

Library of Congress Control Number: 2016902109

Print information available on the last page.

iUniverse rev. date: 2/9/2016

Also Available from Author Louis Paul DeGrado

Savior
Finalist, *Foreword* magazine's Book of the Year Contest!
Glimpse the future in this exciting science fiction thriller!
How far will we go to save ourselves? Faced with its own demise, humankind turns to science for answers, and governments approve drastic measures in genetic testing and experimentation.

Battle lines are drawn when a religious crusader and the medical director of the largest research firm clash over thousands of people frozen in cryogenic stasis who are being used as human test subjects. Caught in the middle is Kyle Reed, the director of the company, who has been brought back after two hundred years to face his greatest dilemma: support the company he founded or expose the truth behind its plans.

The Questors' Adventures
The Round House and *The Moaning Walls*
What do you call a group of boys who set out to explore the unknown? They call themselves the Questors, and they're ready for excitement, adventure, and mayhem. Join the adventure as the boys, ages ten to thirteen, must overcome jittery nerves and active imaginations to investigate a haunted house in their neighborhood. An engaging series for young readers!

The People Across the Sea
Editor's Choice, iUniverse
Within the towering walls of the city by the sea, a dark secret is kept. The city's history was wiped out by foreign invasion, and even now, the city stands poised to repel another attack from the dreaded people across the sea.

A culture based on fear and the threat of invasion has spawned a leader, a council, and the Law of Survivors. Aldran Alfer is now the Keeper of the law and the council leader. He knows the hidden terror that threatens to rip the city apart.

The sons of Aldran, Brit and Caln, find themselves caught in a web of danger and mystery. Brit finds himself on the run from the Black Guard, veiled men who prowl the streets and crush any who oppose the council's will.

While Caln remains in the city, struggling to hold his family's position on the council, Brit heads to the forbidden desert to seek out the Wizard, a man with strange powers who was banished from the city. In the company of the Wizard and a mythical desert wanderer, Brit will find his destiny. He must cross the land of the Sand Demons, fierce predators who stalk the desert, where he searches for a way to carry out his father's plan to lead their people to safety and end the threat from *The People Across the Sea*.

The 13th Month
Editor's Choice, iUniverse

Have you ever wondered why bad days linger or why moments of regret stick with you and bad situations seem surreal? What would you do if you found out that evil exists in these moments of time and forces of evil were working to control and extend them by warping reality? Would you have the faith to stand and fight? Evil once controlled the 13th Month and is looking to do so again!

When a revered priest, Father Frank Keller, investigates a tragic murder in his parish, he is thrust into a covert battle between forces of good and evil.

Seeking answers, Father Frank is contacted by a group consisting of a holy man from India, a Native American Shaman, a college professor, and an attractive middle-aged psychiatrist. The group's mission is to fight shadows: parasitic creatures that lurk in moments of time and warp reality to take control of their host.
The leader of the group, Adnan, is convinced that the shadows, once banished from the world, are gaining a foothold. The only way to stop them is to go to the place where the shadows come from and turn the tide.

Father Frank must face his own insecurities and desires in order to find the faith to combat the evil that threatens those closest to him and help the group. To do so, he must prepare himself to cross through a portal where the shadows come from; a portal that may lead him directly to the gates of Hell!

Exist to Inspire

www.Literarylou.com
Home of Author Louis Paul DeGrado

Make a Difference

Contents

Chapter 1
The Dawn Patrol

C hief crouched in the predawn hours, ready to pounce at the
first sign of trouble. He was out before any of the guests
would awaken. He scanned the concrete sidewalks and
pathways of the Dollar Inn, the three-story motel he guarded,
and listened for scratching or scurrying sounds. He sniffed the
odors of cigarettes, day-old microwave dinners, damp laundry,
and sweaty socks. One smell previously on the menu was missing:
the wet, hairy stink of rat.

He approached the corner that led to an alley between the
buildings. His heart beat rapidly, and his tail flicked back and
forth, keeping time until the moment arrived. He jumped around
the corner to surprise his prey. But …

"*Nothing!*" Chief said to no one in particular. He knew that
people couldn't understand what he was saying anyway. Sam
seemed to understand him more than anyone, though, and would
follow him if Chief indicated the need.

His lean muscles flexed and worked in harmony as he continued his patrol route and ran up the staircase; he would start at the
top row of rooms and work his way down. He reached the third

floor and ran down the halls checking for anything out of place. He stopped at a vacant room and peeked inside. Nothing.

Instinct overtook him as he raced forward, examining each of the three levels of the motel. Then he went back to the alley, checking each Dumpster and crawl space along the way. Senses beyond sight and hearing, those of the mind and inner sight, reached out in front of him like sonar guiding his lightning-like moves. They were the senses of the Protectors, those who were called to protect humans against all that is evil.

After running around for hours, he stopped at the doorway of the only place he hadn't checked—the basement. His nose twitched at the smell of moldy, dusty air coming up the stairwell. He looked back. At one time, his owner, Sam, would have been right there to back him up, and every patrol would have been a fight. Now all was clear. It had been that way for months, as Chief had driven all the vermin off the property.

Chief casually trotted down the steps. *How rats can live in such places is beyond me,* he thought. Sam had said the owner was coming by today, so Chief was going to be thorough about this and make sure nothing was out of place.

Suddenly, Chief stopped in his tracks. The hair on his tail thickened and stood on end, making his tail look twice as big. He pointed his ears forward and peered out across the distance, noticing something new. "Humph," he said, relaxing his stance. "Someone put a water jug down here." He continued down the stairs toward the jug. He recognized it as a replacement for the water dispenser in the lobby.

"Okay, tough guy, want some of this?" Chief flexed his front claws and bared his teeth. "You weren't around when I took care of those rats down here—were you, tough guy? They don't call this the Bronx for nothing. You gotta be tough to hang down here."

The water jug didn't reply as Chief kept his eyes fixed on it. He could make out his reflection in the water as he approached.

He reflected back to a time when the place hadn't been safe, remembering the day he'd scared the rats away.

Chief had hissed and jumped high, dodging a shadowy attacker. He'd flung his right paw across his body, followed by his left as he'd rolled and came back to his feet. Pearly white teeth had flickered in the single phosphorus bulb that had remained on in the four-bulb fixture.

"Not so fast," he'd called out as he'd jumped across the landing in front of the stairwell. He'd turned, teeth bared, and pounced on the invisible attackers. Then he'd stepped back and put his right paw up. "Tell all your friends," he'd said through his teeth while extending his claws, "there's a Protector in this motel, and this will be the last thing they see." He'd swiped his right paw across his front like a sword cutting through the air. "That is, if they venture here."

Chief remembered the rats quivering in front of him. They hadn't dared to move. "This is the last warning. Next time I see any of you, I'll be cracking skulls. Now *get*!" The rats had scurried up the stairs, and Chief had taken a swipe just over the head of the last one, causing it to squeal and run over the rat in front of it in panic. One rat had gone down a drainpipe that Chief looked at now. Since then, Sam had capped the pipe so no rats could crawl up it.

"Nothing here now," Chief said, "but a bunch of boxes. And you." He pounced, landing directly in front of the water jug. "I guess I'll let you live." He started walking away and then swung back around, admiring his profile in the reflection.

"Chief?" Sam called, his voice traveling across the parking lot and down the steps. Chief headed outside and ran back to the small single-bed room he and Sam called home. The sun had risen, and as Chief approached, he recognized the fancy black sedan parked alongside Sam's rusty faded-green pickup truck as that of Bill Ryan, the owner of the motel.

"Ah, there you are," Sam said, patting Chief on the head as

he entered the apartment. Chief rubbed up against his leg. "This boy's always hard at work, Mr. Ryan," Sam said from under a raggedy brown felt cap in which he shoved the mats of his curly black hair. His thick shoulders and callous hands were that of a working man. He stood nearly six feet tall. His small brown eyes looked about sharply but were often aimed at the floor.

Chief looked at Mr. Ryan, his blue suit, city shoes, and thin necktie. He thought the tie would be fun to play with.

"Sam, that's exactly what I'm here to talk to you about," Mr. Ryan said. "You and that cat have done wonders for this place. And that's no easy task down here in the slums."

Mr. Ryan waved his hand, motioning for Sam to follow, and looked outside the large single window. "The curious thing is since you fixed up the place and had your cat drive out all the mice and rats, we've enjoyed a better clientele. And we made the environmentalists happy because we used what they would call a 'green' alternative to poisons and traps."

"Environmentalists?" Sam rubbed his chin.

"Don't worry about that right now."

Mr. Ryan reached into his suit pocket and pulled out two cigars. He handed one to Sam. He patted his pants pockets, checked his coat, laughed, and then looked at Sam. "I guess I forgot my lighter. I don't suppose you have some matches?"

"Chief don't like it when I smoke," Sam said.

Chief's ears perked up, and he stared at Mr. Ryan, who looked at him and smiled.

"Well, that's probably better for the both of us." He put the cigar back in his pocket. "He's a smart cat."

"Thank you, Mr. Ryan," Sam said, peeking out from under his cap. "My boy Chief is as tough as they come." Chief purred a little as Sam patted him on the head.

"That's why I think you and that cat of yours deserve a promotion, Sam." Mr. Ryan looked directly at Sam, whose mouth stood wide open, revealing two broken teeth. "That's right. I have a new apartment building uptown, and, well, I have some problems. Wires are shorting out, stuff's missing in the basement, and people are reporting noises in the walls."

"Sounds like rats to me," Sam said. Chief walked over and curled up on an old towel he used for a bed.

"The building wasn't cheap to build. It's in a nice part of town, a part where people don't expect there to be rodents. We charge a higher rent and have clients that live there on a permanent basis. If I can't keep it occupied, I can't pay for the costs. Today is a new age, and folks are turning back the clocks, looking for more environmentally friendly, down-to-earth ways to handle stuff. Exterminators, poisons, and traps just won't do. How would you and Chief like to move to a better place?"

Chief lifted his head, and his ears perked up.

Sam removed his hat, scratched his head, and looked over at Chief. "We're pretty comfortable here, Mr. Ryan. I couldn't afford no rent uptown."

Mr. Ryan laughed and patted Sam on the shoulder. "You'd have your own apartment, Sam, two bedrooms that are bigger than this room, rent-free, and an office that would read 'Maintenance Man.'" He gestured widely in front of Sam, outlining the imaginary sign. "I can't very well keep you at the same salary if you're going to be the maintenance man at a classy, new uptown apartment building, can I? Oh, and you'll be carrying double your current salary. Whaddya say?" He put his hand out in front of Sam. "Job starts tomorrow if you accept."

Chief got up, went over to Sam, and rubbed against his leg. He thought it would be great to explore somewhere new. Sam seemed to get the message and shook Mr. Ryan's hand, saying, "I guess the Chief here thinks it's a good idea. Thank you, sir, thank you."

"He's a Siberian breed, isn't he?" Bill Ryan said. "I can tell by the muscular tone and size."

"I don't know much about that," Sam said. "Found him wandering about as a kitten, and we've been together since."

"Well, he's quite a prize. They're known to be good hunters. My wife's a cat fan and has a Persian herself. I would prefer a good guard dog, but that's hard when you live in the city. Now, we've made some modifications to the complex; there are pet doors in the storage rooms and select apartments to accommodate the cat's patrolling. You'll be in one of three buildings on site. Report to Ms. Sorenson tomorrow," Bill Ryan said. "She's the manager of the complex." He raised one eyebrow and nodded. "She's a stickler for procedures and rules and a little particular about details, but you two should get along fine. See you, Chief." Mr. Ryan saluted with two fingers in Chief's direction and left the apartment.

Chief heard the large engine of Mr. Ryan's car start and pull away.

"Did you hear that, boy?" Sam said, whistling through his two broken front teeth. "We're going to the big time." He went to the refrigerator and opened the door. Chief jumped on the table and went to his place where Sam fed him.

Sam took out a can of cat food, popped it open with his knife, and poured half of it into a bowl. Then he smiled at Chief, winked, and poured the rest. "No limits tonight." He pushed the bowl in front of Chief and took a seat at the table. He reached down and stroked the yellow-and-orange stripes on Chief's back as Chief ate.

"This will keep you strong, boy. You and me, we're a team. That's what we are. No more cleaning bathrooms and laundries for Sam. No, I'm gonna hire someone to do that. That's right." Sam sat back in his chair, crossing his hands behind his neck. He grinned, showing several fillings among the teeth that remained. "Maintenance man—that's what Mr. Ryan called me."

Chief ate half of the food and then stepped away. "What is it, boy?" Sam asked. Chief licked his paws and groomed his face. "Oh, that's right. Don't want to get too full. Lean and mean, that's it, isn't it?" Chief continued his grooming ritual. "Well, better start packing," Sam said and went outside.

Later, as Chief drifted off to sleep, he could hear Sam packing. He thought about where the move would take him but didn't worry. He trusted that Sam would always be there for him.

The next morning, Chief took one last lap around the three-story motel. The place remained free of any vermin. He didn't bother going in the basement this time. "Chief," Sam called in the distance, and Chief headed back to the apartment.

Chief ran around to the front of the motel and spotted Sam's truck. In addition to the dents and peeling paint, the truck now bore all the possessions Sam had acquired over his thirty-seven years of life. The bed overflowed with multiple tools and toolboxes of all sizes, an old orange lounge chair, a table, a television, and Sam's favorite lamp. Chief jumped in the passenger side, put his paws up on the dash, and looked over at Sam.

"This is it, kid," Sam said. "Our chance at the big life. Hold on."

The old engine sputtered to life, and with a puff of exhaust, the two headed down the road. Chief looked back and watched the motel fade into the past. It wasn't long before he noticed changes. The road lacked potholes, and instead of being parked on the side of the road, cars lay neatly tucked away in garages. The homes were bigger with neatly trimmed lawns and painted fences, and the trash cans had lids. All the dogs in the neighborhood were fenced in, and those being walked had leashes.

Sam whistled a fast, happy tune, nodding in approval. "Whoa, look how clean everything is," Sam said as the houses gave way to taller and taller buildings. He reached into his shirt pocket, pulled out a slip of paper, and looked down at it. "This is the one." He pulled into the parking lot of a tall apartment complex and found a space at the front. "Wow," Sam said. "Must be fifteen stories tall, maybe more."

Sam parked the truck and opened the door. Chief jumped

onto his lap and held his head high in the air. He sniffed. *Fresh,* he thought. He jumped down and turned back to Sam.

"Stay close," Sam said, "until we know what we're dealing with here."

The two walked through the double doors into a lobby that was twice the size of the old motel's lobby. There was a receiving counter, mailboxes, and a sharply dressed lady behind the desk. Chief looked at the lady in the gray suit and slacks and then at the counter. He didn't see the bell he had been accustomed to seeing on the desk at the old motel. Several sets of eyes stared out from behind papers and magazines at Chief as he trotted alongside Sam, who introduced himself to the woman behind the counter. Chief took the opportunity to look around the lobby area.

All leather chairs and couches with wooden legs with no place for mice to hide. Good, he thought. He reached out with his senses. He heard the chattering of tenants and spotted some motion, mostly adults and no children. No scent of dogs or other pets. The lobby was well kept.

The sitting tenants were engaged in business, and those walking about moved with purpose, as though they had places to be. *It looks organized,* Chief thought.

"Wait!" His nose twitched as the smell of sanitizers and perfume gave way to something more distinct. "Smoke!" Chief jumped up on the counter where Sam waited, executing a perfectly balanced turn as he landed and pointed in the direction of the smell.

"What is it, boy?" Sam asked.

Chief looked at a woman in a tight red dress wearing black three-inch heels and furs wrapped around her neck. Underneath a black lace hat complete with white flowers, two eyes peered out from thick-framed eyeglasses that sat upon her pointy nose. Blonde curls framed the edges of her face, and protruding from her bright-red lips was a long holder that contained a burning cigarette.

"You must be the new maintenance man." She held out a white-gloved hand. "I am Ms. Sorenson, the apartment manager."

Sam grabbed her hand firmly and shook it, causing her hat to tilt and the cigarette to fall from the holder. He picked up the cigarette and offered it to Ms. Sorenson. "I didn't know they allowed smoking in the building," Sam said.

"We don't," Ms. Sorenson responded. She looked at Chief, who stood on the counter at eye level with her. She raised an eyebrow. "Humph" was all she managed in his direction. "Come with me; I'll show you to your office."

Chief had no trouble keeping up with Ms. Sorenson. Her heels clacked against the tiled floor, announcing her every move. Chief cataloged everything he could sense: the number of entrances into the main lobby, how clean the floor was (cleanliness was a definite line of defense in rodent control), and more. High in the air he smelled the aroma of food: chicken, veal, assorted breads.

"There's a cafeteria in the complex," Ms. Sorenson said. "You can take your meals there. Laundry is on the fifth floor, extra storage in the basement."

Having a cafeteria on the premises would be an additional challenge for Chief as he monitored the building.

"Here is your office," Ms. Sorenson said, opening a door and handing Sam the key.

"What about my apartment?" Sam asked as Chief nudged by to get a good look around the office.

"It's all one unit," Ms. Sorenson said. "Your office is attached to the apartment, which has two bedrooms, a living room, and a kitchenette. If you please." Ms. Sorenson led the way into the apartment, which was three times the size of their old apartment. "This is your office area." She pointed to a room where a desk, a phone, a notebook, and a wastebasket stood. "This is the living room, and the kitchen area is in there." She smiled through smoke-stained yellow teeth.

"This sure is a nice place." Sam smiled, took his hat off, and ran his fingers through his uncombed black hair. "Mr. Ryan said it's rent-free. Is that right? I can't afford rent in a place like this."

"Part of your salary," Ms. Sorenson said. "Other than the office furniture and that old couch, it's unfurnished. I hope you won't have any children running all about the place." She raised her eyebrows.

"No, ma'am. Only family I have is Chief there." He pointed.

"Right. As you will notice, your front door has a pet door on it. There are several doors like that throughout the building. This whole environmentally friendly thing of using cats instead of poisons to rid the apartments of critters was not my idea."

"We're here to do our best," Sam said.

"Yes, I'm sure you are," Ms. Sorenson said. "My room is down the opposite side of the first floor. If you need anything, just tell Debra at the front desk."

Ms. Sorenson left, her high heels tapping down the hall away from the apartment. *I'll know when she's coming,* Chief thought as he pranced to the bedroom doorway and glanced in before going back to the front door. He meowed and looked at Sam.

"You take the first patrol," Sam said. "I've got to get our things unpacked, and then I'll be out to take a look around myself. Now go to work."

Sam, not accustomed to the pet door, opened the door, and Chief sprang out. He headed down the hallway, ears forward, nose activated. He wouldn't eat dinner until later—that way his senses would be heightened. *Let's see what we're up against,* he thought as he went to the elevator and waited for it to open. When the door opened, he jumped in and was surprised to find a man by the buttons.

"Oh," the young man said, "you must be the new tenants." He held the door open as if expecting someone else to come into the elevator and then looked back to Chief. "Ms. Sorenson doesn't allow pets to travel in the elevators. Not without an owner." He reached down to pick up Chief.

Chief went into action. Crouching down and lowering his tail, he let out a hiss and swiped his right claw at the attendant. The lanky, freckled-faced attendant stepped to the back of the elevator. Chief remained defiant and hissed again. The attendant moved out of Chief's way and to the opposite side.

Chief moved to the buttons. *I'll save the kitchen for later. Let's start top down.* He jumped up and hit the largest number with his paw. The doors closed, and he rode to the top floor without incident. The elevator attendant remained quiet as Chief exited on the fifteenth floor.

There's another cat in the building, Chief thought as he sniffed the air. *But the scent isn't fresh.* He walked around the fifteenth floor. *Hmm, only one apartment up here. No scent of rats.* He went to the end of the hall. Access to the stairs was open, with no doors, so he took the stairs to the fourteenth floor. He crept along the closed doorways until he spotted one that was open.

He approached the room and peeked inside. Boxes filled the room, and some men were unpacking. In the background, an elderly woman sat in a recliner sleeping. Beside her chair a birdcage rested on top of a three-foot-tall circular table. In the cage, a small yellow canary looked directly at Chief.

"Hello," the bird said. "I am Ladie."

"I'm Chief," he said and headed down the hall. He quickly decided the bird would be of no use since it was in a cage. He traveled down the stairs, stopping at each floor and going down each hallway sniffing and observing. He didn't find any new scents worth worrying about until the fifth floor.

Definitely rats. The scent is new, and they're moving in a straight line—exploring but not settled in yet. There's still time. He stopped and sniffed the air. He followed his nose down the stairwell back to the first floor, stopping in front of another set of stairs that led down. *There.* Chief nodded. *They're coming up from the basement, probably through a drainpipe just like the last place. I still have time to stop them before they get spread out.*

🐾 II 🐾

Tired from the day's move, Chief knew he needed rest before he started clearing the place, so he went back to his and Sam's apartment. The smell of fresh fish entered his nostrils as he got closer to his new home.

"Ah, there's my boy," Sam said as Chief ran in the apartment and to his dish. "Thought you'd like some of the real stuff tonight." Sam sat on the couch. Without anything to set it on, Sam's favorite lamp, a single bulb with a rainbow-colored shade over it, sat on the floor by the couch. "I've got the truck all unpacked." He slid off his boots and lay back. "Quite a place here. Fifteen floors. They got permanent tenants here, Chief. And a cafeteria with pie for dessert."

Chief ate lightly. Still licking his lips, he looked up. Sam's eyes were closed.

"Yep, we're moving up. You and me." Sam's snores let Chief know he was fast asleep.

Half-unpacked boxes filled the apartment. Apart from Sam's old orange lounge chair, a brown leather couch, and a small table with two chairs in the kitchen, the brown, shaggy-carpeted apartment was void of any other furnishings.

Chief spotted his towel slightly sticking out of one of the boxes. He tugged on it, freeing it from a few magazines, and hauled it beside the couch where Sam rested. He put it on the floor, circled twice, and plopped down. He looked at Sam, who was still dressed in the same clothes he'd worn all day, and smiled. He knew Sam would take care of him. Chief slept deeply that night, knowing it would be the only full night of sleep he'd have for some time. *Tomorrow*, he thought, *the work begins.*

Chief woke hours before the sun would be up, fully alert and ready to hunt. He checked on Sam, who remained sleeping, and then headed out into the quiet hallway. He immediately went to the elevator. There was no attendant on duty this early, and he rode easily to the fifteenth floor. He wanted to investigate the scent of the other cat in the building.

I need to make sure it knows who's in charge around here, Chief thought as he exited the elevator onto the fifteenth floor. "Must not be much of a cat if it's let the rats go about as they please," Chief said, digging his claws into the carpet to test its depth as he started down his patrol. *Carpeted hallways. This will make it easier to pick up the scent and easier to corner without slipping.* Picking up speed, he tested his ability to maneuver. He noticed this floor was different from the other floors, shorter and with only one apartment at the end of the hallway.

Suddenly, Chief spotted something moving toward him. It was white and fluffy. He stood his ground as the figure got closer. He recognized his target—the cat whose scent he'd followed.

"You must be the new building cat. My name is Charlene."

Chief looked upon the fluffy solid-white Persian cat. Unable to speak, he had a sudden urge to lick his paw and clean his face but resisted. He'd gotten up early to look over the building and had not taken the time to groom. He knew he must look terrible.

"I've never met a Protector before," Charlene said from smooth pink lips. She moved closer to Chief. Her long eyelashes flickered over sparkling blue eyes.

"You know what I am?" Chief asked.

"Yes. Not every cat has the calling of the Protectors, but I know about their heritage. All cats do. You are a descendant from those who've protected humans since ancient times."

"I don't know much about all that," Chief said. He caught himself staring at her long eyelashes and the beautiful face behind them. He shook his head to clear it of the fog he found himself in. "Chief's the name. Pleased to meet you, Mrs. Charlene."

"Oh, please, not so formal. Call me Charlene, and it's *Ms.*" Her eyelashes flickered as the words left her mouth.

Chief blushed; he'd never met a cat so beautiful. He didn't

know what to say, so he stuck with what he knew best, his job. "Yes, of course, Charlene. I wasn't aware that there were other cats in the building."

"Yes, several, but we're all pets. None of us are allowed to go out where we please like you."

"But you're out now?" Chief asked.

"Yes, several of the apartments and storage rooms have pet doors on them, including the penthouse. But if my owner knew I was out, she would be furious. I just had to come out and meet you. I was curious." Charlene came so close it tickled Chief's whiskers. Then she turned away and pranced down the hall.

Chief stared for a moment and then took off after her. Coming up beside her, he tried to think of something to say. "Can you tell me about the place?" Chief asked. "I mean, strictly business, you understand." He looked away, pretending to pay attention to a particular piece of the carpet. "Why is there only one apartment on this floor?"

"Oh, you mean the penthouse. Well, it's supposed to be the best, but I think it's too far removed to be desired. I've been here about six months," Charlene said. "Mrs. Ryan is my owner. She keeps me in the apartment here but is never around. She travels a lot. They are always busy buying new buildings. I get moved around a lot. I think Mr. Ryan asked your owner to feed me while they're out."

"Sam?"

"Yes, that was his name. It would be nice to have him taking care of me. Ms. Sorenson doesn't like cats."

"Right. Ms. Sorenson, bright-red lipstick, tight clothes, high heels, and smells of smoke."

"You've met her." Charlene laughed.

"I've never wanted to scratch a human before but ..."

"Chief!" Charlene scolded. "She's not that bad. She just overdoes it a little."

"Sorry," Chief said. "Didn't mean that last part. Sam's the best. We'll take good care of you."

"We?" Charlene stopped at the only apartment on the floor and smiled.

Chief smiled, and for some reason he didn't feel as nervous. "Can you tell me about the rats? Have you seen any?"

"They showed up about two months ago," Charlene said. "I haven't seen any, but I can smell them. They don't come this high, but they are in the walls. Well, guess I'll see you later?" She blinked her eyes slowly.

Chief stared at those blue eyes framed by perfectly combed hair. "Thank you for the information," Chief said. "I'll be taking care of this problem shortly." He turned and started to walk away.

"Come by if you need help," Charlene said.

The offer caused Chief to stumble. He whirled around. "Excuse me?"

"I can take care of myself," Charlene said. She put up her paw and extended her claws. "I may be a pet, but I still have these."

Chief's chin dropped. "I'll remember that," he said, watching Charlene until she passed through her pet door. He was trotting down the hallway smiling when suddenly his senses alerted him of danger. His hair stood up on his back. Still thinking about Charlene, he'd let his guard down. Instincts beyond his consciousness kicked in, and his heart raced.

"That dame can cause a traffic jam," a voice in front of Chief said.

Chief pointed his ears and eyes forward and raised his hair to give the appearance that he was larger. He went into his attack stance with claws extended, ready to pounce, but he could not make out who addressed him. His eyes caught movement of a dark shadow at the end of the hall standing under the window.

"It's a trick I learned," a deep voice said. "Stand under a window with the sun at your back; that way what's in front of you can't tell you're there until it's too late. By then, you have the advantage."

"I see." Chief watched closely as a short-haired black cat,

larger than him, emerged from under the window. Chief kept his stance, making sure not to let the larger opponent get to his side, where he could use size to his advantage. "That's a good trick. I didn't know there were any other male cats here," Chief said. He took stock of the cat's muscular frame and noticed by the scars on his ears that the cat had been in a fight or two.

"There aren't. Relax. Name's Baxter. I run the building next door. It's new just like this one. Carpets on every floor, air-conditioning, and an elevator. I just wanted to come over and introduce myself." Baxter sat down in front of Chief and lowered his head to signal his nonaggression.

Chief relaxed his stance. "Name's Chief."

"I heard about you," Baxter said. "The Bronx Bruiser, here in my neighborhood."

Chief raised his eyebrows. "The Bronx Bruiser?"

"That's what they call you. I guess you cleaned up your old neighborhood. Even chased some alley cats out of there from what we heard. Word gets around. They say you got the fastest right hook on the continent."

"Well, I don't know about that," Chief said. He flexed his right paw out in front of him, admiring it as he extended his claws.

"The alley cats are plugged into the pigeon network," Baxter said. "They get news from all over the place. That, and Ladie: she knows more about what's going on in this neighborhood than anyone. She's the bird up on the fourteenth floor with Ms. Doris."

"The canary?"

"You know her?" Baxter asked.

"Saw her yesterday. Birds are harmless. What about the alley cats?"

"Those guys amaze me." Baxter shook his head. "You might want to introduce yourself to them sometime. Sikes is their leader. He can throw one wild party."

"Not in my building. Alley cats were trouble where I come

from," Chief said. "Always trying to get in on your territory like you owed them because they were cats."

"No offense, Chief, but it's not like that here. You might be fast, but these are big territories we've got to cover. These boys are great. You never know when you're going to need some allies."

"I'll take my chances," Chief said.

"Hey, how about I show you around?"

Chief nodded. He followed Baxter to the stairwell, out an open window, and to the fire escape that ran along the side of the building. They climbed along it until they reached the top of the building. Baxter jumped on a two-foot-wide wall that bordered the flat roof.

"What's wrong?" Baxter asked as Chief stopped and looked around.

"It's just"—Chief looked down—"I've never been so high before."

"It's exhilarating, isn't it?" Baxter said. "Sikes and his boys hang out in the alley, down there. Sikes has kinda taken the others in like their father. He leads them and keeps them outta trouble. They just want to be left alone. They don't cause any problems, and they provide an extreme benefit."

"Benefit?"

"They keep the street rats in check by keeping them out of the alleys and Dumpsters." Baxter took a few more steps and turned around. "Here's the spot. Now look out there."

The wall was wider where they stood at the center of the building. "Wow, you can see the whole world from up here," Chief said. He looked across the rows of buildings, many of which were still under construction.

"It's a big place, Chief. Fifteen floors, twenty rooms each floor. Lots of territory to cover. That building over there is mine," Baxter said, gesturing. "And the one to the right back there is Paggs's. His building was the first one built, but all three are the same design. He's an older cat. He used to be tough and still is, but I check on him once in a while. Back there, that building's a black zone. Don't go there."

"A black zone?"

"Means stay out. They're using rat poisons and all kinds of chemicals."

"Any kids back there?" Chief asked. "Those chemicals are dangerous."

"Yep, kids all around this neighborhood. Rich kids leaving toys everywhere and not picking up after themselves. Parents buying stuff all the time that ends up in closets and storage rooms. A haven for rats and mice."

"No wonder there's a problem," Chief said.

Chief looked down as he walked back and forth along the wall. "If this Sikes has the alleys, and the buildings on either side of this one don't have problems, then the rats must be coming up through the basement."

"Through the sewers." Baxter nodded. "We don't dare go down there. Not enough room to fight."

"Then we need to draw them out in the open or keep them in the sewers," Chief said.

"What's that?"

"I got work to do." Chief walked back to the fire escape. "Thanks for the tour."

"Hey," Baxter said, catching up to him. "We kind of got a thing going, me and Paggs. We help each other out when we need it. Once one building is infested, it'll be harder to keep them out. Heck, when word gets out that the Protector from the South Bronx has moved to town, those rats will be packing their bags."

Chief sat down and considered what Baxter said. "Who was here before me? Did he work with you?"

"Nobody was here. You got the newest building. No infestations yet, but they must be having some problems."

"Why do you say that?"

"Because they got you," Baxter said, his face relaxed.

Chief looked out at the huge buildings, the clean streets bustling with people, and felt good. He relaxed and thought about Charlene for a moment. Then his mind snapped back to work.

"Thanks for coming by, Baxter," Chief said. "I got some work to do now."

"Gonna start clearing the building, are you?"

"Top down, I'm gonna drive those rats and any other pesky varmints right out of here," Chief said with his teeth bared.

"Ooh," Baxter said, "eviction notices are being served." He slapped his paws together.

Chief looked at him, raising one eyebrow.

"If you need any help, just call on me," Baxter said and trotted by Chief, heading down the fire escape.

Chief followed him and jumped down in front of him to show off. "I found you earn more respect by doing the job yourself. If I show any weakness or those rats think I need your help, then they'll get wise and try stuff when I'm alone. Nope, I'm going to do it myself."

Baxter jumped over Chief and slid down to the next floor, stopping abruptly and causing Chief to halt. "I didn't mean I'd help with the rats." Baxter grinned. "I meant if you need any help with Charlene." He winked at Chief and started walking.

Chief cleared his throat and followed Baxter down to the end of the fire escape. "She's not, uh, your girl?"

"No way. I'm a bachelor and proud to stay that way. Besides, that's one classy cat. You might, and I say *might*, win her over if you live up to the reputation that preceded you."

"Very funny," Chief said. "Does, well, does Charlene know about my reputation?"

"Of course," Baxter said. "Thanks to Ladie, everyone around here knows." The two were at the bottom of the fire escape that ended at the alley running between buildings. "Well, gotta get back to my own place. See ya, Chief."

Chief watched Baxter disappear down the alley, wondering if

he should have accepted the help. *Baxter's right. It's a big building. Lots of places to hide.*

Chief threw out his right paw, flexing his claws. "Fastest right hook on the continent." He looked at his paw. "We attack at dawn!"

Chapter 2

A Saucy Chase

C hief stood at the top of the stairs, his pupils dilated, the hair on his back straight up, and his ears locked forward listening to the scratching sounds and squeaky voices. So far, he'd taken the rats by surprise, but he could no longer count on it this time and suspected they knew he was coming. He'd spent the last week chasing them out of the pantries, the stairwells, and the elevator shaft. He'd killed three in the ventilation system and another in a storage room.

"Only one place left to go," Chief said as he moved toward the basement entrance. A gurgling sound emerged from his stomach. "Slim and hungry," he said, licking his lips. "No slack!"

He flexed his front claws, feeling each individual one hit as he walked down the stairs to the dimly lit basement. Storage containers, a few lockers, a large sink and a washbasin, and the Trane water chiller were all down there, and the rats were among them.

His nostrils twitched, and his elite senses picked through the smells—detergent, sanitizers, sewage, and mothballs—until he honed in on the one he wanted. *There it is!* Chief thought.

But there was something other than the smell of rats that came through, and he tried to place it. So far, everywhere the rats had been, he had smelled something else, something familiar that he couldn't quite place. Then, it came to him: *Spaghetti?* Chief shook his head to regain his composure.

Carefully, Chief came to the end of the stairs. When his foot came off the last step, a large rat emerged from his right and jumped at him. Chief dodged to his left, surprising the rat, which missed its target and glided by. Chief's right claw stopped the rat in its tracks and reversed its direction, slinging the rat across the room from where it had come with four fresh claw marks.

Chief braced for impact as another one charged him. He waited until the rat got close enough, and then Chief pounced high into the air, coming down on the rat with his full weight and disabling him with one blow. He was readying for the next attack when he heard a voice.

"Enough!" Four rats emerged from the shadows in front of Chief. The light from the stairwell illuminated them. Chief stood poised to attack, but the rats backed away from him, and a large brown rat emerged. "Enough, cat. No more fighting."

"Watch out, Wilber!" one of the other rats yelled out. "His right paw is fast."

Chief immediately recognized that the strong smell of spaghetti sauce he'd been chasing all day was from the large brown rat. "Spaghetti?" Chief couldn't help asking. Long whiskers protruded from the face of the rat, and unflinching black eyes stared back at Chief.

"Hey, some of us like certain foods," Wilber said, sitting back on his hind legs. He used his front hands to gesture and shrugged his shoulders as he spoke. "I'll have you know my family hails from a long generation of Sicilian rats. Good food is in my lineage. What? You think we all eat trash?"

"I didn't say anything," Chief said.

"That's just like a cat." Wilber shook his head.

"I can't believe this," Chief said. "I'm actually standing here talking to a rat. Usually they run away so I don't kill them."

"We have names, and mine's Wilber. This is my associate, Quido." The largest of the other four rats, who stood a half step back from Wilber, nodded.

"I'm not interested in a history lesson or your names. I'm interested in your leaving." Chief kept his attention on his surroundings, sure the rat was stalling while the others plotted to get behind him.

"I suppose you think you cats are the only ones that come from something."

"You better start marching back to where you came from," Chief said, tightening up his stance, "before I give you a lesson you don't want to learn."

"I think you misunderstand me," Wilber said. "I know all about your kind, Protector of the light, descended from cats that were treated like gods, from Egypt. Hey, you win." He waved his hands in front of him. "I don't want to lose any more of my guys. This place is a gold mine, but we can take a hint, cat. We'll step off your turf if you lighten up."

"Are you actually trying to call a truce? I must have fallen asleep. This can't really be happening." He shook his head. "Wake up, wake up."

"As I said, name's Wilber. I'm the head of the family." Several of the rats flanking Wilber nodded as if this confirmed he was an important rat. "Look," Wilber continued, "we don't want any more trouble, but I need to know you'll respect the deal."

"What deal?" Chief asked while baring his teeth. "This is my place now. The deal is you leave or die." He swiped his claws in front of Wilber.

"Hey," Wilber said, "no need for any more violence. We'll stay clear of here if you agree to stay out of the sewers. They're ours." Wilber's eyes were solid, and he turned sideways and nodded to the other rats, who then disappeared through a pipe under the utility sink. Wilber moved forward until he was within Chief's reach and lifted up his paw.

"Huh?" Chief raised one eyebrow and lowered the other.

"Oh, sorry," Wilber said. He spit on his paw and held it back out.

Chief considered pouncing now that Wilber was vulnerable, but he didn't. "How do I know I can trust you?"

Wilber looked down at his paw, wiped it on his belly, and stepped back. "You don't," he said. "But I own the streets around here. You keep to your place, and you and your family leave my family alone, and I promise you, you'll never see any of us messing up your place. *Capisce?*"

He doesn't know I'm alone, Chief thought. "I suppose I can take a chance and trust you. But I don't want you just out of my building. If you tread on any of the buildings in this complex, if I even smell you near me and my brothers ..."

"We won't come back. You took out four of my boys already and disabled two more. From what I've seen here, any rat would be stupid to take you on. You're not just an ordinary hunter. You're a descendant of the ancient Protectors. The family's run into your kind a few times, and it always ends badly. I have no appetite for that. Have a good life, cat, and don't bother to write." Wilber turned and slowly walked to the drainpipe and disappeared down it.

Chief sniffed. *Smells like they've gone.* Then his ears caught a distant voice.

"By the way, *cat*, in the end, the Italians became more powerful than the Egyptians. Come on, Quido. Bring the boys."

Chief stood in the dark for a minute, ears and eyes scanning the room. Nothing moved, and he stood alone.

"I thought you were Sicilian," Chief muttered to himself, still confused about what exactly had taken place. What he did know was that the rats had left. He sniffed around to make sure the basement was clear. Then he stopped in front of the pipe where

Wilber had crawled away. *Sam will have to fix the hole in this grate.* He stared into the darkness beyond. "I wonder how many of them there are." He sniffed the edge of the pipe, and his face went sour. "Eww! I'm not going down there."

He ran up the stairs and down the hall, stopping to prance just before he entered his apartment. Evening was approaching, and he was happy his mission to rid the place of rats hadn't gone into the next day.

"Job's done. The building is clean," Chief said. He smiled and licked his paws, slicking his hair back. No one was there to notice. Sam was gone.

"I didn't realize the rats here had such a long family history," Chief said. He took a long drink of water and ate some of the dried food Sam had left out for him. "Family? Hmmm." Chief sat in the apartment for a moment and thought about Charlene. It was quieter than the motel and, without Sam around, seemed lonely. Chief left the apartment and went to the stairs. He was about to go up to visit Charlene when a thought occurred to him. *First, let's get everything in place.*

Chief went out the back door and headed into the alley. His ears went forward and then sideways, and he scanned the alley in front of him. His nose reacted first. "Whew," Chief said. "Garbage and, wait, I smell—" He froze in place as a large, unkempt gray cat with black stripes emerged from behind one of the Dumpsters. The tabby cat, who was as tall as Chief, moved toward him. He looked fit and lean. His brown eyes were unflinching, and his striped tail flicked slowly back and forth.

"Yo, you must be the new kid in town. I'm Sikes. It's an honor to meet the Bronx Bruiser," the cat said.

"Bronx Bruiser, right." Chief raised his eyes at the compliment and cleared his throat.

"That's kind of a nickname we came up with for you," Sikes said.

Chief smiled. "I approve." Then he remembered something

he'd learned at his old place: not to trust alley cats. His eyes narrowed. Maybe Sikes was just trying to flatter him so he wouldn't come down on the alley cats so hard. "Look, Sikes, I've got a job to do. I keep the building clear of all varmints and rascals."

"Hey," Sikes interrupted, "me and the boys heard you've been clearing out the building. It's a big place, and we wouldn't mind helping, you know, for some table scraps or somethin'. I mean, the food in the Dumpsters is pretty good and all, but it would be nice to eat somethin' before it's considered garbage."

Chief stuttered, "N-n-no, thanks for asking. I took care of the problem. I appreciate the offer, but where I come from, the alley cats were smooth talkers. When I turned my back, they were moving into my territory expecting handouts. Then, you know, too many hens in the henhouse and all that."

"Hey, Sikes." A skinny, short-haired calico cat emerged from behind Sikes. "Did he just say you was a smooth talker? He doesn't know you then. And what's this about handouts? Man, around here we don't even let the people know we're here, or they call animal control."

"Chief, this is Rascal, my right-hand man," Sikes said.

Chief kept his eyes forward. He was tired from the fight with the rats, and now there were two alley cats in front of him. He geared up to make a stand, and his tail went up.

"Yo, boys," Sikes called out, "come and meet the Bronx Bruiser." Two large cats emerged. One was dirty white with gray stripes and the other gray with dirty-white stripes. "This is Dazzle and Scratch." Both cats nodded in Chief's direction.

Unable to tell which was which, Chief nodded back. He had tangled with alley cats before but never four of them at once.

"We respect your job," Sikes said, coming up beside Chief. "We have no desire to be inside that building. We want to live free. All we ask is to be left alone. You see, we've been chased all over the place."

"Yeah," Rascal said. "Some-a the boys didn't make it this far."

"Poor Traz," Dazzle said, lowering his head.

Sikes walked closer to Chief and sat. He lifted his left paw out in front of him and waved it across the alley. "Here, we got a nice, new neighborhood. Animal control ain't moved in yet. The trash cans are full of food. We don't need any handouts, and we'll help you. You keep the building clean; we'll keep this alley clean."

Sikes moved even closer so that he was right beside Chief. Chief took his eyes off the other three cats to eye Sikes. "No rats in the Dumpsters or in the alley, just us. We can keep a low profile." Sikes turned and looked to the Dumpsters. "See?"

The other three cats had disappeared. Chief blinked twice and looked again but couldn't find Scratch, Dazzle, or Rascal.

"No problems," Sikes said.

"Very discreet," Chief said. He thought for a moment, sniffing the air one more time. The odor of food and trash hid the smell of cats. "Deal," Chief said. He noticed it was getting dark outside. "Now I've got important business to attend to." Chief whirled about and ran back to the apartment building.

"Wow, he sure is fast," Chief heard Sikes say as he went into the building.

Chief hurried to the top floor. When he reached the hallway he paused, wet his paw, and slicked back his hair. *I hope she's still up,* he thought as he pranced down the hall. Then he stopped. *Am I sure about this? Everything else has fallen into place today. Why not this?*

"I wondered if you were going to come by," Charlene said.

Surprised, Chief stifled a reflex to jump.

"I've been waiting for over a week for you to come see me," Charlene said. "Did I surprise you?"

"Sort of," Chief said. "It's been a long week. Things jumping out at me haven't been, well, as friendly looking as you. What are you doing out in the hall?"

"The missus is away. She's been away a lot lately. Sam let me out. I think he feels bad that I'm cooped up all day. You drove the rats out, didn't you?" Charlene passed on the right side of Chief close enough that he could almost feel her.

Chief turned to follow her. "Yes," he said, coming alongside her. "Strange bunch of rats. I didn't know they had a family history."

"Well, so you settled it yourself. I guess there's nothing exciting left to do," Charlene said, sitting down. She started grooming her fur.

Chief looked down the hall toward the apartment where Charlene stayed. "Were you waiting out here to help me?"

Charlene stopped grooming. "I'm not supposed to leave this floor, but if you had needed any help …"

Chief considered his next words wisely. "That was very thoughtful. But, you know, I had to do it myself to show those rats who runs things around here."

Charlene didn't respond.

"I mean …" Chief paused, searching for words. "I didn't even let that big cat Baxter help me."

Charlene smiled. "Baxter's just like an alley cat, tough and free-spirited."

"If you go for that type of stuff," Chief said.

"Do I detect jealousy?"

"It depends."

"Baxter's not my type." She stretched out her left paw in front of her, examining the tips of her claws. "I prefer the strong, gentle type—someone who knows how to handle a tough situation with tact."

"Come on," Chief said. "I've got something to show you." He raced by Charlene, who followed him step for step. He took her to the stairway, out the open window, and onto the fire escape.

Charlene hesitated, so Chief stopped. "I'm sorry; is it too late?"

"No, that's not it," Charlene said. "I'm just not used to being outside."

"Come on. Your owner's away, and Sam won't mind. It's safe. Just watch your step, and follow me." Chief led her to the roof where Baxter had taken him and stopped at the side that over-looked the city.

"Oh my," Charlene said. "It's so beautiful. I never knew the world outside was so big! I mean, I can see a little out of the apartment window, but out here, the air is so ..." She stared at the stars.

Chief watched Charlene's eyes sparkle as the starlight light reflected off them. He sat down, yawning.

"Long day?" Charlene asked.

"Yes. Now that the rats are out of the building and I don't have to worry about alley cats, I can take a breath," Chief said. "I didn't know I was so tired."

Charlene sat down by him. "Sounds like you need a break. So how is it you just happened to be on the top floor after such an exhausting day? Did you forget something?"

Chief smiled. "No, I came to see you."

"Oh. I guess now that the missus is never around, I'm getting lonely being by myself."

"Then it's a good thing I came by," Chief said.

"Do you think the rats will come back?"

"No," Chief said. "In my experience, they'll stay away as long as they sense me."

"So you've made the building safe already," Charlene said. "What will you do now?"

"There's always the chance of other rodents," Chief said, "other dangers. Who knows?" He moved closer to Charlene.

"Then you better stay close," Charlene said and smiled.

"Being a Protector is all I know. I thought it might be nice to make a friend."

"Friend?" Charlene said.

Chief touched Charlene's tail with his, and the two sat there looking out across the city as their tails danced with each other.

Chapter 3

The Smallest One
of the Bunch

"**C**hief!"

Chief's ears perked up. He recognized the alarm in Sam's voice and raced up from the basement where he'd been patrolling. It had been over two months since he'd last seen any rats, but he still patrolled the area daily.

"Chief!" Sam's voice rang out again.

Chief turned the corner toward Sam, who stood outside their apartment.

"There you are, boy. It's time."

Chief raced into the apartment and up to the table where Charlene was lying. A lady in a white lab coat whom Chief recognized from her previous visits stood over Charlene.

"You're too late," the veterinarian said to Chief. "She's already done."

"Thank you, Dr. Burgess," Sam said to the veterinarian. "I'm glad we have a vet in the building."

"Yes," Dr. Burgess said, "glad it happened before I was off

to the office. She should be fine. I'll check on you when I get back."

"Thank you, Doctor." Sam closed the door as Dr. Burgess left. "You and me, we're going places; that's what we're doing," Sam said to Chief. "We're a team all right. My first grandkids." Sam smiled from ear to ear. The light glimmered off the silver caps on his front teeth.

"Ah, look at my boy," Sam said. He patted Chief on the head as Chief raised up on his hind legs to look into the cat bed on the table. Four kittens were curled next to Charlene. "It's only been three months since we moved here, and things keep getting better. Now you're a big family man, mister." Sam took a new pet bed out of a paper bag. He went to the second bedroom, picked Chief's old towel up from the floor, and put the new pet bed down.

Chief followed him. Purring, he rubbed against Sam's leg and then hopped into the new pet bed, examining it. Sam put two new pet blankets on the floor and lay out a few new cat toys. Sam went back into the kitchen and returned with the pet bed that held Charlene and her kittens. He put it by Chief's bed. "Oh, my boy." Sam patted Chief's head again and smiled before he left the room. Chief could hear him putting away groceries, humming as he did so.

"He sure is happy for you," Charlene said.

"I've never seen him so excited," Chief said. "Are you all right?"

"I'm fine. Just tired," Charlene said. "They're so cute."

"And small," Chief said.

"What did Sam mean that you're going places? Are you leaving?"

"No. *No*," Chief said. "It's more like he means we're getting a better life than what we had. When Sam first got me, we lived in a basement. He had a cot and a locker. I had an old towel to lay on. Not much to live with. Then we moved up to our own motel room. It was better than the basement but not as good as this place. Now he has his own apartment that's not the size of a closet and an office, and you and I have our own room." He raised his nose in the air. "I smell fresh fish again. Fourth time this week."

Chief went to the blankets Sam had laid out and pulled one across the room to cover Charlene and the kittens.

"You lived in a basement." Charlene pricked up her ears, her eyes wide with concern.

"Yes. Those were tough times. I had to keep on my guard—the rats, you know, they don't sleep."

"Oh, dear, don't tell your story in front of the children."

"Sorry," Chief said, licking the head of one of the kittens. One of the kittens was shaggy with orange-and-yellow fur like Chief, another was white like Charlene, one was orange with black stripes, and the smallest of the group had fluffy black-and-white fur.

"You've never talked about where you and Sam came from," Charlene said.

"It's not exactly the kind of thing a guy tells a girl he's trying to impress. Besides, that's in the past. I left all that bad news behind me. Speaking of bad news"—Chief twitched his nose—"I smell smoke and perfume. That means Ms. Sorenson's on her way." He shook his head and moved where he could see into Sam's office and watch the conversation.

"Sam," a high-pitched, whiny voice rang out. Ms. Sorenson entered the room. "Sam?"

"Yes, Ms. Sorenson, here in my office," Sam said.

"Well, I heard your cat and that cat of Mrs. Ryan's have had kittens. I'm not running a boarding house for cats," Ms. Sorenson said with her chin and nose in the air.

"I'm sure we didn't think that, Ms. Sorenson," Sam said, sitting back in his chair. "Those little kittens won't hurt anything, and they can help keep the place free of varmints. Besides, Chief's eventually going to age. He'll need to train one of his kids to take over and keep the place safe."

"There haven't been any rodents around here since the first week you moved in," Ms. Sorenson said. "I don't know why you can't just let him out at night when everyone is asleep. We can't have all those cats running around this complex. But if you must, keep one. Just don't let it run all over the building."

"Thank you, ma'am," Sam said, smiling.

Ms. Sorenson frowned, and her eyes went to the ceiling. "I want the rest gone by Friday."

"They have to stay with their mother for six to seven weeks, or else they can die," Sam said. "I'm sure you wouldn't want that."

"Of course not; I'm not heartless. But do it fast."

Sam looked around the apartment and back at Ms. Sorenson. "Will there be anything else?"

"I've had complaints from several tenants about the hot water not being hot enough. Please adjust the thermometer."

"You mean the thermostat," Sam said.

"Yes, well, whatever it is, just get it done." Ms. Sorenson spun around, nearly falling in her high-heel shoes, and marched out of the apartment, her footsteps echoing down the hall.

Chief looked at Sam, who smiled momentarily and came into the bedroom with the cats. "That lady drives me crazy."

Sam leaned over Chief and watched the kittens sleeping. "Don't worry; we'll find good homes for them." He walked back to his office.

Chief followed Sam and rubbed his leg, purring.

"You heard the lady, Chief; pick one." Sam took his keys from the table without petting Chief and walked out of the apartment and down the hall.

Chief went back to his room and looked at Charlene. She cuddled around the little black-and-white cat, the smallest of the litter.

"I take it you heard that?" Chief asked. "He's right. I will need someone who can take over, one of these days."

"Is that all you heard?" Charlene asked.

"I'm sure Sam will find good homes for them."

"I'm sure he will for the rest of our children, but this one won't make it out there. We're keeping her."

"That one?" Chief looked at the kitten. She had fluffy hair like her mother, a white chest, black hair on her back, white paws, and a small spot of white on her tail. "That one will never be able to fend off a rat. She's not even as big as a mouse."

"Why, that's a perfect name for her, since she's so small," Charlene said and turned her head away from Chief.

"What?"

"My little Mouse," Charlene purred and pulled the little kitten beside her.

Chief sighed. "I'm going on patrol." He needed some time to think and decided he'd patrol from the top down as he headed to the elevator.

Bing. The bell rang, and Chief stepped in.

The attendant backed up immediately. "Right. Going up." He kept his distance from Chief and hit the button for the top floor.

"How's the smallest of the litter supposed to grow up to take my place?" Chief muttered to himself. "Now I've just got something else to worry about and protect. Mouse … Well, at least the name fits."

Seven weeks passed, and Chief kept busy doing patrols while the kittens grew. Soon, all the kittens were gone except the one Charlene clung to. She never left the kitten's side or the apartment and continued to call her Mouse.

Chief watched from the doorway of the apartment as Charlene cleaned the little kitten, whose eyes were wide open, curiously looking around the room. The eyes stopped at him.

Chief looked around the room and back to Mouse. Her eyes remained fixed on him. "Wait a minute," Chief said and approached Mouse. "Her eyes ..." Mouse's left eye was blue, and her right eye was green.

"Yes, isn't it great?" Charlene said. "That just makes her even more special."

"Well, I got to do my rounds," Chief said and turned around. Before he could leave the room, two heads peeked through the door and around the corner from where Charlene and Mouse sat.

"Yo, Chief, me and the guys wanted to see how the kid was doin'," Sikes said.

"May we come in?" Baxter asked, poking his head around the corner.

"Come in, boys." Charlene's soft voice carried through the room.

Before Chief could protest, Baxter and Sikes went past him.

"Hello there," a large, slightly overweight yellow cat said to Chief.

"Hi, Paggs," Chief said, greeting the cat who ran the building behind his.

"Sorry that I haven't been by, but I am getting up there in years. And although you cured us of our rat problem, we must be ever-vigilant, and patrols take time. May I remind you that my building was the first one finished, so the varmints had more time to settle."

"We understand," Chief said.

"Your boy is getting, uh, fluffy," Baxter said. His whiskers twitched, and he turned sideways, looking at Chief. He moved back a few steps. "I mean, there's nothing wrong with that. Kids got a lot of hair."

"That's because *he* is a *she*," Charlene said.

"Oh. *Oh!* And, a-a fine one she is. Really, right, Sikes?"

Chief glared at Baxter as Baxter looked around the room as though trying to find another exit.

"Yeah, a real fine girl she is. Wow, I never thought I'd see a little snapper running around again." Sikes wiped his eyes. "I'm sorry, Mrs. Charlene. I just get all choked up when I see these little ones. She's a cute one."

"Thank you, boys, for coming by," Charlene said.

"Come on; let's give the lady some privacy," Chief said and herded Baxter, Paggs, and Sikes to the hallway.

"I hope you don't mind me coming in here to check on yous, Chief," Sikes said.

"I don't think Charlene minds if you guys come by," Chief said. "She likes the attention, especially because her owner is never around anymore."

"All feminine types are like that, Chief," Sikes said. "They gets happy when they get attention about stuff—like what they've changed around the house and what the kids is doing and all. Hey, me and the boys are going down to the park later to chase some pigeons. I'll bring you back some flowers for her. The ladies always like flowers. See yous later." Sikes jumped out an open window.

"I better go too. Good evening," Paggs said and followed Sikes.

Chief kept walking to the stairs and started up to the next floor.

"No elevator today?" Baxter asked.

"I need the walk," Chief said. The two cats slowly walked up the stairs.

"Ah, that's Sikes," Baxter said. "He sure is a character. Always up to something; if he's not attracting more homeless cats to help out, he's in the park chasing pigeons."

Chief didn't respond.

"Look, I'm sure Charlene understands," Baxter said.

"Understands what?" Chief stopped. He perked up his ears and looked at Baxter.

"Oh, you didn't tell her you wanted a boy, did you?"

"I didn't have time. She was worried that the smallest one wouldn't be tough enough to survive without our protection."

"Sounds like the wife of a Protector," Baxter said. "She's right, and you know it."

"I'm trying not to show her I'm disappointed," Chief said. "Do you think she knows?"

"Even I can tell something's not right with you. I noticed you standing out in the hall like you're afraid to go into the room, and I know you aren't."

"I've been worried that Charlene's owner will come back and take her, worried that I won't be able to take care of her and that kid. I guess I expected her to pick one of the kittens that I could train to be a Protector," Chief said. "Instead, she picked the smallest of the litter. I don't know how to act."

"Well, ain't that something," Baxter said. "She's married to a Protector, and here she is playing the role of Protector by taking care of her smallest child. She was right to pick that one. It needed the most care. You should be proud of her."

Chief's eyes grew wide. "Guess I didn't think of it that way."

"Besides," Baxter said, "even the smallest offspring from you two is going to have a lot of spirit. Come on; I'll race you to the roof."

The two zipped along the stairs out to the fire escape and all the way to the roof. Chief stopped at the ledge to catch his breath and looked around at the other buildings. "I guess I never thought I'd have more than the apartments to protect."

"We've got the safest block in the city," Baxter said. Putting his left paw around Chief's neck, he spread his other paw out and waved it across the skyline. "Look at that view."

Chief grinned.

"Of course, now that you've got all this extra responsibility and such, I guess it will be up to me to do the tough work around here," Baxter said. Chief tackled him, and the two cats wrestled to the ground, pouncing and practicing their fencing moves. Then they sat and looked down to the street below.

"Maybe Charlene is right," Chief said, catching his breath.

"There's nothing wrong with a girl. She can be as gritty and tough as her old man."

"Maybe?" Baxter said. "In a couple of months, that kid's going to be more than you can handle. A real fighter. I can tell."

"Thanks, Bax."

"For what?"

"Helping me put things into perspective. Guess I needed to step back and take a look at what I have and realize how lucky I am."

"That's the spirit, Chief," Baxter said. "Some of the dames are born killers."

Chapter 4
Power Sliding

Mouse tore around the corner of the fourth-floor hallway and zeroed in on her target. Glancing over his shoulder, Chief noticed she kept her claws out just enough to grip the carpet but not too much to get them stuck, just as he'd taught her.

"I'll get you this time," she said, closing in on him.

Chief rounded the corner and stopped.

Mouse tore around the corner faster than Chief expected. "Wait!" she called out as Chief came at her. She tried to dodge to the right, but he was too fast.

"Got you!" Chief said as he pounced on Mouse and gently tackled her to the floor.

"Oh, *Dad*! That's not fair," Mouse protested as she got up. "I was supposed to be the attacker."

"Just trying to teach you one more lesson: don't cut the corners too sharp. You might run into something unexpected," Chief said. "What was that you were doing to come around the corner so fast?"

"I call it my power slide," Mouse said. "But I'm still working on it."

"That I can tell," Chief said.

Mouse hung her head low, breathing heavily.

"Chin up, kid. You did a good job loosening up at the end. I bet that tackle didn't even hurt."

"No," Mouse said, "it didn't hurt." She kept her head low.

"You bounced right back!" Chief put his paw under her chin and lifted the fluffy little black-and-white head. "Okay, you caught me. Look, the only reason I stopped around this corner was because I couldn't run anymore. You're too fast."

Mouse smiled. Then she yelled, "Uncle Baxter!" and ran down the hallway, pouncing on Baxter.

Baxter rolled over and let Mouse tackle him. "Oh, you win, kid."

Mouse stood on Baxter and held up her paw in victory and then jumped down. Baxter rolled back to his feet.

"My, you are getting so big," Baxter said.

"Sam says I've only grown an inch in three months," Mouse said. "He says that's not much."

"Sure seems like a lot to me," Baxter said.

"Watch this, Uncle Baxter!" Mouse yelled as she ran down the hall, stopped, and rushed right back. "Dad's teaching me to run and pounce. I'm almost as fast as him." Mouse bounced in a circle around Baxter.

"Wow. Look at that," Baxter said, grinning. "You got the fire of the Protectors in you."

"The Protectors?" Mouse asked.

Chief shook his head at Baxter, indicating he didn't want to talk about it.

"Well, that's something your father's going to have to tell you about."

"Your mom's probably wondering where we are," Chief said. "Go tell her I'll be done in a little while."

"Bye, Uncle Baxter," Mouse said and ran down the hallway.

"Go get 'em, tiger," Baxter said.

Chief watched Mouse disappear down the stairs.

"Man, just like her dad," Baxter said.

"What's that?" Chief asked, coming up beside Baxter.

"She's got your speed, Chief. I can see it, and only six months old. She's getting big."

"Almost seven now," Chief said, turning around. He and Baxter trotted back to the small room where Chief stayed.

"Wow, has it been that long? Seems like just yesterday she was a rookie."

Chief frowned and lowered his eyebrows. "You really think she looks bigger?"

"Not so much," Baxter said. "Just trying to cheer you up—and her. She is fast and has a lot of spirit. That's got to count for something."

Chief lowered his head again. "Not if those rats come back. One day they will."

"Look at it this way." Baxter stood in front of Chief. "She's still fast, and you should be proud of that, you know. You should savor the moments of her childhood. She isn't going to be that cute and cuddly forever. She's the offspring of a true Protector, not just a bruiser like me. I was hired for my muscle, not my skill. Eventually she'll have the calling, and it's for a reason. You'll have to explain it to her. Have you told her anything?"

"No, not yet. She's spirited enough already without me telling her about our mission to protect humans. I didn't want to add to her little ego. You should have seen the way she chased after me today."

Baxter laughed. "See, I told you she had spirit."

"Are you hungry?" Chief asked as they entered the apartment. Charlene and Mouse were there, but Sam was out. Chief looked around the kitchen but didn't find anything to offer. "Sorry, Baxter, I don't have any food out. Sam's been busy. Ms. Sorenson has him jumping all the time. He doesn't seem as happy lately."

"I give that lady a wide berth when I see her," Baxter said. "She's probably driving him crazy."

"That doesn't sound hard for her. She wears enough perfume; it's like a beacon warning that she's getting near. And the smell of smoke." Chief shared a laugh with Baxter.

"Don't worry about it," Baxter said. "I'm not hungry anyway. Besides, you got a family to feed, and I need to stay in shape. I don't get as much activity since you ran all the live food out of here. It has me kind of worried."

"What do you mean?" Chief asked.

"Maybe you did too good a job," Baxter said. "My landlady keeps talking about tough times and the economy. Whatever that means. Even told me I needed to stay in my room when I'm not out patrolling. People are complaining about allergies and stuff."

"Allergies?" Chief said. "You'd think they'd be grateful that we keep the rats away so they don't die of the plague or some other disease."

"Or wake up to mouse droppings all over their food," Baxter said.

"Or worse," Chief said, "there could be spirits."

"*Ooohh* ..." Baxter shivered. "I guess that's the nice thing about being in a new building. We don't have any of them to deal with yet."

"Come on," Chief said. "There's a good window on the second floor overlooking the main street. You can see lots of action outside."

The two cats sprinted to the second floor, went to the end of the hallway, and jumped to the window ledge. The window faced the main entrance to the apartment complex. The ledge was wide enough for them to sit upon as they watched the people coming and going on the sidewalk below.

"Come to think, I haven't seen a rat since you made that deal with Wilber. I can take it if people don't want me out in the halls all the time, but this boredom is killing me." Baxter rolled over, put his paws up in the air, closed his eyes, and hung his tongue out.

Chief laughed. For a moment, he forgot that his daughter was small and fluffy and that he worried about protecting her more than he worried about protecting his building.

"How could they buy all that stuff?" Baxter asked, bouncing back to the window. "Bags and bags of stuff. They use it for a few months, and then it all ends up in the basement in storage boxes and gives those rats a good place to hide." He looked down the hall. "It's so quiet here. You've got yourself one classy place, Chief."

"Yeah, clean and quiet. Not like the old days," Chief said. "Sam and I, we came from a motel. People didn't stay there for more than a few days at a time. No cafeteria and only three floors. It was in an area Sam refers to as the slums. I didn't know places like this even existed."

"That's where Sikes came from. He and Rascal came up here from the neighborhoods right around your motel."

"I worry about them," Chief said.

Baxter raised his eyes and looked at Chief. "What about them?"

"People around here are getting so picky lately. Ms. Sorenson, she's a mean one, and if she finds out they're out in the alley, well, they're dead."

"I guess you got a point. Things are changing."

"You ever wonder if the day will come when people won't want us around?" Chief asked.

Baxter didn't respond right away. "If people get a little ignorant for a while, then so be it. When our time is over, their time will be up, and it won't matter."

"Is that what you believe?"

"That is what is foretold. I might not be a Protector, but my father told me all about them," Baxter said, "all the legends … the special senses and the ability to ward off evil, the heightened speed and agility. He said when the humans no longer need the Protectors, the Protectors will cease to be, and so will humans. Are you going to tell Mouse about her heritage?"

"She's just so small. I worry about her all the time. Not every cat gets the calling, and if I tell her about them and she doesn't get the calling, she'll be crushed."

"Well," Baxter said, "I better get back and patrol. I'll tell Sikes to watch out for Ms. Sorenson."

"Thanks for coming by."

"No problem," Baxter said. "It gave me something exciting to do. Now I have to go back and do my patrol. My booorrriing patrol."

Chief didn't follow Baxter. He stayed at the window watching. He sensed something behind him and whipped around ready to defend himself. His eyes forward and claws out, he searched for a threat. He caught a whiff of a foul sensation in the air, but nothing was there. "Hmm," Chief said, "I'm sure I felt something for a moment." He trotted back to his apartment.

Down he went in the swirling water, spitting, choking, and not knowing if he would survive. *The humans will pay*, Bragar thought as he closed his eyes. If he survived, they would pay. His thoughts turned cold like the inside of his cage. Cold and alone. That's how they had kept him locked up for years before they had flushed him down the toilet. He remembered a conversation his captors had had as they'd watched him in his cage.

"There's something wrong with that one, Pete," the short, stocky man in the lab coat had said. "He sits there in his cage, staring at us all the time. He doesn't scurry around like the others do. He does the mazes as fast as any of them but doesn't eat at the end. He just sits there, glaring. It's like he's mocking us."

"Stop it, Joe," Pete had said. "You're creeping me out. He's a rat. An ugly one, but just a rat."

"Look at him," Joe had said. The two men had glanced into the cage.

Bragar had stared back at them, his red eyes unflinching. He'd hated the way they treated him.

"There's no telling what all that stuff he's been injected with has done to him," Pete had said.

"Kind of makes you glad you're not a rat, doesn't it?"

Pete had shivered and backed away from the cage. "We're done with our tests on him, and we have plenty of other rats. Throw him out if he bothers you that much."

"My pleasure."

"And, Joe," Pete had said.

"What?"

"Quit smoking down here. It'll ruin the experiments."

Bragar remembered being afraid as the gloved hand had reached down and taken hold, squeezing him, holding him tight as he'd been lifted out of the cage. He remembered the foul breath and odor of smoke. The other rats had looked on as the man had walked him into another room. There, in a round bowl with water turning and spinning, the man had dropped him.

Now he struggled to stay above the water, but he couldn't keep his eyes open to see where he was going. There was nothing to grab on to, and he went down with the swirling water. The light faded. He continued to spin in the darkness, choking in the water.

"They're going to pay for this!" Bragar yelled out before he lost consciousness.

Chapter 5
A Canary Told Me

In the early morning, Mouse nudged Chief's head with hers. "Dad, did you call me?" she asked.

He opened one eye and then shut it, hoping she would go away.

She nudged him again. "Dad, can we go on patrol? We're burning daylight."

"What?" Chief said, opening both eyes. "Burning daylight? Where did you hear that?"

"I heard it off a television show Sam was watching last night."

"You know you're not supposed to stay up late watching television," Charlene said.

"Well, I guess since the whole family is up anyway, I'm going on patrol!" Chief said.

"I'm ready for an adventure!" Mouse saluted her father and perked up her ears. She fluffed her tail and marched to the door.

Chief didn't follow.

"You told her you would let her tag along today," Charlene said and winked. "She's all yours."

"You're right," Chief said. "I guess there's no real danger. Come on, kid." He headed out the door, and Mouse followed.

"First thing we have to do is stretch out," Chief said.

Mouse pushed her paws out in front of her and lowered her body to the ground, yawning.

Chief took off down the hall, and Mouse raced after him as he zigzagged around the corners and up the stairs. He looked back at her and smiled, proud that she was keeping up with him.

Chief didn't stop until they reached the fifteenth floor and exited the stairway. Mouse came up beside him in the hallway.

"That's what I call warming up." Chief breathed heavily from the early-morning run. "We can train up here since no one else is around."

Mouse didn't stand still but bounced around on her feet. "Why doesn't anyone live up here? Why is there only one room on this floor? What floor are we on? I lost count."

Chief smiled. "You do have a lot of energy. We are on the fifteenth floor. This is what they call the penthouse, the top room that's bigger than the other rooms. Mr. and Mrs. Ryan live up here, but they have many buildings, so I don't think they stay here much. That's why your mother stays with us now."

"Why don't they come here more?"

"I don't know. Off building some other building I guess. Enough with the questions; let's start our lessons today. Remember what I told you: when running, make sure you don't get your claws too far out on the carpet, or you'll snag going around corners. Use your pads when you're on wood or slick floors like the lobby area. Rodents can't run well on slick floors either. Speed and stealth are your friends."

"What is *stealth*?" Mouse asked.

"It's the natural ability of all cats to sneak up on someone or something without them knowing it and then *pounce!*"

Mouse jumped back as Chief pounced high into the air and then landed with a thud.

"In your case, stealth is something we need to work on," Chief said. "First, you've got to learn to stand still."

Chief knew Mouse was trying to stay still, and she managed to stop bouncing, but her tail swished back and forth as though independently following its own instructions.

"Your biggest advantage is jumping or, as we call it, pouncing."

Chief's eyes narrowed, and he lowered his front legs and leaned back. His tail flew in one direction and then the other, keeping his body balanced as he shifted his weight. Mouse looked behind her, trying to find the invisible opponent he was homing in on. He waited until she turned around to face him, and then he jumped right over her to tackle the unseen foe.

"Wow, Dad." Mouse grinned, her eyes wide. "Great *pounce!*"

"That was a tuck-'n'-roll pounce," Chief said. "The key is to use all your body weight when coming down. You can take the air out of your opponent. Come on; you try." Chief backed up and sat down. "Pretend I'm a rat. Lower your front legs so you can push off with them, and put the weight on your back legs."

Mouse did as instructed.

"Good," Chief said. "Now narrow your eyes; that'll let 'em know you're serious. Focus on the moment you'll come down on your target. Once you feel it, pounce."

Mouse quickly jumped high. Chief tried to get out of the way, but she came down on him with a thump and rolled him over. He wrestled with her a moment and then lay back down on the floor.

"You win," he said.

Mouse bounced around celebrating her success.

Chief stood. "Fantastic." He grinned. "Did you trade those legs in for springs?" He looked at Mouse's feet. "I better check that you didn't get rabbit legs accidentally."

"Oh, Dad," Mouse said. "Did I do good?"

"You did great!"

"Can we pounce on some rats today, Dad?" Mouse's tail flung back and forth in the air.

"No, we won't see any today," Chief said. "I've run them out of here. Besides, it's not all fun, hunting rodents and stuff. It's dangerous work, and you need to leave it to me until you grow up. Understand?"

Mouse bounced up and down on her feet around her dad facing him. Chief wasn't sure she had heard a word he'd said. In a flash, he reached out his front paws and pinned her to the ground. "Listen," he said.

"Okay." Mouse's muffled voice came out from under his paws.

Chief relaxed his paws, and Mouse looked up at him.

"There's one place you must promise me you'll never go by yourself. I never want you to go to the basement without your mom or me. No, I take that back. You are never to go to the basement period."

"Why?" Mouse asked.

"That's where all the bad things hide out. Rodents, insects, snakes. They all find their way to the basement. It's just a bad place to be for a little cat. So promise me." Chief patted her head with his paw.

"I promise," Mouse said. Her head drooped with her voice.

"Hey, none of that," Chief said. "Come on; I'll take you to meet Ms. Doris. That'll be an adventure for you."

"Are we going to see Uncle Baxter today?"

"Patience, son—I mean, daughter. One thing at a time." Chief led her to the stairwell and headed down to the next floor.

They came off the stairs and went down the hallway of the fourteenth floor. At the end of the hall was a room with the door cracked open. Chief said, "Ms. Doris's apartment has a pet door, but she usually leaves her door open in the day anyway. I always go in to check on her. She's going to want to pet you, so purr and show her some manners."

"Oh, there's my hero," a woman called out. "And you've brought your little one, how sweet."

"That's Ms. Doris," Chief said, nodding to a white-haired,

plump, short lady with wrinkles. He was pleased that Mouse purred just as he had told her to when Doris petted her head.

"Come in," Ms. Doris said, leading them through a door into the kitchen, where she opened a can of tuna, put it in a bowl, and set it down on the floor. Then she sat down at the table, watching them eat. "Did your father tell you how he saved me?"

Mouse licked her lips and looked at Ms. Doris.

"Well," Ms. Doris continued, "one day I took an awful spill. Your father came by and noticed I was lying on the floor. He went to get help. Oh, dear, what a mess I was in. I might not be here today if it wasn't for him. He's a real hero."

Mouse looked at her dad and smiled. "Wow, Dad, you're a hero."

A whistling sound came from the other room.

"Dad? Do you hear that?" Mouse asked.

"Let's go into the other room and see what it is," Chief said. "Curiosity is natural in a cat. Don't be afraid to explore; use your senses to keep you safe."

Chief let Mouse lead the way, knowing there was no chance of danger. He followed her into a room full of afghans and brightly colored throw pillows that covered the couch and chairs. A knitting basket with multiple colors of yarn sat alongside a rocking chair. Chief stepped into the room and watched Mouse as she carefully approached the source of the sound: a little yellowish bird in a tall cage near a window. The bird was moving her head up and down as she sang. The bird stopped whistling.

"That was beautiful," Mouse said. The bird noticed Mouse and went to the edge of her cage.

"Hi, Chief," said the little bird that had fluffy yellow feathers, a small beak, and an orange spot on her chest.

"Hello, Ladie," Chief said. "This is my daughter, Mouse."

"My, you are a little fluff ball. You're so precious and cute," Ladie said.

Mouse narrowed her eyes and frowned. "I am not cute. I'm a hunter."

"I'm sorry," Ladie said. "I can see, yes. You look very brave and formidable."

"Formidable?" Mouse said, cocking her head sideways.

"It means tough and vicious," Ladie said.

"Oh," Mouse said. "I guess you're right."

"Well, it's a pleasure to finally meet you, Mouse," Ladie said. "I've heard all about you since the day you were born."

"You talk to my dad?" Mouse asked.

"I do sometimes," Ladie said. "But I also heard about you through the pigeon network."

"Pigeons?"

"Yes," Ladie said. "No one really pays attention to them, but they are everywhere and gather a lot of information."

Mouse smiled. "Oh, well, I don't know what a pigeon is. But you're a bird, aren't you?"

"Yes." Ladie laughed. "A canary to be precise. A fancy one at that."

"Why are you in a cage?" Mouse asked and jumped up on the chair next to Ladie's cage.

"Mouse," Chief said, "stay off the furniture."

Ladie backed into her cage away from Mouse. "My, you are a curious little one, aren't you? And straight to the point, just like your dad."

Chief nodded at Ladie, and Mouse jumped down beside him.

"It's safer in here, and I have everything I need," Ladie said.

"Safer?" Mouse said. "I guess that's true for a small bird. I'm not too worried about that."

"Oh no?" Chief said, smiling.

"I'm a prowler." Mouse crouched low and moved stealthily about the room, her eyes low, as though expecting something to jump out at her. "I need space."

"Okay, that's enough," Chief said. "We need to go. Ladie, make sure you call me if Ms. Doris needs anything."

"Yes, of course," Ladie said. "I'll sing you a song."

"Just whistle," Chief said. "A nice, short, crisp whistle will do."

"Chief, there's a boy on the fifth floor who lost his fancy pet mouse. I heard his mom talking to Sam about it. And please check on the baby while you're at it. He's in one of the apartments close to the laundry room."

"Great, a mouse in the building. Maybe someone will step on it."

"Chief!" Ladie scolded. "It's a pet."

"Well, I'll try not to kill it if I come across it, but I haven't sensed it around. We'll check on the baby later."

A pigeon flew up to the window and landed on the sill but did not come in.

"Uh-oh. A customer," Ladie said. "Chief, would you mind?"

"Hmm?" Chief said.

"You make my customers nervous," Ladie said.

"We were just leaving," Chief said. "Don't let that thing fly around in the building." The pigeon flew in and landed on the stool across from Ladie's cage where Mouse had sat.

"Come on, Mouse," Chief commanded.

"Dad, Ladie can talk."

"Yes, but we're cats. Remember what I told you: if the eyes face forward, it's a predator, a hunter. Animals that have eyes on the side of their faces are prey. We are hunters. Birds are prey. Cats don't associate with prey."

"But we talked to her."

"That's because I was being polite. Besides, it was business. She knows a lot about what's going on around this complex."

"She hears it from the pigeons," Mouse said.

"Cats chase pigeons."

Mouse looked back to the apartment. "Oh, I didn't know."

"Well, that's just the way things are," Chief said.

"She could sing, and it was lovely," Mouse said. "I don't know if I could ever eat such a lovely bird, even if I was really, really, really hungry. Nope, not even then."

Chief frowned down at her and shook his head. "Yes, canaries sing." He stopped in the hallway and looked at Mouse.

Mouse sat back on her legs and put her chest out.

"If you are going to be a Protector, you better learn how it works. Our job is to keep the building clear of vermin," Chief said.

"Vermin?"

"Yes. Most anything that crawls around and is not a cat is considered a disease-carrying, disgusting vermin," Chief said. He tilted his head and added, "Unless the humans keep it as a pet. Then you have to be careful, because they get upset if you kill one of their pets."

"Like Ladie?"

"Yes. If it's in a cage or has a collar around its neck, there's a good chance it's a pet."

"Is that why Ladie doesn't fly away?" Mouse asked. "Because she's a pet?"

"I don't think Ladie can fly. Otherwise, she wouldn't be in that cage," he said. "It's a waste. She sits there all day letting those pigeons come into her place. They sit on that stool talking, and then they go back outside. I guess even humans don't want them around."

"At least we can roam about, right, Dad?"

"Enough about that, we need to get back to our lesson. Attention!" Chief commanded. He paced back and forth in front of Mouse. "Ears forward. Chest out. Now back to vermin. Mice are small and harmless, but they are pests just the same and must be dealt with. Snakes are rare but dangerous. If you ever see one, you are to get me immediately. Lizards, moles, big spiders, and anything that's crawling around on the floor that looks like it doesn't belong here needs to be dealt with. Finally, the worst of all and our main enemy is the rat. They are dirty, diseased, and lazy, and people hate them."

"Right, rats are bad," Mouse said.

Chief walked in front of her, and she put her chin up and chest out.

"The alley cats are not allowed to stay inside the building. When Sam has extra food, I try to give a few pieces to Sikes. He's the leader. They help keep the rats under control in the alleys and stuff. I've let them come inside on occasion, but I never let them stay. They'll move in, and they don't have manners. That'll make the people mad, and then we'll all be out on the street."

"No alley cats inside," Mouse said. Her eyes moved back and forth as though connected to a pencil that was jotting down notes.

"Now are you ready to continue our patrol?"

"Yes, sir!"

Chief bolted across the hall, looked back at her, and winked. Every day with her was a new adventure, and she had lots of energy to keep up with him.

They went into the storage rooms and into the kitchen. They went to the lobby and into the vacant apartment on the fifth floor where Sam stored extra furniture. Every so often, they'd stop, and Chief would teach her something new.

"Some people don't mind having us around," Chief said. "They leave their doors open and will even give you treats. It's okay to eat, but never stuff yourself. Otherwise, you won't be able to run and pounce. Make sure you check any areas where food is stored or thrown out—pantries, garbage cans, stuff like that."

"For vermin, right?"

"Right," Chief said. "They need to eat too, so those are common places where they hang out."

Chief taught Mouse how to pounce when running and how to get the high ground on stairs in case she ran into trouble.

"That's a good day on patrol," Chief said, catching his breath as they came to their apartment.

Mouse jumped up and down with excitement.

"You sure have a lot of energy, kid," Chief said.

"Am I ready to be a Protector now, Dad?" Mouse asked, her tail moving back and forth behind her.

"Attention!" Chief commanded. "Eyes and ears forward. Chest out. Now the question was, are you ready to be a Protector?"

"Dad," Mouse asked, "what's a Protector?"

Chief moved close to her and sat down. "The Protectors are as old as life itself," Chief said. "We were chosen among all animals to protect people from all evil in the world. It's a battle from ancient times."

"Is every cat a Protector?"

"No, not every cat, only those descended from the chosen ones. But all cats have a responsibility to help the Protectors. It's our destiny."

Mouse stared down the hallway. "What was that?" Mouse stiffened. "Dad, I think I saw something move down the hall."

"What did you see?"

"Something weird," Mouse said. "A black shadow."

Chief ran down the stairs to the first floor. Mouse followed.

Once at the bottom, Chief stopped. *The spirit of the Protectors here?* Chief thought. "Mouse, what did you see?"

"Nothing, Dad. I thought I saw something. But it was just a shadow."

"A shadow?" Chief said. "Are you sure?"

"Why, Dad? What does it mean?"

"When I was young and the spirit of the Protectors first came to me, it was in the form of a shadow dancing along an alley. It called to me. After that day, I changed and had the instincts of the Protectors."

"What instincts?" Mouse asked.

"Nothing you need to worry about now. I'll tell you more about the Protectors later. As of today, you are an official Junior Protector. You are hereby assigned the fourteenth floor."

Mouse's eyes grew wider, and she smiled. "You really think I'm ready?"

"You can be anything you want to be," Chief said. "All you have to do is believe. Now, you are to check on Ms. Doris three times a day, morning, after lunch, and after dinner. Once you have fulfilled your mission, I will tell you more about what being a Protector is all about. Now get some food, and then it's time for bed."

Chief and Mouse walked back to the apartment. The door was half-open as Chief peeked in.

"Mom! Mom!" Mouse yelled as she ran by him and entered the room. "I'm an official Junior Protector."

Chapter 6
Never Try; Never Fail

Deep in the sewers below the apartment complex, two rats broke away from the rest of the pack—one short and stout with small feet, whose body and hefty appetite had earned him the nickname Slim, and a tall, thin, lazy fellow with a long nose by the name of Slouch. In the dark tunnels, they made a peculiar pair.

"Hey, what you got over there?" Slim asked.

"Another one of these things!" Slouch said, holding up the white wrapper.

"Oh, another diaper."

"Don't those people read the directions? They're not supposed to flush 'em down the toilets."

"Lucky us! Save some for me," Slim said.

"No. What I mean is that they'll clog up their drains. Then when the water won't drain, they'll pour all those cleaners down them." Slouch screwed his nose up and winced.

"Yeah, right. That would make it stink down here." Slim kept a straight face for a moment and then slowly grinned. Then the two rats broke out laughing.

"Oh, that was a good one," Slim said.

"My sides hurt," Slouch said, pawing his side.

"Mine too," Slim said, and they kept laughing.

"You're so round you don't have sides," Slouch said, and the two laughed some more.

"Sometimes you get me going," Slim said, wiping the tears from his eyes.

"Hey, Slim," Slouch said, "have you noticed a few more rats hanging out down here than was here before?" Slouch pointed to several clusters of rats nearby in the same tunnel.

"Yeah, now that you said so, I did notice that. That old Wilber is sure getting tough with all his rules. Now he has all the buildings and alleys, and guys like us get stuck down here in the sewers." Slouch leaned up against the wall, his body resting against it as though he were holding it up.

"Them were the good ol' days then," Slim said. "When we were with Wilber, we had plenty of food. Good food. Pastas and sauces." He licked his lips as he sat down against the wall.

"Too many rules," Slouch said. "It was always 'Do this; do that. Comb your hair. Don't burp at the table. Don't pee upstream of the camp.'"

"Yep, I'm sure glad we're out on our own. No more rules. No more responsibilities."

"You said it. Too much to do and not enough fun then. Well, no more. Never try; never fail—that's my motto," Slouch said.

"Your motto?"

"Yes," Slouch said. "You see, too many people wear themselves out trying to get somewhere. I say, if you try once, that's enough." Slouch spread his hands wide. "Anything that don't come easy ain't meant to me."

"Ain't meant to *be*?" Slim said, puzzled.

"That's right," Slouch sang out as he snapped his fingers. "You see, it's a philosophy."

"A what?"

"A philosophy." Slouch sang:

Hmm, hmm.

Everyone wants to be happy.

They spend their time running around.

I say, what's the hurry?

Kick back and settle down.

Slouch pulled up a piece of wood and offered the seat to Slim, who sat down as Slouch continued to sing:

Life's better when you gots no worries.

That's the way it should be.

You can live life to its fullest

When you gots no responsibilities.

Slim snapped his fingers along with the song and got up from his seated position. "Oh, now I see; it's a philosophy," Slim said. "Puts it all into perspective."

"Into what?" Slouch asked.

"The way you see things."

"Oh, well, that's what I'm telling you," Slouch said and started singing again.

When everyone's trying to get ahead,

always worried about being behind,

I say it's time to just let it go,

Nothing wrong with the back of the line.

What's the point of working so hard

When you could take a nice, long nap?

Is it worth all the worry and hurry

For the better part of the table scraps?

Slim took over the song and sang:

Life's better with no one to tell you,

"Go and clean up your room."

I say, "I gots plans," and hang up that ol' broom.

"What plans do you gots?"

"Doing nothing."

Slouch took the lead again:

They'll say we're lazy.

I say they're crazy

Thinking they are free.

It's my philosophy.

Life's better; you'll live longer …

When you gots no responsibiliteeeeeeeeeee.

"Oh, you make me laugh," Slim said.

"We got each other now. That's why we got to stick together," Slouch said wisely. "You and me. We look out for ourselves. We'll make our own rules and make sure these rats don't move in on our territory."

"We got territory?" Slim shrugged his shoulders as he sat down, his paws open in front of him.

"Of course. These lower tunnels down here is our territory. Let Wilber have the part under the restaurants; that's fine. This cave, those pipes, that water running through the tunnel, even that junk floating in the water that looks like—" He stopped for a moment, and Slim followed his stare.

"Hey, what is that?" Slim asked. "Looks like a deranged bunny rabbit or something."

Slim and Slouch ran to the water's edge. "Looks kinda like us, but it's white," Slim said. "And ugly." The mass of soggy hair floated to the edge and stopped in front of them. "Give me a hand." Slim waded out and pulled the mass out of the water.

"Aaah!" Slim and Slouch both screamed and jumped back as the thing moved.

Beady red eyes peered out at them. "It's alive!" Slouch said.

"Do something—mouth-to-mouth, beat on its chest." Slim spun in circles.

Slouch raised his leg and kicked the creature in the chest. The thing sputtered, and water flowed out of its mouth. Its eyes focused on Slim.

"We thought you were dead, dude," Slim said.

"You," a raspy male voice said. The creature coughed, and congested words sputtered forth. "You … come here."

"I think he means you," Slouch said, backing up a step so that Slim was in front of him.

"No," Slim said, stepping back and pushing Slouch forward, "he means you."

"You," the thing said, struggling to stand, "fat one."

"Me?" Slim said, pointing his finger at himself and looking around as though trying to find someone else to be him. "I'm not fat—slightly overweight and metabolically challenged, you know, slow metabolism."

"Tell me your name!" the creature, now recognizably a rat, commanded.

"It's Slim. Are you okay, dude? I mean, what happened to you? You look like you fell into some bleach or something."

"I'm Bragar," the white rat said, not answering the questions. His eyes glared, and he growled through his teeth. Standing up, he stretched out to his full length and let out an awful, unnatural growl. Slim and Slouch cowered against the wall and started edging their way away from their find. Bragar was bigger than they were, not fat like Slim or tall and thin like Slouch, but long and muscular with long, sharp teeth. The big rat shook the water out of his fur.

"Where are we?" Bragar asked, moving toward Slim, who stood on his hind legs and pushed his back against the concrete to no avail.

"We're in the sewers?" Slim replied. "Below the city?"

"Is that a question?" Bragar's tone increased as he towered over Slim.

"No, no, dude," Slouch said, trying to help Slim. "We are in the sewers, below the city. Ain't you never been down here?"

Bragar's nose twitched back and forth as he sniffed the air around him.

"It's a good thing we found you when we did," Slim said.

"Down that dark tunnel you were heading is Plummeting Falls. No rat's ever come back from there."

"Yeah, we should know. That's where we used to send the rats Wilber didn't like when we worked for him," Slouch said.

"Wilber?" Bragar said.

"He's the rat that's in charge down here," Slim said.

"But we don't work for him anymore," Slouch said. "We're independents."

"Hmmm." Bragar looked around and pointed to the other rats. "And them?"

"They're independents too," Slouch said. "Wilber controls the territory around us, but he doesn't come down here much. Rats live in the sewer, but Wilber, he's, like, classy and stylish and such."

"I can understand," Bragar said. "It's dark, smelly, and scruffy. What are you two doing down here?"

"Us?" Slouch said. "Man, we own this place." He crossed his arms and nodded. Slim nodded back. "We're, like, in charge of all those rats over there. Hey, you," Slouch cried out to the group of rats. The rats looked up at him for a moment and then continued ignoring him.

"That's right, as you were." Slim nodded. "They're, like, on break. Good help's hard to find, you know."

Bragar's red eyes shifted between the two of them.

Slim felt the eyes penetrate through him, and he trembled. "Okay, okay, we're outcasts," he said. "Wilber threw us out of the pack. We live down here in the drainpipes."

"Yeah." Slouch nodded. "But we don't care. There's more space down here. Uh, who are you, anyway?"

"I ..." Bragar started to say and then cleared his throat. "I come from above. I am ... an outcast too."

"Hey, just like us," Slouch said, happily grinning. He moved from the wall and over to Bragar and patted him on the back. "Where'd you get those cool eyes, dude? They're, like, red. I've never seen a dude like you. Most of us have boring black eyes. Except Slim. If you look real close, one eye's bigger than the other."

"Hey!" Slim said, elbowing Slouch. "You're not supposed to tell." Then he turned to Bragar. "What's up with the whole white fur thing? You look like you got too much sun up there."

Bragar's eyes narrowed, and he stood up, sniffing the air. "There are no people down here?"

"No," Slouch said. "That's the beauty of it all. The only time they come down here is if they're building something new or fixing something. So don't break anything."

"Hey." Slim scratched his head as though he had to rub the next sentence out. "You can hang with us. We gots plenty of room. You can be part of our pack. I mean, although you're, like, a weird color and all."

Slouch smacked Slim on the back of the head.

"What did you do that for?" Slim asked.

"Be nice to our guest." Slouch shook his finger and his head. Then he looked at Bragar. "You're cool, dude," Slouch said. "That color does you good and all. In fact, you'd be easy to find in a crowd, and it does get crowded down here once in a while."

Bragar came back down on all fours and looked at the two brown rats in front of him. His stomach growled.

"Man, I bet Wilber's guys wouldn't mess with you," Slouch said. "You're huge, dude. We should, like, hang out. You know, stick together. Safety in numbers and all that." He leaned back against the wall.

"Are you in some type of exercise program or something?" Slim asked. "I mean, I could go for something like that, you know, maybe like ten minutes a week or something."

"Hmmm," Bragar said and started walking in the opposite direction that the water flowed.

"Where you going?" Slouch asked. He left his leaning position against the wall and hurried to catch up with Bragar. Slim followed.

"You want to hang out?" Slouch asked. "We got some food back there stashed in the pipe. It's getting close to dinnertime, and people flush all kinds of food down the sewer. I bet we can get a good spot by the drain tonight if you stick with us."

Bragar continued walking. "You would let me be part of your pack?"

"Oh, yeah, you know, it's exclusive and all, but we could waive the membership fee for you. We can show you around and stuff," Slouch said.

Slim scratched his head. "Our own pack. That sounds cool." He stopped walking and watched as Bragar continued up the tunnel. "Hey, you don't want to go that way. That's Wilber's territory."

Bragar turned and stood on his hind legs, showing his full height. Slim saw other rats in the area turn and take notice of Bragar. Bragar murmured, barely audible, "An army, just waiting to be led." After a moment, Bragar said louder, "You say there are no humans down here?"

"Nope," Slouch said.

"None of you have run a maze, been given shots, or been shocked?" Bragar asked.

"No idea what you just said," Slim said.

"Perfect," Bragar said. His eyes narrowed and glowed. "But you are not free to go where you want if this Wilber doesn't let you. Does Wilber have more rats in his pack than are in this tunnel?"

"Not if you count the vile rats," Slouch said, scratching his head. "Wilber's rats are just tougher. You know, work out more and stuff."

"Ah," Bragar said, "they know how to fight." He began walking up the tunnel again.

"Wait," Slouch said. "That's Wilber's territory, remember?"

"You can stay down here if you like," Bragar said loudly. "Or you can follow me, and I will teach you how to fight and give you equal shares in everything I come upon." His raspy voice echoed off the sewer walls. Then he turned and looked at the other rats clustered throughout the tunnel. "That goes for everyone." He started walking again.

"Hey, who's that guy?" a small, scruffy-looking rat asked.

"Oh, hi, Darts," Slim said. "We just found him floating in the water."

"If he's not from around here," Darts said, "maybe he knows where some food is."

Darts and several brown rats passed by Slim and Slouch and started following Bragar. Slim and Slouch looked at each other, and Slouch shrugged his shoulders. They ran in front of the herd of rats now streaming from the tunnel.

"Hey, we saw him first. No cutting in line," Slim said as he and Slouch did their best to push their way to the front of the pack and catch up to Bragar.

"What's the plan then?" Slouch asked as he finally reached Bragar.

Bragar looked behind him and smiled. "I've found my flock. Now I'm going to make those people pay."

"What people?" Slim asked.

"All people," Bragar said. "They treat us like garbage. I'll show them."

"What is that look?" Charlene asked, stepping beside Chief, who was watching their daughter sleep. "It almost looks like you're happy."

"What do you mean?" Chief asked.

"Well, you never look at our little girl that way," Charlene said. She lay down on a fluffy white matt. "Like you're satisfied. You usually stare at her as if doing so would make her grow more."

Chief looked at Charlene and then back to Mouse. "I don't mean it. I just don't know how to treat her at times."

"You treat her like your parents treated you as a kid?" Charlene asked.

"My parents?" Chief said. He felt embarrassed. "I grew up on the streets until Sam took me in."

Charlene moved closer to him. "Surely you remember something."

Chief tried but couldn't think of anything. "Well, it doesn't matter. She's got a lot of spunk and energy. I told her she did good today."

"That's nice," Charlene said. "I take it since you've been out all day you don't need to patrol tonight."

"No patrol tonight," Chief said. "She wore me out." He smiled, and he and Charlene lay down next to each other.

Charlene fell asleep, purring beside him. He was tired, but he couldn't sleep. Instead, he watched Mouse sleeping. He realized the feeling he had was something new. For once, he wasn't disappointed that she was so small. Mouse had been wonderful all day. She'd listened to his instructions and excelled at everything he'd asked her to do.

Hours passed, and Chief was still unable to sleep. He sat up and walked out into the hallway. "Maybe I've been too busy to pay attention," he said to himself. "But busy doing what? Avoiding being part of the family I wanted? The apartment is safe … What am I worried about?"

"You're worried about not being a good father," a voice said from down the hallway.

Chief jumped to his feet, and his eyes immediately fixed on the figure on the floor. "Ladie? What are you doing down here?" Chief walked down the hallway to where the little bird stood.

"Sorry, Chief," Ladie said and backed away from him. "I spend all day giving advice. I just couldn't help but do it for you as well."

"Is that what you do? I never imagined. Why are you here? Is there something wrong with Ms. Doris?"

"No, Carl told me something I thought you needed to know."

"Carl?" Chief asked. "The pigeon?"

"Please don't call him that. He's very sensitive. He's a cockatoo."

Chief shook his head. "Get to the point. What's so important that you'd risk coming all the way down here?"

"You need to check on Paggs," Ladie said. "That's all." Ladie turned and raised her wings to fly.

"Wait!" Chief said. "Why? Why do I need to check on Paggs? Is something wrong with him?"

"I thought I'd be brief since you wanted me to get to the point."

Chief looked around, making sure no one else was listening to his conversation. "I'm sorry. What is it?"

"Paggs is fine," Ladie said.

"Then what? What is it?" Chief shook his head as Ladie looked around the hall, repeating what he'd done just moments before. "There's no one else awake at this hour."

"Well, I don't want to start a panic if someone overhears us talking," Ladie said. "There's something going on in his building. There's word on the street that some rats are moving underground. It might be best if you check it out."

Chief chuckled. "So that's what you do all day: give advice and gossip."

He started walking back to his apartment. Ladie flew over him and landed so close in front of him that her beak touched his nose, causing it to twitch. Ladie's eyes narrowed, and Chief backed away.

"Look," Ladie said, "you just go check on him tomorrow, and I'm sure you'll find out all you need to know. Then you can thank me. You saved Ms. Doris once, and I'm paying you back. Now we're even." Ladie jumped up and flew down the hall.

"Does Ms. Doris know you can get out?" Chief called out.

Ladie winked back at him and kept on flying.

"Why, that little faker," he muttered. Then he went back to bed.

The next morning, Chief took Mouse on a patrol while he thought about how he would handle Ladie's warning.

"Dad, what's that sound?" Mouse asked. The two cats traveled down the hall on the fifth floor. "It sounds like someone's in distress."

Chief curled his lips. "That is a baby, a little person." Chief moved to the side of the hallway as the stroller went by. "They are annoying, slobber a lot, and are noisy. But it's our job to watch out for them too. We need to keep a close eye on that one. His mother is always on the phone and doesn't pay attention to her surroundings."

"They sure do cry a lot," Mouse said as the mother and baby continued down the hall.

"As long as they're in the stroller or in a crib, they're harmless. But if one gets out on the floor, look out." Chief licked his paw and groomed the side of his face and head. "Whatever they grab on to goes in their mouths."

"Eww!" Mouse cringed.

"I know," Chief said. "It's disgusting. If that happens to you and the mother is around, you've just got to take it. If the mother's not around, hiss a little or give the kid a little smack with your paw, and he'll learn his lesson. Now let's get on with our patrol."

"Are we going to stay out all day again today?"

"I don't suppose it will hurt anything. Why, did you have plans?"

"No." Mouse's eyes grew wide. "I think I prefer being out here with you instead of in the apartment all day with Mom."

"Really? You don't think it's fun to sit for hours in the warm sun coming in from the window?"

"Nope." Mouse kept her chin up and marched beside him.

"You wouldn't rather be chasing around the apartment playing with all those toys Sam bought for you?"

"It's boring," Mouse said. "I want to get out and explore."

"Well, that's just like a Protector," Chief said. "I'm gonna show you something today, but you have to promise me you won't ever go on your own and that you will never, ever leave this building." He stopped walking.

Mouse stopped. "Oh, I promise," she said, smiling from ear to ear.

"Follow me," Chief said and raced out the window onto the fire escape. He looked back to make sure Mouse kept up and led her all the way to the roof.

"*Wow!*" Mouse said, looking down at the alley and around at the other buildings. "This is great!"

"Over there is Uncle Baxter's building." Chief pointed. "And there is Paggs's building."

"You can see forever from here." Her nose twitched back and forth. "And there's a lot of smells out here that are different from inside."

"I've got to go see Paggs today," Chief said. "We'll have to finish up our patrol first."

"Can I go with you?"

"Not today," Chief said.

Mouse hung her head.

"Chin up; let's take things one step at a time. This is your first time outside. I don't need you getting lost," Chief said, putting his paw under Mouse's chin. Her bright eyes looked up at him, and he smiled.

"Can we stay up here just a few more minutes?" Mouse pleaded.

"Sure," Chief said and sat down.

"Where does Uncle Sikes live?" Mouse asked.

"Down there between the buildings." Chief pointed with his

paw. "Where those big green-and-black cubes are; those are the trash Dumpsters."

Mouse looked out across the skyline at all the buildings. "I never knew the world was so big. Are there cats in all these buildings?"

"Most, I think," Chief said. "Not as many as there used to be."

"Why not?"

"At one time, people depended on cats to keep the rodents away. This prevented disease and kept their food safe. Now they have other ways: poisons, traps, and even dogs."

"What's a dog?" Mouse asked.

"You'll know if you see one," Chief answered. "Most of the time, your senses will kick in if it's a mean dog and tell you danger is at hand."

Mouse squinted and cocked her head to one side.

"Okay," Chief said, "if you see some goofy, furry animal walking on four legs that does everything people tell it to do and hangs its tongue out of its mouth a lot, then that's a dog. Oh, and they bark at everything."

"Oh," Mouse said. "And they don't like us?"

"Nope. They're not quite as classy as us," Chief said. "And they're jealous, so they're usually not in a good mood. Come on, kid. Let's go."

The two cats raced down to their apartment, where they stopped for a drink.

"Oh, Dad," Mouse said, "can't I stay out for a little while longer?"

Chief sighed. "Well, I guess we haven't checked the bottom four floors. I'll make you a deal."

Mouse pranced around in a circle and settled back in front of her dad.

"If you promise to stay off the elevator and don't go higher than the fifth floor except to check on Ms. Doris, you can stay out until dinner. But keep it to the first five floors, and make sure you're home in time for supper. I've got to go check on Paggs," Chief said and headed down the hall. He turned around before he reached the staircase and called back, "Don't go near the basement!"

"Thanks, Dad!" Mouse said.

Mouse ran to the fifth floor and into the furniture storage room. She'd already decided it was her favorite place in the building because of all the stuff it had to explore. She jumped across mattresses, bed frames, dressers, chairs, and all sorts of furniture.

Suddenly, Mouse stopped. She sensed something. Her ears perked up, and she inhaled deeply as she moved to the doorway. She looked down the hall. Her ears stretched out, and she heard a faint noise.

"The laundry room," she said and crouched down to her best stealthy stance. She crept along the wall until she came to the edge of the room and stopped. A shuffling of plastic came from within, but there were no people present.

There's no one else around, so it's up to me to get to the bottom of this, Mouse thought. She pounced through the door, fluffing her tail and raising the hair on her back to make herself appear larger to whatever lay inside the room. Claws out, she stopped just inside the doorway and prepared to attack.

Mouse carefully scanned the room, but nothing appeared out of the ordinary. In the middle of the laundry room, some clothes had been spilled onto the floor, including a pair of short blue pants that were inside out. A small piece of partially wrapped candy stuck out of a small hole in one of the pants pockets. Mouse noticed bite marks on the candy. *Something's been in here eating,* she thought. She kept her eyes forward on the evidence, scouting for any motion.

There! The jeans moved. *There's something under them!*

Mouse closed in. Her tail twitched to give her balance, and she prepared to pounce. She kept perfectly quiet and reached out, putting her left paw on the corner of the pants. The lump underneath stopped moving.

Mouse held her position and waited. The small lump moved down the leg of the pants to the end and then paused. Suddenly, a tiny pink nose with whiskers emerged from under the pants and stopped. It twitched around. Then a fuzzy black-and-white body appeared with large ears. *That's not a rat or a snake or a lizard. Is it a mouse?*

"Stop, you!" Mouse called out.

Bulging, beady black eyes perched on a small, curious face turned slowly and looked at Mouse. The whiskers and nose went totally still, as if by remaining motionless the mouse thought it would make itself invisible.

"I can still see you!" Mouse declared.

The eyes closed tightly and then peeked again.

"Still see you," Mouse said.

"Who, me?" the creature asked in a little voice.

"Yes, you. Why aren't you running?" Mouse lifted up one paw to show her sharp claws at the end.

The little creature stood up on her hind legs and peered behind Mouse to the door. "Why? Is there someone scary coming?"

"Me, you silly little mouse."

"Mouse? Where?"

"You," Mouse said. "I'm sure that's what you are. You're not big enough to be a rat, and you're definitely not a dog or a bird. I've met a bird."

"Oh"—the little creature looked down at herself—"I guess I'm a mouse. What are you?"

"I am a cat. A Junior Protector," Mouse said, narrowing her eyes. "And I am fori … forma … *formidable!*"

"Hmm. I've never seen a cat. I'm definitely not a cat. You're kind of fluffy and cute. Maybe we could be friends. I'm Little

Foot. I don't have any friends. And no one comes down here but those people and their big feet. *Stomp, stomp, stomp!*" Little Foot walked in a circle with large steps.

"Friends?" Mouse said. Her eyes grew large, and her tail lost its twitch. "I'm a cat. You're a mouse. How can we be friends?"

"I don't know much about being a mouse," Little Foot said. "I've never met anyone like me. I've always wanted to have a friend. Those people and their big feet, always stomping. It's nice to meet another floor dweller. I hide a lot, so I don't get many chances to meet anyone. I can be your friend, if you want. It's easy. Just tell me your name."

Mouse relaxed and sat down. "You don't have fleas, do you?" Mouse asked.

"What are fleas?"

"Well, they carry diseases and are dangerous to people. And I … well, I'm supposed to protect the people in these apartments."

"I don't know anything about fleas," Little Foot said, looking around the room and behind her. She held her tail nervously in her hands.

"Do you have to itch a lot, I mean, like something is crawling on you?" Mouse asked.

"No," Little Foot said, twisting her tail around. "I did have a boy that picked me up a lot, but he held me too tight all the time. I don't know where he went. I think these were his pants."

"Well, then you don't have anything to worry about." Mouse looked at Little Foot, who smiled at her. She was confused about the whole situation now and didn't know what to say to the tiny little creature. Unlike the rats that her father had told her about, this little mouse seemed harmless, and she couldn't bring herself to kill it. "Curious."

"What?" Little Foot asked.

"I said *curious*. That's something my dad says when I do something that he can't figure out."

"What does he do after he says *curious*?" Little Foot asked.

"He just says *curious* and then goes on doing what he's doing."

"Oh." Little Foot nodded as though she'd found some new wisdom. "So what's your name?"

Mouse looked back to the door and listened. She heard nothing. She turned back to Little Foot. "I'll tell you, but you better not laugh. It's Mouse."

"Pleased to meet you, Mouse," Little Foot said. "That's a fine name. Oh!"

Mouse noticed Little Foot looking at her eyes. "Yes, I know; I have two different-colored eyes. Kind of strange."

"I think they're lovely," Little Foot said. "It makes you unique and special."

"That's what my mom tells me."

Suddenly, Little Foot stood on her hind legs and twitched her ears. "Shh! Someone's coming down the hall. Follow me." Little Foot ran around the washers and dryers to a set of shelves and wiggled in between some boxes.

Mouse followed as best she could and squeezed into the tight area. She listened. "I don't hear anything," she said.

"Wait." Little Foot moved her ears forward.

Mouse perked her ears up and finally heard footsteps, human footsteps. They passed the laundry room and headed down the hall.

"We're okay," Little Foot said and stroked her tail with her tongue.

"You have good ears."

"Great ears. I can hear anything," Little Foot said, raising her head.

"How come you didn't hear me coming?" Mouse asked, walking out from among the boxes to the middle of the laundry room.

Little Foot walked out as well and examined Mouse's paws. "I think it's your feet." She poked at one. "They're padded, so you don't stomp, and your hair is fluffy. I did hear a sound, but it was faint and didn't sound dangerous."

"Humph," Mouse said. She fluffed her fur and snapped her tail back and forth. "Not dangerous? I am a hunter. I have the heart of a lion and the speed of a cheetah. The reason you didn't hear me is I was in stealth mode."

"Wow, stealth mode! That sounds wonderful," Little Foot said. "I bet we can be best friends."

"We can't be friends. I'm telling you, I'm a cat. I'm supposed to eat you."

Little Foot lowered her head and sat back on her hind legs. She took her tail in her front paws and wiped her eyes, shedding a small tear. "Well, then, you can eat me if you need to. I mean, if you're hungry." She sniffled.

Mouse looked at the pathetic, small creature. "I don't think I can eat you. Maybe I can just chase you out of the building or something."

"You can't eat me? Why not?" Little Foot stood up on her hind legs to look at Mouse at eye level.

"Because you're not trying to get away. I'm supposed to chase you first. And then pounce on you."

"Oh, I can run a little." She moved around Mouse in a circular pattern. "I'll try not to go too fast; that way you won't get hurt."

"Hurt! Ha, I'm a predator. I laugh in the face of danger. Ha."

"You seem very brave." Little Foot stopped running. "I wish I could be that brave." She lowered her eyes to the ground.

"You must be brave," Mouse said. "You are standing here talking to one of the most formidable hunters the world has ever known."

"Forma-formidable ... I mean, me? Brave?" Little Foot's ears perked up, and her eyes no longer drooped.

"Yes," Mouse said, happy to see Little Foot wasn't so depressed. "In fact, you're so brave I don't think I can eat you. Besides, I've never eaten anything still moving. I don't know if my stomach would agree with it, and I can't patrol on an upset stomach."

"Even if I run, like this?" Little Foot trotted a few steps.

"No, no, no," Mouse said. "That won't work at all. Too slow. Besides, you're too small, and I don't even know if you would taste good."

"That's not a very nice thing to say," Little Foot said. Turning back around, she went up to Mouse. "How do you know I won't taste good?"

"I'm sorry," Mouse said, noticing Little Foot was upset. "I'm sure you taste good. I'm just full, and I'm not interested in eating something that has so much fur anyway. It might cause me to have indigestion."

"Oh," Little Foot said, stepping back from Mouse. "In that case, can we be friends?"

Not knowing what to say, Mouse said nothing.

With ears drooping and smile gone, Little Foot slowly turned and walked away. "I guess I'll just be on my way then, just me, *all alone*, not a friend in the world. No family, *no* friends. Poor, *loooonesome* me." She looked back at Mouse one more time.

"Oh, stop that," Mouse said. She went to the doorway and looked down the hall. She knew her dad would not approve. "As long as he doesn't find out."

"As long as who doesn't find out?" Little Foot shot across the room, crawled up under Mouse's head, and then looked down the hall.

"My father," Mouse said. "He's the cat in charge in this building, and if he knew you were in here, he would make you leave, and that's to say the least." Mouse had no idea what to do as the little mouse looked up to her with bright eyes and a smile. She knew her father might kill Little Foot if he found out she lived in the laundry room. Mouse thought about it and reasoned that one little mouse could not be dangerous.

"We can be friends, Little Foot. But we've got to get you somewhere with less people around and somewhere my dad doesn't go often."

"Oh, yes. That would be nice," Little Foot said. "No more having to dodge the big feet." She marched around, stomping her feet. "Look at the size of some of the socks that come into the laundry." She ran to a laundry basket and held a large sock in the air.

"I know where we can go! Be right back." Mouse took off down the hall and then raced back to the laundry room. "The hallway's clear. Follow me."

She led Little Foot to the furniture storage room. "This is one of my favorite places. There's a lot of room to play and plenty of places to hide. No one will find you in here."

"*Wow!*" Little Foot stared for a moment and then disappeared into the room.

"I'll be back after I have dinner. When you're not with me, you have to promise to stay in this room. And if anyone comes but me, you need to stay out of sight."

"Okay," Little Foot said from somewhere hidden in the room.

"If my dad finds out …" Mouse said under her breath. She feared what might happen but was excited to have a new friend. And as she walked away, she couldn't wait to get back and play with Little Foot.

Chapter 7
Paggs's Pad

"There's no doubt about it," Chief said. "That's rat scent. Maybe two days old." He sniffed around while Paggs and Baxter kept watch in the basement of Paggs's building. "They're not here now."

"Thanks be," Paggs sighed. His gray fur stood on end. "Perhaps it was just a scouting party, and they've realized a cat is here."

"They've definitely been here and up to the second floor at least," Chief said. The three cats huddled.

"Definitely a scouting party," Baxter said.

"Why would Wilber's boys break the truce?" Paggs asked.

Chief looked into Paggs's tired eyes and shook his head. "I don't know. For a rat, he seemed very organized and in charge. I think he would stick to what he said."

"Maybe he's not in charge anymore," Baxter said.

"Could be," Chief said, turning around. "But those rats had structure. If Wilber died, I think they'd still respect the truce or at least tell us."

Paggs and Baxter looked at each other and then back at Chief. "You're kidding," Baxter said. "You think that?"

"If you would've met Wilber, you'd understand. But that's not the only reason. Come here." Chief pointed to a spot on the wall. "Smell along here."

"Whew," Baxter said. "Smells like a sewer rat all right."

"My point exactly," Chief said. "Wilber's rats had class. They smelled like pizza, spaghetti, or perfume. They wouldn't smell like, well, like sewer rats."

Paggs's head went sideways. He closed one eye, and looked toward the ceiling with the other. He lowered his eye back down before shaking his head and looking at Chief. "I'm not following you."

"I get your point," Baxter said. "You're suggesting these rats aren't respecting the truce because they're not with Wilber."

"Exactly. They're either passing through or scouting out the place," Chief said. "The first choice is no problem. If they're just passing through, they may have smelled that there's a cat in here and moved along. The second choice—well, it may mean Wilber's not in charge anymore or that another group has moved in. If so, they might come back and in greater numbers."

"Then we should all be on the lookout," Baxter said. "Let us know if anything else happens, Paggs."

Paggs nodded.

Chief and Baxter ran up the stairs and outside to the alley. "We'd better increase our patrols," Chief said, "just in case something's changed. These rats came in through the basement, so we need to start there."

"Agreed." Baxter nodded. "I'll talk to Sikes and let the boys know what's going on. Maybe they can help watch the alley and stuff."

Chief kept walking down the alley.

"You still don't trust them?" Baxter asked.

"Who?" Chief asked.

"Sikes and his boys. You don't trust them."

"Look." Chief stopped walking. "Where I come from, alley

cats were nothing but trouble. Sikes and his boys are fine, but I don't know that I'd count on them to help out if things get tough. They'd probably move to another alley."

"I think you got him all wrong," Baxter said. "You see, Sikes was someone's pet at one time. Had a house to live in and all."

"He did?" Chief's ears perked up. "What happened?"

"Well, you won't get it out of him, but Rascal and Sikes were neighbors. One day, Rascal's owner moved away, leaving him out on the street. He told me that he went to Sikes's looking for something to eat. Sikes's owner closed the door on him. So Sikes left his owner and decided he'd had enough of people. Rascal and Sikes have been together since."

"And Scratch and Dazzle?"

"True alley cats. Some kids were picking on them one day, and Rascal and Sikes let 'em have it. Sikes decided they weren't safe out on the street without a leader, so he became their leader and takes care of them."

"Wow, what a story," Chief said. "I guess it couldn't hurt to let him know what's going on. It's getting late. I better get going. See you tomorrow."

Chief headed down to the alley. The apartment complex consisted of three buildings. Baxter and Chief's buildings were side-by-side off the main road and Pagg's's building was behind Chief's. Beside the building Paggs guarded was a parking lot. The parking lot and Pagg's building were surrounded on three sides with a five-foot wall that ran behind the buildings, dividing them from the land behind them. Between the front two buildings was an alley wide enough for vehicle access and to hold the trash Dumpsters. In front of the Dumpsters was a single row of parking for staff. This was where Sam parked.

The walls separating the complex from the undeveloped land behind made Chief feel closed in but secure. He stretched his hearing and sight as far as they could go but didn't sense anything among the multiple Dumpsters.

"Hmm." Chief sighed. "Plastic, cardboard, glass, paper. That's a lot of recycling." He slowed his pace. "Sikes, Rascal, you boys around?"

A slender gray cat with dirty-white stripes and paws emerged. "They're not here. They went off to the park to chase the pigeons."

"Scratch?" Chief asked.

"No, I'm Dazzle," the young cat said, tiptoeing around and spinning. "Ta-da!"

"Nice dance move," Chief said, lightening his tone. "Do me a favor, Dazzle. When Sikes comes back, tell him we suspect a new group of rats may have moved into the area. I would like you guys to keep your eyes peeled. Let Baxter or me know if you see or hear anything."

"Maybe I'll just have to go talk to Streets," Dazzle said and tapped out a rhythm with his paws. "He knows the lowdown around here with the rats."

"Streets?"

"Yeah, he's like us. Out on the road."

"Great. Anything would help," Chief said. "Hopefully it's nothing." He headed back to his building and then turned around. "Thanks, Dazzle. And nice work with those dance moves."

"Come by sometime, and I'll show you a few."

By the time Chief finished his patrol, it was night, and he went straight to the apartment. Mouse and Charlene were there sleeping, and Sam was sitting in his chair with his eyes closed. Chief brushed against his leg.

Sam reached down and stroked Chief's back. "Hello there, boy. Guess I must have fallen asleep in this chair. You and me both know there's many a night I've done that. This place is much bigger than that old motel. I'll just have to get used to it."

Chief sat on Sam's lap and purred. It reminded him of old times back at the hotel when he and Sam were with each other most of the day. With more territory for the both of them, they were not working together as much, and Chief missed the closeness they used to have.

"Dad?" Mouse opened one eye in the early morning and spotted her dad walking toward the door.

Chief turned and looked at her. "You must've played hard yesterday, I didn't think you were going to get out of bed."

Mouse struggled to her feet, a little off balance as she shook the sleep from her head, and fumbled across the floor through the crinkle sacks and fake mice Sam had scattered about the floor. "Ready to patrol," Mouse said.

"Not before breakfast you don't," Charlene said.

Mouse ran over to the food dish, chomped her food, and drank some water.

With water still dripping off her chin and food still in her mouth, she ran back to the door, where her mom and dad were sitting.

"Weady for batrol," Mouse garbled, still chewing. She snapped to attention.

Chief didn't say anything, but he didn't need to. Mouse had seen that look before and knew it meant something was wrong.

"I have to go do some things today," Chief said. "We are not going to patrol."

"Can I go with you?" The words jumped out of her mouth.

"*No!*" Chief said harshly. "I need you to stay close to home today."

Mouse drooped her ears. She finished chewing and swallowed. She turned away from her dad and looked around the apartment. After days of excitement exploring the apartments, it was back to staying home and playing ... by herself.

"But ..." Chief said.

Mouse immediately turned, and her ears perked up.

"You can still check the fourteenth floor for me today," Chief said. "And not just Ms. Doris, the entire floor."

Mouse spun around and jumped. "Can I check the fifth floor too?" she asked, knowing that Little Foot was there.

Chief raised one eyebrow, and his eyes shifted left then right. "You like that furniture storage room, don't you?"

Mouse nodded.

"I don't see any reason why not. Just make sure you don't scratch up anything, and stay away from the basement." Then Chief leaned in to whisper, "And no going on the roof without me. Your mom still doesn't know about that." He kissed Mouse on the head and took off down the hall.

Mouse watched her dad from the door until he went up the stairs. Then she turned around to the apartment.

"You're not upset?" Charlene asked.

"No way. I'm going to patrol all by myself." She thought about it and then looked at her mom. "Mom, you don't mind staying in the apartment alone?"

"Cats don't mind being alone. That's one of the good things about being a cat," Charlene said.

"Don't you get tired of staying in this room?"

"I go out from time to time. I used to be Mrs. Ryan's pet. She kept me inside all day, and I got used to staying in one apartment. It doesn't bother me."

"I need to explore," Mouse said.

"I know," Charlene said. "You get that from your father."

"You just let me know if you ever want to go on patrol, Mom. I'll show you what to do."

"I'm sure I'd appreciate it, dear."

"Well, I guess I should be going," Mouse said and headed for the door.

Charlene raised her eyebrows and smiled as Mouse walked in front of her and out the door. "You are just like your father, can't sit still. Make sure you're home in time for lunch."

Mouse called back, "Okay, Mom!" as she raced down the hallway as fast as she could. It felt good to run. In addition to everything her dad had taught her about how to run on the smooth floors and on carpet, Mouse had made up her own technique to go faster on the smooth tile. She sailed down the hall, not slowing down one bit until the end by the stairwell. She put her paws out and executed a perfect sideways slide, angling her body to face the stairs, and took off running up the stairs without missing a step.

Mouse didn't slow down until she reached the fourteenth floor and Ms. Doris's apartment. She entered through the pet door and listened for any movement. *She must be sleeping still*, Mouse thought when she didn't hear Ms. Doris about. Mouse headed to the bedroom. She jumped lightly on the bed, went up to Ms. Doris's face, and monitored the breaths as they went in and out of her mouth. The pace indicated she was fine.

"Rest well, Ms. Doris," Mouse whispered. She jumped off the bed and went through the kitchen. As she approached the doorway to the living room, she heard Ladie's familiar voice. Mouse went to the edge of the kitchen. Seeing a pigeon on the stool across from Ladie, Mouse waited, but she couldn't help but overhear the conversation.

"Oh, honey," Ladie said, "he's just saying that because, deep down, he's insecure. I think he does it on purpose to ruffle your feathers. Here's what you do. You stay out all day. I don't care where. Go watch people shop or something. Find yourself a nice group to hang out with, and you don't go back until tonight. The later the better. You give that Bo time to think about it. By the time you get back to the nest, he'll come cooing back to you. And don't give in too easy. Make him earn it. Now run along."

Mouse waited until the bird flew away and then pranced into the room. "Hi, Ladie." She looked around to make sure nothing was out of place.

"Hello there. To what do I owe the pleasure of your company?" Ladie asked, coming to the side of her cage.

Mouse got closer to the cage and looked up. "Oh, Dad put me in charge of checking on Ms. Doris and you. I'm supposed to do it three times a day. In fact, I'm in charge of the whole fourteenth floor now and the fifth floor."

"That sounds important," Ladie said.

"It is," Mouse said. Holding her head up, she marched around the room. "Pretty soon I'll be doing the whole building by myself. Maybe even the basement."

"Thank you for keeping us safe and checking on Ms. Doris for me," Ladie said.

"Just doing my job." Mouse looked about the room once more. She didn't want to leave but didn't know what else to say. She slowly walked toward the door, stopping occasionally as if she'd spotted something important. "Everything's fine in here. Guess I'll be going." She started walking again, slowly.

"You're welcome to stay awhile and visit if you like," Ladie said.

Mouse shot across the room and jumped onto the stool across from Ladie, causing the stool to wobble and Ladie to back up in her cage. Mouse looked at Ladie. "I guess I can stay for a minute or two."

"That would be nice," Ladie said, taking a few steps forward.

"Wow, Ms. Ladie, you sure have pretty feathers. The color is so bright."

"Why, thank you, Mouse. I think that's why people like to have us as pets—to brighten up their homes."

"Do you ever get sad sitting in your cage?"

"Oh, no," Ladie said. "I get plenty of food and sunshine. I can sing whenever I want to. It's nice and warm in these apartments. I'd rather be in here than outside where there are so many predators."

"Hmm, you sound like my mom. Don't you get lonely?"

"Honey, I don't have time to be lonely. You see, that stool you're on"—Ladie pointed with her wing to the black-and-white cloth-covered stool Mouse sat on—"usually has someone sitting on it every hour. I got friends from here to Miami."

"Wow," Mouse said. "I don't know where Miami is, but it sounds neat. You and my dad are a lot alike then."

"How so?"

"You both help others," Mouse said. "He keeps you, me, my mom, and the rest of the people in this building safe, and you help other birds and Ms. Doris."

"Hmm," Ladie said. "I guess I never thought of it that way. I just wouldn't go telling your dad that we are alike."

"He doesn't much care for birds," Mouse said.

"Most cats don't," Ladie said. "I can see you have your dad's sense and courage, but you have something else that's unique."

Mouse leaned her head closer and pointed her ears forward. "You mean something unique besides my eyes?"

"You are polite and pleasant," Ladie said.

Mouse's ears flicked back, and she scowled. "Pleasant? What good is that for a cat?"

"Oh, it will do you wonders. Don't knock it. I've learned we can use all the friends we can get."

Mouse leaned in again. "What do you mean? How can we be friends if you're a bird and I'm a cat?"

"Sometimes we complicate things more than we should. You wonder how we can be friends because you look with your eyes and not with your heart. You are only looking at my appearance."

Mouse's nose twitched, and she turned her head sideways.

"Why don't you sit in the rocking chair and make yourself comfortable," Ladie said.

Mouse stepped off the footstool and onto the padded rocking chair and lay down.

Ladie began with a light, pleasant whistle and then started singing:

Here I am.

I come to you with an open heart.

Does it matter what I am?
I could be your friend.
What is there to hide?
It's more important what's inside.
Here I am.
I could be your friend.
It's an amazing thing to have someone bring
smiles to your heart.
When you have a friend, you're never too far apart.
See me now.
All I am I give to you.
It's a bond that never ends
Between friends.
When the water, land, and sky unite,
they grow the trees so tall and the flowers
So beautiful and bright.
If we too worked in harmony,
What a wonderful place this world would be.
Here I am.
Won't you be my friend?
Here I am.

"That was wonderful," Mouse said, sitting up in the chair.

Suddenly, she caught a flash of movement to her right. Something flew in the window and headed straight for her. Mouse remained still as her ears perked up and her tail twitched. Her first instinct was to pounce on it, but she remembered that Ladie often had visitors. The winged yellow-and-white creature zipped in and landed on the stool facing Ladie.

"My, oh my, oh my," the bird said, shaking his feathers and scratching his neck. "I say, there must be a dozen weddings today with all the doves flying around."

"Is that right, Carl?" Ladie said.

"If those people knew all the problems those doves had getting along, they'd think twice before calling them lovebirds," Carl said. He kept cleaning himself and rambled on, "I mean, they're so fickle about where to nest, what to name their children, whether they should fly south with everyone else. On and on and on."

Mouse sat very still on the rocking chair observing Carl, who hadn't seemed to notice her yet. Then, as Carl reached to clean one of his back feathers, he locked eyes with her. Mouse smiled encouragingly.

"Carl, I'd like you to meet someone," Ladie said. "This is Mouse."

Carl didn't move. From his position on the stool, his eyes were right in line with her teeth, and Mouse realized that her smile might not be as encouraging as she'd hoped. She snapped her mouth shut.

"It's okay, Carl. She won't eat you."

Mouse remained still, afraid that she might scare Carl into flight.

"Pfft! Oh," Carl said, his voice muffled as he blew a feather out of his mouth. Color returned to his face as he turned completely around to look at Mouse and put out his wing. "Pleased to meet you." He bowed with the wing going across him like a cape.

"I'm Mouse." She waited to see if Carl would laugh at her name. He didn't. Mouse felt relieved that she'd met another friend, even if he was a bird. "Are you a pigeon?" Mouse asked.

Ladie laughed.

"Surely you jest," Carl said, puffing out his chest.

"Sorry, Carl," Ladie said. "She's just a kid. She's Chief's daughter."

"Oh, in that case, let me introduce myself." Carl spread out his wings, and some orange feathers on top of his head stood up. "Carl's the name. I am a free-flying cockatoo—noticeably different from a pigeon by my refined feathers and coloring and the sound of my voice." Carl whistled a short tune.

Mouse smiled and closed her eyes as she listened, rocking her head to the song. Ladie joined in, and Mouse thought it was the most beautiful thing she'd ever heard. She opened her eyes when they finished singing.

"Clearly, I am descended from a superior line of birds and hail from a lost kingdom where birds reigned supreme. Stolen when I was a child, I have broken free of my captives and blended in with the natives of this land until such time that I can return to my native land." Carl finished and bowed his head.

"The great cockatiel race," Ladie said. "Oh, I've heard that one before. Are you still living with the pigeons, oh great and mighty bird?"

Carl glowered at Ladie and then turned back to Mouse. "I don't mind the pigeons. I am outnumbered and far away from home. One must improvise if one is to keep his freedom."

"Don't you like pigeons?" Mouse asked.

"They're the seagulls of the inland. Pooping on everything, leaving their feathers lying about, nesting wherever they like. No class I tell you. But one can't be too choosy when he needs allies. You do understand the importance of allies?"

Mouse cocked her head. "Ladie, you're friends with my dad, and he's a cat. That's like an ally, right?"

Carl and Ladie exchanged glances. "Well," Ladie said, "I wouldn't exactly call us *friends*. But I don't think he'd ever hurt me."

"But it's okay to be friends with other animals that are not the same as you?" Mouse looked up at the two birds.

"Of course, sweetie," Ladie replied. "We all share this one world."

"Yes, absolutely," Carl said, "one can never have too many friends. They are your allies through the trials of life, those you call upon in times of need."

"Mouse is a Junior Protector," Ladie said.

"Joined the corps, have you? Bravo." Carl saluted Mouse with his wing. "Following in the footsteps of your old man. Your dad's a hero."

"I've heard," Mouse said.

"Well, then, I am at your service," Carl said. "I can bring you information. Reconnaissance is my specialty."

Mouse heard movement in the kitchen.

"Ms. Doris is up," Ladie said.

"Time for me to go," Carl said. "Mouse, keep up the good work." Carl saluted again and flew out the window.

"Well, I better get back to patrolling," Mouse said.

"You sure you don't want to stay and say hello to Ms. Doris?"

"I'll be back later," Mouse said. "Ms. Doris will want me to stay and have some milk, and that will slow me down." She realized she'd been at the apartment for a long time and was worried that Little Foot would probably be waiting for her. "Thanks, Ladie."

"The pleasure was all mine," Ladie said.

"We sure showed them rats," Slim said, waving his hand. They entered the large sewer pipe with several dozen rats.

"Yeah, who's the boss of these sewers now?" Slouch said, folding his paws together as he slumped against the wall. "Wilber thought he was so smart sending us away, saying we had no respect." Slouch farted loudly enough for the others to hear and laughed. "Respect that!"

"Gross, Slouch! Dude!" Slim held his nose and waved his hand. "It stinks down here enough already."

"Ummm!" Bragar looked around the dark tunnel with his red eyes, his nose in the air.

"It sure was a good idea to go get these other rats," Slim said. Bragar didn't respond.

"How did you know there were more rats down in those deeper tunnels?" Slouch asked. Bragar still didn't respond. "They don't look so healthy, though."

"They're vile rats," Bragar finally said. "But they'll do."

"Ooh!" Slim moved quickly, catching sight of something, and went across the tunnel. He grabbed a half-eaten slice of pizza and brought it back to Slouch.

"All right, dude, it's one of Wilber's food stashes. We got the good stuff now," Slouch said.

Slim moved back to a pile of food scraps and started digging around until he found an orange peel. "Hey, get back," he said as other rats came closer. "Get your own food." He walked back to where Bragar and Slouch were standing.

"Hmmm," Bragar said and turned to the group of rats behind him.

Slouch greedily grabbed the orange peel from Slim, drawing Bragar's gaze. Noticing this, Slim smacked Slouch, grabbed the orange peel, and offered it to Bragar, who showed no interest in it.

"Hey!" Slouch said, still gripping the pizza in his other hand.

"Sorry, what was I thinking?" Slim said to Bragar. He stepped aside and pointed to the pile. "Here, eat up. Your idea got us all this stuff. We'll let you go first."

Slouch offered Bragar the pizza. Bragar took it and tossed it to a group of rats that tore it apart. Slouch's mouth hung open, and he licked his lips.

"Sorry, boss," Slim said. "I can find you something better."

"Listen," Bragar said softly.

"Listening," Slim said immediately. "We're listening, right, dude?" He looked to Slouch, who nodded multiple times.

"*Listen!*" Bragar said loudly, and the other rats turned to him. "We have won nothing. We took more territory, but it's still a sewer."

"Make way, make way, coming through," a voice said. A scrawny gray rat Slim had never seen before approached Bragar. The rat had knotted fur and an unusually long snout. Slim's eyes twitched, and he looked back and forth between Bragar and Slouch.

Bragar and the new rat huddled together, whispering.

"Who's that?" Slim asked.

"That's Streets," Slouch said.

"One of Wilber's guys?"

"No, he's independent now. He roams the streets getting information." Slouch stepped closer to Bragar.

"Oh, that must be how he got his name, Streets." Slim smiled at the revelation. "Hey, his whiskers are longer on one side. Makes him look odd."

"*Shhh!*" Slouch scolded. "I'm trying to listen."

"Just as I suspected," Bragar said and patted Streets on the back. He turned to Slim and Slouch and smiled a crooked, curling smile.

"Are you hungry?" Bragar asked in a loud voice. Ten rats nodded along with Slim. "I know where there's food. Not out of the garbage but fresh in the package. So much food you couldn't eat it all."

More rats moved in, and Slim backed up to make room. Slouch grunted and joined the other rats moving closer to hear Bragar.

"Sweet food?" Slim asked. "I love sweet food."

Bragar's thin lips spread in a wide grin. He lowered his eyebrows and said, "So much sweet food that it'll make you sick to your stomach."

Slim's tongue looped around his lips. Cheers erupted, and more rats moved into the tunnel. "What are we waiting for? Let's go," Slim said. Then he stopped. "Uh, where are we going?"

"It's up there," Bragar said and raised his finger, pointing upward.

Slim heard his heart beating in the silence that engulfed the tunnel. He looked at Bragar, whose hand remained raised. Bragar's eyes narrowed, the grin still firm upon his face. Slim realized he wasn't kidding.

Slouch laughed and rolled on his side. "You had us going

there. And I didn't think you had a sense of humor." No one else joined in, and Slouch stopped laughing.

Without blinking, Bragar turned and started moving down the tunnel. Slim watched as most of the other rats followed him as though hypnotized by his red eyes. Slim looked back at Slouch, who had recovered his position against the wall and was dusting himself off.

"What? You and the others been calling him boss," Slouch said. "That's how we ended up in this mess."

"Bragar's got a plan and food," Slim said. "I say we follow him."

"Okay, but he's not telling me what to do all the time," Slouch said.

Slim shrugged his shoulders and headed off toward Bragar. When Slouch didn't follow, he walked back and grabbed him. Unwillingly, Slouch's legs moved forward.

Chapter 8
Hide-and-Seek

"Mouse?" Chief called out from inside the apartment. He heard the crinkle sacks in the bedroom rattle.

"Yes, sir." Mouse came out of the bedroom. Charlene looked up and smiled at her.

"Good," Chief said. "Clean and snappy."

Mouse came to attention as her dad approached.

"Show me your fighting stance," Chief said.

Mouse stood on all fours, put her head and ears forward, and narrowed her eyes.

"Hmm, I suppose your fur is so fluffy it's hard to tell if it's standing on end," Chief said. "Keep your tail at the ready. Remember—a rat might try to sneak up behind you and grab on to your tail. You'll need to be ready to flick it away."

Mouse flopped her tail right and then left.

"Good," Chief said. Mouse smiled. "Now show me your pouncing stance."

Mouse lowered her front legs and bent down, putting more weight to her back legs, which began to twitch. She made a chattering sound.

"Excellent!" Chief said and walked in front of her, exposing his side.

Mouse grinned and pounced. Rolling over him, she pinned him to the ground.

Chief laughed before getting back up. "Now," he said, "go and check the areas I've assigned you, and report back here. Don't stay out all day like you did yesterday."

"Yes, sir," Mouse said and raced away down the hall.

Chief shook his head as he watched her go. "Looks like a little ball of fur charging down the hall. How is anything supposed to be scared of that?"

"She's the daughter of a Protector," Charlene said. "I thought in the history of the Protectors it was the calling that mattered, not the size of the cat."

Chief smiled at Charlene. "There were a few times I faced danger when a little more size would have been nice. Besides, I don't know the history as much as you think, only what I've heard around here and there."

"Yes, I remember," Charlene said. "You weren't raised by your father. You're not going with her today?"

"No, I need to go check on Paggs," Chief said. "And then I need to check our basement."

"Is something wrong?"

Chief thought before he answered. He remembered the night the two of them had sat on the roof and life had seemed perfect. That feeling remained, and he didn't want to spoil it. "No. I'm sure everything is fine. It's just that Paggs hasn't been feeling well, and Baxter and I decided to check in on him."

"Well, that building he's in was the first one built," Charlene said. "My owner toured it years ago when we still lived in a house, and Paggs was there then. He's getting older, I suppose. What time should I expect you back?"

"I won't be gone long," Chief said and headed down the hall. He started to turn back to tell Charlene the whole truth—that there was a scent of rats in Paggs's building—but he decided he wouldn't worry her. Still, he was worried about Mouse and wondered if he'd made a mistake letting her patrol alone when she was so small.

"She'll be fine," Chief said to himself. "First sign of rats in this building, I'll confine her to the apartment." As he approached the entrance to the basement, he didn't smell any scent of rat. Despite this, he had an uneasy feeling that he couldn't place, a feeling that something bad was about to happen.

As much as Mouse wanted to go straight to the laundry room to see Little Foot, she knew her responsibilities came first. Besides, she had played with Little Foot most of the previous day. She charged up the stairs to Ms. Doris's apartment and ran through the slightly opened door and into the bedroom. She watched the covers rise and fall. "Yep, she's breathing," Mouse said and ran into the living room, startling Ladie.

"What is it?" Ladie asked. "Is something chasing you?"

"No," Mouse said. "Sorry. I'm just in a hurry today; that's all."

"Oh, important business to attend to?"

"You can say that," Mouse said, walking toward the door. "I'll be back later. If you need me, just whistle out a note."

Mouse ran down the stairs toward the furniture room. She stopped at the laundry room after hearing a sound from within. She looked up and down the hall to make sure no one was watching before she went in. As soon as she entered, the sound stopped.

"What are you doing in here?" Mouse asked.

Little Foot came out from behind one of the dryers. "Looking for food. Sometimes people leave stuff in their pockets, especially the little people. It's usually something sweet or mushy."

"Oh." Mouse sniffed the air. "Let's go down to the furniture storage room," she said. "It's not as busy there, and we won't have to keep ducking behind the machines." Mouse looked out into the hall. "Okay," she said. "The coast is clear."

The two ran to the furniture storage room and began bouncing on furniture and playing.

"I know! Let's play hide-and-seek," Little Foot said.

"What's that?" Mouse asked.

"I'll hide my eyes," Little Foot said, "so I can't see you. You have to find a place to hide. Then I'll come and try to find you. Then we'll switch, and I'll hide and you'll seek."

"Okay, sounds like fun," Mouse said. "So hide your eyes."

Mouse ran across the large, open room and crouched behind one of the many couches. She giggled, sure Little Foot would be unable to see her.

"Got you!" Little Foot said, coming up behind Mouse, who jumped.

"How did you find me?"

"I could hear you giggle all the way across the room," Little Foot said. "You have to be quiet when you play."

"Oh, I guess you do have good ears."

"See, told you so. You should use your stealth mode like you did in the laundry room."

"Oh, okay," Mouse said.

"But now it's my turn to hide," Little Foot said.

Mouse went back to the front of the room near the door and counted. When she was done, her instincts took over. She immediately headed back to the spot where she'd left Little Foot. *Hmm, she didn't stay here.*

Mouse sniffed the floor, and her senses led her to a reclining chair. From underneath, a little tail was sticking out. "Ha, found you!" Mouse said.

"What? I was totally silent."

"I used my nose," Mouse said. Then, as Little Foot came out from under the chair, Mouse thought of something. "If I can smell you, then so can my dad." She went to the doorway.

Little Foot followed, and the two looked down the hall.

"You must stay back in this area, away from the stairs. The smell of all the detergents in the laundry room will keep him from noticing you as long as he doesn't come down this far."

"Okay," Little Foot said. "It's your turn to hide. Try to stay quiet this time."

They played hide-and-seek in the room for hours until they were tired, and then they sat in the warm sun coming in through the window.

"That was fun," Mouse said. "Too bad we can't play through the whole building."

"It would take forever to find you," Little Foot said. Then she perked up her ears. "What's that sound?" Little Foot stood on her hind legs and went still.

Mouse went to the door and looked down the hall. She spotted a baby sitting outside of the laundry room. "Oh, that's one of the little people. My dad called it a baby. The mother must be doing laundry."

"Let's get a closer look," Little Foot said and charged down the hall.

Worried, Mouse quickly overtook her and ran to the doorway of the laundry room to look in. The baby's mom was folding clothes and had her back turned to the door.

"You can't just come down the hall," Mouse scolded Little Foot. "If someone sees you, we'll both be in trouble. The coast is clear, but be quiet." Mouse crept up to the baby, who sat on the floor in a little springy seat.

"Mmm?" the baby said as Mouse and Little Foot walked closer.

"How cute," Little Foot said, stepping even closer.

"Hey, watch out. He has hands," Mouse warned.

"Yuck, what's that smell?" Little Foot asked, curling up her nose.

"See that white thing around it?" Mouse said. "Babies aren't smart enough to go in a litter box. Their parents wrap those things around them, and they go in that."

"That's disgusting. It's not natural."

"Don't!" Mouse said as Little Foot stepped too close.

The baby swooped an arm down and grabbed Little Foot. Mouse closed her eyes, too afraid to watch at first. Then she opened her right eye slightly to see what was happening. Little Foot was laughing as the baby held her.

"He's still cute," Little Foot said.

Mouse's heart skipped a beat as the baby moved Little Foot into his mouth.

"Don't eat her!" Mouse cried out, but she knew the baby couldn't understand her. She looked around for someone to help, but the mother was too busy on her phone.

The baby curled up his face, took Little Foot out of his mouth, and put her down before spitting up.

"Gross," Little Foot said, shaking the slobber from her fur.

Mouse rolled over and couldn't help but laugh. "I told you not to get too close."

"Watch out!" Little Foot said as the baby reached for Mouse's tail.

With lightning-quick reflexes, Mouse swatted the baby's arm away from her, taking care not to use her claws as she cleared the grasping hand. "Whoa, that was close," Mouse said.

Startled, the baby started crying, and Mouse heard the mother's footsteps coming to the door. "Stand still," Mouse said to Little Foot, who cringed as Mouse pounced on her, covering her completely. Mouse looked up as the baby's mom peeked out to see what had caused the baby to fuss.

"Oh, hi, little kitty," the mother said.

"Meow," Mouse said. She waited until the mother picked up the baby and, holding him, went back into the laundry room. Then Mouse whispered to Little Foot, "Keep low and stay under me."

"You don't think they'll see me?" Little Foot said.

"As long as I stay low, you should blend in. Humans are tall; looking down, they shouldn't see you." She walked away slowly with Little Foot directly under her, hidden from view.

Once they made it back to the furniture storage room, Mouse broke out laughing. "I guess that baby doesn't think you taste good either."

"Yuck," Little Foot said, wiping her face with her paws. "I'll need some disinfectant. He tried to eat me."

"My dad said all babies do that. They put everything in their mouths."

"Well," Little Foot said, "that's the last time it will have a taste of me. I don't care how cute they look. Thanks for covering for me."

"No problem," Mouse said. "It's just a good thing we're the same color. You blend right in. What should we do now? Want to play hide-and-seek again?"

"How about going to see that bird you're always talking about?" Little Foot suggested.

"I don't know." Mouse jumped down from a couch and looked at Little Foot. "Playing in a room with a bunch of furniture no one uses is a lot different than sneaking up to the fourteenth floor."

"But I want to meet the bird," Little Foot said. "I'll just hide under you like I did in the hallway. You said I blended right in."

"If my dad found you, and I convinced him not to eat you, he would at least throw you out of the building," Mouse said. "And there are alley cats out there. You don't want to be out there."

"Oh," Little Foot said as she turned away from Mouse. Her ears dropped. "I understand. I should be happy to have at least one friend. And you are a good friend and all."

Mouse shook her head. "Okay, let's go. But you have to stay close to me, and if we run into anyone, you hide under my fur."

The two friends headed down the hallway. Mouse went cautiously and listened at every turn. They entered the stairway and got off several times to let people pass.

"Whew," Mouse said. "That last one was close. Those people could have seen us. Only five more floors to go; stick close." Mouse moved forward, but Little Foot didn't. Her little body went completely still. She raised her ears and looked to the stairway. Mouse stopped and listened.

"Quick," Little Foot said as she ran down the hall, "we need to hide." They found a small broom closet with the door ajar and entered.

"What is it?" Mouse asked.

"Shh," Little Foot said. "It's Slim and Slouch." Little Foot ran over to the door and pushed it closed so only a crack remained. Then she bent down and put her right ear to the crack.

Mouse hesitated. Then she remembered she was a cat and that she was still in her dad's apartment building. "There's nothing to fear, not here, not in my dad's apartment building."

"Shh," Little Foot insisted.

Mouse walked up behind Little Foot, summoning her courage. She pointed her ears forward and listened. She heard two low, squeaky voices.

"You sure he's gone today?" one rat asked.

"That one's Slim," Little Foot whispered to Mouse.

"I saw him go to the other building, just like Bragar planned," the other rat, Slouch, said.

"What if he comes back?"

"He will, so let's make it quick. Bragar wants a report."

The voices faded down the hall.

"We're okay now," Little Foot said. "They're gone."

"This is my dad's building," Mouse said. "Are they bullies or something? You don't need to be afraid. I'll teach them a thing or two." Mouse put out her paw, opened the door, and looked down the hallway.

"No," Little Foot said. "Those rats are dangerous. You have to warn your dad."

"What?" Mouse said. "Rats! Who are they?"

"Slim and Slouch. They work for someone named Bragar."

"Bragar? Who is he?"

Little Foot looked at Mouse. Then she looked up as if searching the ceiling for an answer.

"Little Foot," Mouse said, looking at her friend, "what do you know?"

"Okay, I'll tell you," Little Foot said, sitting down. She grabbed her tail and held it between her paws. "I haven't always been in the laundry room or on the fifth floor. The little boy that had me would take me to the basement and put me in a ball to roll around. It was there just last week I ran into Slim and Slouch. They told me if I spoke to anyone about them ..." She drew her paw across her throat in a slashing motion.

Mouse's voice came out in a high pitch. "It's dangerous out there. You could have gotten hurt."

"I'm ... I'm a lot tougher than you think," Little Foot said, making a fist with one of her paws. "You see, being this small, I've learned how to hide and be quiet. And when you are good at that, sometimes you hear things. Bad things."

"Tell me. I have to know if there's something going on in the building. I'm responsible for this building."

"Well, I've never met Bragar," Little Foot said. "But Slim and Slouch told me he's coming to take over the buildings."

"You're just telling me this now?" Mouse said.

"I was worried at first because they threatened me. But I feel safe with you. I mean, if they mess with you, your dad would eat 'em, right? Anyway," Little Foot said, stroking her tail and looking up at Mouse, "they talked about how Bragar is going to take over the place. He's recruited the worst of the rats, the vile rats. Some of rats at the pet store used to tell scary stories about them. Bragar's not just after this place but all the apartment buildings. He's already taking over the sewers."

"How am I going to tell my dad about this? He'll want to know how I found out," Mouse said. She started walking down the hallway back to the stairs.

"Mouse." Little Foot put her paw on Mouse. "There are a lot

of rats down there. What are we going to do? You're not mad at me, are you?" Little Foot walked underneath Mouse and came out under Mouse's head. "I'm sorry I didn't stay in the furniture room like you asked. But now we know some important information, right?"

Mouse looked down at Little Foot and her tiny, curious eyes and cute nose. She couldn't imagine how a cat could ever eat something so cute. She thought for a moment and watched the hall as if she expected the two rats to come walking down it.

"I'm not mad at you," Mouse said. "I shouldn't have treated you like you're helpless. My dad does that to me, and it makes me mad. But I am worried about you. I'm worried about the rats or my dad finding you. I'm not sure how I'm going to tell him about all of this."

"What are we going to do?" Little Foot asked.

"We're going to see Ladie. She's good at figuring things out. But it's later than I thought, and it will have to wait until morning. I've got to get back to my apartment. Let's get back to the furniture room where you'll be safe."

Mouse returned home to find her dad there. After dinner, they wrestled before they went to bed. Although tired, Mouse tossed and turned with the information she held. She knew Ladie could help her decide how to tell her dad.

Chapter 9
Bragar's Diabolical Deeds

"You sure about this, boss?" Slouch said as they emerged from a vent in the wall. Bragar's nose went high into the air as he smelled and looked around the room. "I mean, we're rats. We usually creep into a building through the walls and stuff. We don't usually go out in the open. I mean, what about the cat?"

Slouch crouched as Bragar turned and looked at him. Slim cowered beside him.

"I was right about the food, wasn't I?" Bragar said.

"Yeah, lots of food. All we had to do was take it right out from under the people's noses," Slouch said, nodding.

"And now our numbers have doubled," Bragar said. "I picked this building because you visited and told me the cat here is weak and aged. He won't be a problem for us if we stick together. Now come on."

Slim and Slouch stayed where they were as Bragar stepped forward. He looked back at them.

"Uh, what about the cat?" Slouch asked.

"That is exactly what we're here for, the *cat*! Now go!"

Slim and Slouch remained still, shaking.

"You first," Slouch said.

"No, I insist," Slim said.

Bragar spit. "That's the problem with our kind," Bragar said. "Always cowering, groping about. We outnumber the cats ten to one." He lifted his right claws up into the air. "You see these? We were given these claws. We're not as tender as the mouse or mole. And these"—he bared his teeth, showing his long fangs—"these teeth can rip flesh. We're not going to tangle with the humans, but we can take out their Protectors. And when we do, we're going to take over these buildings."

"Great plan," Slim said. "Really smart. But, uh, before they had the cats, they used poison. If we get rid of the cats, what's to keep them from using poison to kill us?"

"Just leave that to me," Bragar said. "I know a thing or two about their chemicals. They're not just dangerous to us but to the humans as well."

"So why are we here?" Slim asked. "To get more food?"

"This one called Paggs, he's the weakest. We'll start with him. If we scare him out, more rats will join our ranks. As we get mightier, we'll take down our enemies one by one. Soon they'll all fall."

Bragar turned back to the vent they had emerged from. "Come forward, my lab rats," he said, and four large rats emerged.

"Hey, boss, these guys look like you. Where'd they come from?" Slouch asked.

"Just a few of my brothers," Bragar said. "Last night when you slept, I went to get some help."

"They look different," Slim said.

"We've been tested on for years," Bragar said. "I and some of my brothers are immune to their poisons. Our species adapts faster than any other mammal. A few thousands may die, but we'll adapt. The humans will poison themselves in the process of trying to get rid of us. Then all will be ours."

"Hey, I'm Slim, and this is Slouch," Slim said to the group of rats. He walked up to them, but they remained in a catatonic state. He raised his hand and waved it in front of one of the rats but received no response.

"Come, my brothers," Bragar said.

Slim and Slouch backed up and let the larger rats by. "What's wrong with them?" Slim asked.

"Nothing, just a few jolts to the brain and a few poisons to the gut," Bragar said. "It's made them stronger."

The large rats licked their lips and looked at Slim and Slouch, who moved behind Bragar for safety.

"You see the way those guys are looking at us?" Slim whispered.

"Yeah, maybe it's not the cat we should be worried about," Slouch whispered and stayed close to Bragar.

"We will eat soon," Bragar said. "First, let's pay a visit to the cat. Here, kitty kitty."

"This will never do," Mouse said as she stopped to wait for Little Foot to catch up. They were on the stairs and heading to the fourteenth floor.

Little Foot stopped and sat down, taking rapid breaths. "Can we … rest … a … minute?"

"Come on," Mouse said. "We're only halfway there." She grabbed Little Foot in her mouth and flicked her up in the air. Little Foot did a flip and landed on Mouse's back. Mouse charged up the stairs and didn't stop running until she reached the fourteenth floor.

"Hold on!" Mouse said as she headed along the smooth floor. She kept up her speed and executed a slide, scrambling to get her feet into position at the last second to grip and then take off in a new direction.

"Wow!" Little Foot called out.

"I call that my power slide," Mouse said.

Mouse screeched to a stop outside of Ms. Doris's apartment.

"That was wild," Little Foot said. "How did you learn to go around corners like that?"

"Been practicing," Mouse said, holding her head up high. "Saves lots of time getting places. You better hide under my fur. If Ms. Doris sees you, she might have a heart attack or something."

Little Foot climbed down and ducked under Mouse.

Mouse walked as tall as she could, which caused her to look a little awkward as she entered the living room.

"Hello there, sweetie," Ladie said. "I didn't expect to see you back so soon. Are you changing your patrol times like your father does?"

"He's a smart one," Carl said. He sat on the stool in front of Ladie. "Yep, he's a Protector. A warrior of good." Carl turned his head to one side, looked directly at Mouse, and then turned his head to look with the other eye.

Mouse did the best she could to look normal. "Is Ms. Doris around?"

"Oh, no, honey, she goes down to the country club and plays bridge at this time of the day," Ladie said. "I thought you knew that. Is something wrong? You look troubled."

Mouse nodded. "I need your advice."

"Why are you walking so funny?" Carl asked. He kept turning his head to look with one eye and then with the other.

Mouse glanced around the room, causing Ladie and Carl to do the same. Then she walked closer and whispered, "Can you keep a secret?"

"Of course," Carl said. "Have to keep them all the time in the corps."

"Honey, you don't have to worry about us," Ladie said. Carl nodded. "We're here to help you, whatever it is. Now tell us what is going on that has you so wound up."

"Come on out, Little Foot," Mouse said.

Little Foot crawled out into the open. Ladie and Carl looked at each other, then at Mouse, and then back at each other.

"You said that having plenty of friends is like having lots of allies, right, Carl?" Mouse said. "And, Ladie, she isn't hurting anyone, so isn't it wrong for me to eat her?"

Carl cleared his throat. "Well, I did, uh, say something of that sort. But you might want your friends to be someone other than your food. Of course, cats eat birds too, and that wouldn't do." Carl started mumbling, lost in his thoughts.

Ladie flew down from her cage to Mouse's level. "Does your father know?"

"No, I'm afraid to tell him," Mouse said. "He might make her leave. But now there's something important going on, and I've got to let him know."

"Yes, definitely," Carl said. "He's going to want to know about this. Are there more rodents in the building?"

"Rodents?" Little Foot said, frowning at Carl.

"It talks," Carl said.

"Of course she talks," Ladie said.

"Yes, of course," Carl said. He inspected Little Foot. "You have a curious shape to your face, and that tail, hmmm, not a rat's tail. You're one of them fancy mice from the pet store; that's what you are." Carl raised his head in confidence as though he'd solved a great mystery.

"You need to tell your father," Ladie said. "If Ms. Sorenson found out there was a mouse running loose in the building, it could get your father into a lot of trouble. Besides, I believe she belongs to a little boy."

"But if he gets mad?" Mouse said. "Then he won't listen to me."

"I'm sure he'll understand," Ladie said. "You're just a child. You need friends."

Mouse shook her head. "I'm not talking about Little Foot. There's something worse going on, and I think we're all in danger!"

"Something worse? We're in danger?" Carl cleared his throat and jumped down off the stool. "What is it?"

"That's what I've been trying to tell you. Little Foot, tell them," Mouse said, pushing Little Foot forward.

Little Foot looked around the room as though seeking a place to hide and then finally made eye contact with Carl and Ladie. "Mouse has told me so much about you. I'm v-v-very p-pleased to meet you," she stuttered. She sat down, grabbed her tail with her front paws, and held it as she spoke. "I know about the rats."

"Rats!" Carl said. "What rats?"

Little Foot flinched at Carl's quick response. "They are Bragar's spies. They're staking out the buildings and getting ready to move in."

"Oh my," Ladie said. "Now I understand. You're afraid if you tell your father he will want to know how you got the information."

Mouse nodded. Little Foot backed up until she was under Mouse's chin.

"Hmm …" Carl put one wing to his chin. "A very complicated situation. Bragar? A very strange name indeed. Yes," he said with a nod, "very complicated situation indeed. I must inform the pigeon brigade."

"Mouse," Ladie said in a voice that reminded Mouse of her mother's, "you need to tell your father. He's the Protector of this building, and he needs to know. You're his helper, and you were doing your job. He won't be mad."

"But what if he asks how I found out?" Mouse said.

"Then you'll have to tell him," Ladie said.

"If these rats aren't Wilber's thugs," Carl said, "then something bad is going down. You may be worried about your little friend now, but I've seen what rats can do, and she isn't safe if they get into the building."

"We'll help you," Ladie said. She pointed her wing at Carl. "We need intelligence. Contact the pigeons in the park by the old bench, and let them know what's going on over here. See if you can get any information out of them. Chief's going to need all the information he can get."

"Right," Carl said.

"Mouse, you go tell your dad. Then we'll all meet back here during your evening check. You better not bring Little Foot, because Ms. Doris will be here by then."

Mouse leaned down, and Little Foot climbed on. They headed for the door, but Mouse stopped before she went through. She turned around. "Ladie, are the rats that dangerous?"

"Yes, sweetie," Ladie said. "They are dangerous for Little Foot, the baby on the fifth floor, for me, and for Ms. Doris. That's why you and your dad are around."

Mouse debated with herself on the way back to the furniture room. She still wasn't sure she should tell her dad what she knew. "If only there was another way," Mouse muttered.

"What?" Little Foot asked.

"Never mind," Mouse said. "You heard what Ladie said about how dangerous the rats are."

Little Foot nodded. "I'm not worried."

"Please stay in here until I get back," Mouse said as they reached their destination and she dropped Little Foot off in the furniture storage room.

Mouse walked slowly down the hall. An idea occurred to her, and she picked up the pace. Her father wouldn't approve, but she figured if she couldn't go directly to him, she would find another cat to get advice from. Besides that, her curiosity was getting the best of her. She hesitated for a moment at the window and looked back down the hall as she considered the consequences of her actions. She jumped through the window and headed down the fire escape to find the alley cats.

Mouse spotted them by the Dumpsters.

"Hey, guys," Mouse said, approaching two cats—both a mix of dirty white and gray.

"Well, hello, little cat, what's happening?" one of them said.

"What's happening where?" Mouse asked, confused.

"No, that's just a way of saying hello. So next time you come down, you just say, 'What's happening?' Get it?"

"Sure," Mouse said. "So, uh, what's happening?"

"That's the way!" the cat said, smacking his paws together. "Does your pops know you're down here?"

"No," Mouse said. "I don't think he approves of alley cats much. He doesn't like birds either."

"Oh, well, we like birds," the cat said, "especially when they're plump and tasty." He used his paws to outline a plump bird.

"Sorry," Mouse said, "but I don't know your names."

"Don't worry about it, little friend. It's easy to get us mixed up. Just remember—he's Scratch." He pointed to the other cat with him, who had a small guitar. "Nicknamed that because he can sure scratch out a tune on those strings."

Scratch played a few notes.

"And me, I'm Dazzle, because I can dazzle you with my dance steps." He did a twirl and landed with his body twisted and his face toward Mouse.

"Wow," Mouse said. "That's pretty neat. Can you play me a tune and do a dance?"

"Sure thing, little one. Give me a tune, Scratch." He started snapping his fingers. "That's it; bring it down, nice and smooth. That really gets me in the groove." He sang:

> Now you might think I'm just an alley cat,
> That I don't know this from that.
> But I'll tell you they got me all wrong.
> Listen to me. I'll sing you my song.
>
> I never knew my momma,
> My father, or my kin,
> Born into a world
> where I didn't fit in.
> I learned the alley cat,

He knows where it's at.
I said the alley cat,
He knows where it's at.

So I took to the streets
And struck out on my own,
Knowing that I'd spend my whole life alone.
I was down and out, not a bite to eat,
Head down low, watching my own feet,
When I heard this tune that put me in a trance.
My feet went crazy, and I started to dance.
I went to the left.

Scratch joined in, "He went to the left."

"And I moved to the right," Dazzle continued.

"He moved to the right."

"A little bit a grooving, then I realized … that the best time of day …"

"Best time of day …" Scratch echoed.

"Is the middle of the night."

"The middle of the night."

"The best kind of sun …" Dazzle sang.

"The best kind of sun …"

"Is the bright starlight."

Dazzle continued to dance and sing in front of Mouse.

So I sleep all day.
They call me lazy and ignore me,
but I don't let it get me down.
The ladies they adore me
because I got these moves.

He tapped across in front of Mouse and sang, "And I got these grooves." He danced up to Scratch and held his paws out. "And with friends like these, I just can't lose."

He sang, "Yes, the alley cat …"

"The alley cat," Scratch joined in.

"Knows where it's at."

"Knows where it's at."

They repeated this last line several times together until the tune faded.

Mouse sat back and clapped her paws together. "Wow, that was great!"

"Mouse?" Chief's voice rang out from the back door to the apartment building.

"I better get going," Mouse said. "Coming, Dad!"

"What are you doing out here?" Chief asked as she trotted up to the door.

"I was looking for you," Mouse said.

"Well, try to stay out of the alley."

Mouse smiled, the song Scratch and Dazzle had sung still in her head. Worried that her dad was upset that she was outside, she decided it wasn't a good time to tell him about the rats in the building. She would wait until morning.

Chief woke early, as did Sam. Sam busied himself in the kitchen for a bit and then grunted and left the apartment, leaving the door half-open as usual. Chief spotted something coming through the door and said, "Baxter? What are you doing over here this early?"

"Sorry for barging in like this," Baxter said. "No time to knock." He nodded to Charlene and said, "Good morning, Mrs. Charlene."

"Hello, Baxter. Will you be staying for breakfast?"

"No, don't mean to be a nuisance. I just need some advice from the man here. Maybe he can teach me how to get someone as sweet and pretty as you."

Chief smacked Baxter and said, "Let's talk in the hall." Once they were in the hallway, he said, "Sorry about smacking you."

"No problem. Good reflexes."

"Now what's this all about?"

"Paggs was attacked by rats," Baxter said.

"What?" Chief said. "I was just over there yesterday. Is he all right?"

"He'll live, but he's pretty shaken up," Baxter said. "They waited until dark, when they knew he'd be alone, and took him by surprise. We've got to help him. If the apartment manager finds out there're rats in the building, they'll kick Paggs out. That's a failure for all of us."

"Of course," Chief said. "We need to stop them before they spread to your building or mine."

Charlene peeked her head out. "Have either of you seen Mouse?"

"She's probably out checking on Ms. Doris," Chief said. "I'll go find her in a minute."

"What's going on with Paggs?" Charlene asked.

Chief looked at her. "Don't worry," he said. "I guess it's been almost a year since I kicked the rats out of this place. It was wishful thinking that they wouldn't reappear someday. We just need to do some patrols and remind them who's in charge."

"Just don't stay out too late," Charlene said and headed back into the apartment.

"Paggs said the leader was the largest rat he'd ever seen," Baxter said. "And there was something else—he was white."

"That doesn't sound like the rats I chased out of here. I suspect we have a new bunch."

"There's more. The leader of these rats gave his name—Bragar. Told Paggs he wanted us all to get his message."

Chief raised his right paw, extended his claws, narrowed his eyes, and looked at Baxter. "I've never heard of rats attacking a cat in the open. These ones sound aggressive. We'll have to teach them a lesson." He swiped his right claw out across his chest and snapped it back.

Baxter nodded. "Now you're talking. Let's serve us up some rat stew."

"Just let me figure out what I'm going to tell Charlene." He glanced over Baxter's shoulder and said, "You better watch out behind you."

Baxter turned just in time to get out of the way.

"Hi, Uncle Bax," Mouse said as she sped by and slid past the door to the apartment, trying unsuccessfully to stop. She backed up to her dad.

"I told you to be careful how fast you run on bare floor compared to carpet," Chief said. "I'll see you in a—"

Mouse shook off the spill and looked up at her dad, wide-eyed. "Dad," she interrupted, "I have something important to tell you."

"Not now. I'm on my way to help Uncle Baxter. We've got some work to do." Chief started trotting down the hall, and Mouse fell in beside him.

"It's important?" Mouse asked.

"Where have you been this morning? I hope not back down in that alley," Chief said.

"No, I went and checked on Ms. Doris."

"Good. Now go eat your breakfast."

"But, Dad." Mouse stopped.

"Okay, what is it?"

"There're rats in the building," Mouse said.

Chief tried to remain calm. "What did you say?"

"I heard some rats in the building," Mouse said. "They work for someone named Bragar."

"Did you go in the basement?" Chief raised his voice.

"I didn't," Mouse said.

"Sounds like they are watching your place too," Baxter said.

"What's going on?" Charlene walked out into the hallway.

"Stay with your mom today, Mouse; no more patrols," Chief said and then started walking away. "Baxter and I will clear the building when we get done helping Paggs."

Mouse ran up to her dad. "Please, can I go with you? I can help. I'm a Junior Protector. I want to learn to fight like you."

Chief turned around and faced Charlene. "If I'm not back by this evening, will you check on Ms. Doris?"

"Sure, dear," Charlene said.

"But, Dad, I thought I was checking on Ms. Doris?" Mouse hopped beside her dad.

Chief stopped and turned to his daughter. "You are too small to learn how to fight. This is serious business, and you might get hurt. Now go back to our room, and stay close to your mom." Chief regretted the tone and his words as soon they left his mouth.

"We better get going," Baxter said.

Chief looked at Mouse, who stopped jumping. Her eyes dropped to the floor, and her ears drooped as she turned away. His heart sank, but then he remembered the business at hand and took off down the hall with Baxter.

Mouse stood out in the hallway for a few minutes after her dad disappeared with Baxter, his harsh words still ringing in her ears. As she turned to go into the apartment, she noticed her mom was sitting staring down the hall in the direction Chief had left. "Mom, are you okay?"

"Yes, fine," Charlene said. "Come along, Mouse." The two walked back to the apartment.

Mouse walked sluggishly to her blanket and plopped down. She shut her eyes and tried to forget what her dad had said. Suddenly she felt her mom's tongue across her head. Mouse began to purr.

"Don't worry. Your dad's going to be fine."

"Oh, Mom, that's not it. He only lets me do the easy stuff. I thought I was learning how to be a Protector, but it's not real. He just lets me do stuff he thinks isn't dangerous. I never get to do anything dangerous."

"Shh, dear," Charlene said. "Your dad is just worried. I'm sure he didn't mean to hurt your feelings. His instinct is to keep us safe, and that may cause him to overreact. I'm sure everything is going to be fine."

Feeling her mom purring next to her, Mouse drifted off to sleep. When Mouse woke, she went into the living room, leaving her mom still sleeping.

Mouse paced back and forth in the apartment. *Little Foot, Ladie, and Carl are going to be worried when I don't come by tonight,* Mouse thought. *If everything was fine, Mom wouldn't have been staring down the hallway after Dad left … If I leave and get caught, she might be upset. Well, I guess it won't hurt to get a little rest.* Mouse went back to her position by her mom and soon fell asleep.

Chief headed down the fire escape to the back alley. He glanced back at his building. *Maybe I was too hard on her,* he thought. *But this is dangerous work. Why does she have to be so small?*

"Is something wrong?" Baxter asked.

"No," Chief said.

"Then let's quit strolling and turn up the speed."

Chief looked back toward his building once more. "Just giving you time to get ready."

"I was born ready," Baxter said. "If Paggs is right, he's got more than a few rats at his place. It could take us the rest of the day and maybe all night. Not that we can't handle it. It's just a big place."

"Right," Chief said and headed down the alley in a different direction.

"Hey," Baxter said, "Paggs's place is this way."

"I know, but I want to get home fast, and this is the fastest way I know how to get this done," Chief said. "Follow me. We're going to get some help with this one."

Baxter caught up to Chief. "That's why I like you, Chief. You're always thinking."

The two rounded the corner to where the Dumpsters sat. Chief looked around to make sure no humans were around before he called out, "Sikes, I need to speak with you."

"There's nobody here," Baxter said. "They probably went to the park to chase pigeons."

"No," Chief said, "they're here." With his ears pointed forward, Chief listened. He sniffed the air, and his senses reached forward. "Sikes," Chief said. No one responded.

Then Sikes emerged from behind the Dumpster. "Hey, my man, Chief. What's happening?" Rascal's head peeked out from under a newspaper.

"How would you like to score some fresh tuna fish, maybe even some salmon?" Chief asked.

"Yeah, no kiddin'?" Sikes said.

"We need some guys to help us get tough with some rats over at Paggs's building. If you and your boys help, I'll make it worth your trouble," Chief said. "That is, unless you're afraid of a few rats."

"I eats rats for breakfast," Sikes said. "Besides, I'm bored chasin' pigeons. We might just do it no fee, bust us up some rats. Yo, yous guys," he shouted to the trash cans behind him. Two more heads popped out. "Come over here. Looks like we gots ourselves a job to do. Scratch, Dazzle, you feel like breakin' some necks and gettin' rough?"

"Yeah, boss, we've been looking for some action," Scratch said. "Hey, Chief, what's the job?"

"Chief's respecting us and our skill," Sikes said. "He wants our help to rid the building of some rats. Rascal, get the boys ready."

Chief waited until Scratch and Dazzle were on the ground by Sikes. His eyes narrowed. "Here's the plan."

Chapter 10
Battle

"We've got them out of the top floors," Chief said as the others gathered around. "Only five more floors to go."

"They're on the run all right," Baxter said. "Make sure you're checking the pantries for any that are hiding."

Chief noticed Paggs had a large gash on his right shoulder. Pointing at the older cat, Chief said, "Paggs, your building, you know the place better than we do. Check and make sure we didn't miss anything. Now let's split up, take separate floors, and drive this home. Sikes, Paggs, and Rascal, finish clearing this floor and make sure no more come up this way. Scratch and Dazzle, take the stairs and lead in on the fifth floor. Baxter and I will take the elevator to the fifth floor, that's where the storage and laundry rooms are and likely where they will be gathering. Drive them in from the flanks. We'll go floor by floor and start herding them toward the basement. Paggs, you and Rascal catch any retreating the wrong way."

The group of cats took off in different directions, Baxter running alongside Chief.

"You might want to let Paggs call some of the shots," Baxter said. "He's already having a tough enough time accepting all our help."

They stopped at the elevator, and Chief jumped and hit the button for going down.

"He's hurt. Didn't you see the wound on his shoulder? He needs the rest," Chief said.

"Would you rest if it was your building?"

"You're right," Chief said. "I guess I just got caught up in the moment. There are more rats than I expected."

Bing. The elevator door opened, and Chief and Baxter got inside.

"Going down," Baxter said.

Chief smiled. "The building I'm in has an elevator attendant."

"Well, pardon me, then, sir—what floor?" Baxter asked.

Chief grinned before he jumped up and hit the button for the fifth floor. "We can cover more territory if we split up. With Scratch and Dazzle coming down the stairs, we should head to the other end."

"Fine with me," Baxter said. "I haven't seen any action. It'd be nice to have you out of the way."

The two laughed.

The door opened, and Chief shot out ahead. "I'll go to the end and drive them toward you."

It didn't take Baxter long to catch him, and they ran side by side. Chief's nose was going wild with the scent of rats. He increased his speed, heading straight for the furniture room.

"I'll take the laundry," Baxter said.

Chief entered the storage room and immediately spotted a group of four rats facing the door. He hissed, raising his hair up as he approached.

"Finally decided to make a stand," Chief said. "Well, you picked the wrong cat to mess with. I'm not old like that other cat. You think you can just bully your way in here. You should have stuck to the sewers."

Chief formed his strategy. Of the four, one was too thin to be powerful enough for him to worry about, the other too fat to be fast, and another one too scared to be a threat, visibly trembling with fear. His eyes focused on the strange white rat with red eyes. Standing farther away than the others, he looked out of place in the group. He was larger than the others but not fat. Chief sensed no fear coming from this one and knew he was the biggest threat.

"We outnumber you," the white rat said in a raspy voice. "Your overconfidence will end you."

Chief stepped closer. As he did, the trembling rat jumped back and fled to a hole in the wall.

"That coward," the white rat said. "I'll teach him later. You two, stand your ground," he commanded the other rats.

Chief paused before moving forward. The white rat must be the leader Paggs had mentioned to Baxter—Bragar.

"So you must be Bragar," Chief said.

"Yes, I see my reputation precedes me," Bragar said. "Now, why don't you get back to your own building before I have my associates tear you apart?"

The two rats flanking Bragar didn't charge and looked too scared to run. Bragar reared up and bared his teeth, surprising Chief. Chief pounced and dodged the rat's bite, sending his right claws across Bragar's face and tearing flesh.

Bragar howled out in pain. "Get him, you fools," he called out as he retreated.

Chief used his body to knock the other two rats down, and they tumbled across the room. They ran in different directions and darted underneath the furniture.

"Coming your way!" Baxter called as two more rats ran into the room with Baxter in chase.

One of the rats ran right toward Chief, who grabbed it in his mouth and flung it across the room. He watched as Baxter pounced and got the other one. He spotted Bragar and the other two he'd attacked run into a hole in the wall.

"Good catch," Baxter said. "Let's go get those others."

Chief hesitated and went to the wall.

"What is it?" Baxter asked.

"I found their leader. He tried to bite me. He's the largest white rat I've ever seen. Of course, I haven't seen many white rats in my life."

"They're actually very popular," Baxter said as he walked over to Chief. "Some people even have them as pets. What's this?" He pointed to blood on the carpet. "You must've made an impression."

"Let's just say he'll be easier to recognize," Chief said. "And I'm just getting started. Let's go."

Chief and Baxter went to the stairs and headed down a floor.

"They call them 'fancy rats,'" Baxter said, "a name they got because they were first given to fancy people over in Europe."

Chief grinned. "Thanks for the history lesson. I think we've got one of them running with this crowd."

"Actually, I've seen several white rats, and they are all oversized compared to the normal brown rats running around here—that is, the rats running around here before you chased them out and these new ones showed up." Baxter stopped at the next level, but Chief kept going down. "Where you going?"

"We've broken them," Chief said. "They're heading straight down. Get the others and meet me on the first floor. We need to make sure they got our message."

"What message?"

"Don't come back," Chief said, continuing down the stairs. He stopped briefly at each level to sniff the air for the presence of rats but found none. He continued downward until he stood looking down into the basement. "Only one place left to hide," he said to himself. He stared down the hall and spotted two sets of glowing eyes. Then two more sets appeared. They were moving in his direction.

"Where're Scratch and Dazzle?" Chief asked as Sikes and Rascal approached him, Baxter and Paggs close behind.

"Scratch and Dazzle are cleaning up the second floor, making sure we didn't leave anything behind," Sikes said. "Some of those residents didn't seem too happy with us going through their apartments."

"They'd be less happy if they found rats eating their food," Baxter said. "You sure we don't need to check this floor better before heading down to the basement?"

"They're not on the first floor," Chief said. "When we broke them on the fifth floor, they started fleeing. I didn't hear any of them on my way down, but I've overheard plenty since I got here. They're down there waiting to ambush us."

"Where?" Rascal asked.

"The basement," Baxter said, licking his paw. He cleaned a wound on the side of his neck.

"You think they'll leave on their own?" Sikes asked.

"Not this bunch," Chief said. His eyes narrowed.

"They fought us all the way down," Baxter said. "Tough bunch. Don't let your guard down, especially with the white rats."

"They've been down there regrouping," Chief said. "I can hear them shuffling around. The one that's giving the orders, Bragar, I met him on the fifth floor and left a good mark on his face. He'll be easy to find. He's the one we need to get, the one stirring up the others."

"Why is it so dark down there?" Rascal asked.

"They probably chewed through the cords," Chief said. "They know there's only one way down. They'll be waiting for us at the bottom of the steps."

"Then let's not disappoint them," Baxter said and started down the stairs.

"Wait," Chief said. He circled around the group of cats, causing them to move closer together. Then he whispered, "So far we've taken them by surprise. They didn't expect all of us to help Paggs. They may not know how many of us there are, but they'll be attacking in groups. They'll try to divide and surround us."

"What?" Sikes said. "You think they have a plan?"

"Yes," Chief said. "I heard Bragar give some of them orders. They're organized, and, unlike Wilber, I don't think Bragar cares if he loses a few of them in the battle. He's got them convinced they can win."

"What do you suggest?" Baxter asked.

"I'll go down first," Chief said, "draw them out. Once they think they have me cornered, they'll be distracted. I'll draw them to the wall, away from the staircase. Then you guys hit them from behind." Chief paused. "That is, if that's okay with you, Paggs."

"Sounds like a great plan," Paggs said.

Baxter nodded his approval. "It's a great plan, but if Charlene found out that I let you do that, she'd kill me. No way are you going first."

"No offense, Baxter, but I'm the fastest and can dodge their attacks," Chief said. "I need you to back me up. With your size, you can take out more rats when you pounce on them from behind. Besides, I've got a special mission."

"What's that?" Sikes asked.

Chief stretched out his right paw and extended his claws. "I'm going to take out Bragar. He's the one that's caused all of this. I intend to finish what I started."

Baxter nodded. "Okay, but as soon as you draw them out, we're coming in."

Chief went down the single flight of steps. The stairway led to the center of the rectangular basement. There were storage bins for the guests along with water heaters, a water chiller, a furnace, and more spare furniture for the rooms. Chief took every step as though he were walking on ice, slowly, carefully. The basement was dark, with the only light being what filtered down the stairway from above, settling in a rectangle at the base of the stairs.

Chief reached out with his senses, smelling, listening, and even tasting the air. It was rank with rat blood and sweat. One thing missing was the smell of fear. *Soon enough they will fear me,* Chief thought, clearing his mind for the attack.

At the base of the stairs, Chief dodged the first attacker and gashed the rat on its back as it went by. Then he tumbled forward, rolling onto his back so he could use all four paws to fling the next two across the room and into another group of rats. With the rats confused and out of position, Chief stood up and looked for a place to set up a defense against the wall. *I need to get them so their backs are to the stairs. Keep your cool,* he thought. *I need them to think they're backing me into a corner.*

Chief took up a position facing the stairs that kept the rats in front of him and the stairway to their back. No more rats charged him. Instead, they waited for their numbers to grow and surrounded him. Chief hissed and clawed at a few of them as he slowly let them back him into a corner. He counted twelve of the smelly creatures.

"Come on! Who's first to die?" Chief spat. He looked around but couldn't spot Bragar.

"You were a fool to come down here by yourself," a raspy voice called out.

Chief heard the rat in the shadows, just beyond the edge of the light coming down from the stairwell.

"There you are," Chief said, zeroing in on the voice. "Why don't you come out here and show your face? I thought I might give you a matching tattoo on the other side. After those cowards abandoned you, I thought you'd run. But you are a stupid rat."

Two glowing eyes emerged from behind several other rats as Bragar came forward.

"You know, for being the leader," Chief said, "you look like some worn-out old rag that's been wrung out too many times. Heck, if I'd known you were so pathetic, I would've killed you up there and ended their misery."

"You fool, this isn't your building," Bragar said. "This is not your fight. We are taking back some of what is ours."

"What's yours is below ground. You can get there one of two ways—the easy way or," Chief said, slashing his right claws in front of him, "the hard way."

"Why are you taking their side?" Bragar asked. "You protect the people who don't care about you anymore. Soon you'll all be out on the streets, just like us. It's already started. There are cats out on the streets just like rats in the sewers—unwanted and cast aside."

The circle of rats started closing in. Chief couldn't get a lock on Bragar, who was moving back and forth behind the line of rats that were inching forward.

"Wait," Chief said. The rats stalled. "Thirteen? There's only thirteen of you left. That's all you got?" Chief hissed through his teeth, keeping his eyes focused on the movement around him. He spotted four sets of cat eyes coming down the steps. Chief growled and spoke loudly to cover the sound of Baxter and the rest of the cats as they approached. "You're the ugliest one," he said to Bragar. "Is that how you got to be their leader?"

"You think you're so smart, *cat*," Bragar said, slipping between two of the rats in front of Chief. "But now you've made a big mistake. You're going to pay for all the rats you killed today."

"Oh, I doubt that." Chief zeroed in on his target. "In a minute, you're going to find out who made the big mistake." *Come a little bit closer*, he thought. *You're almost in range.*

Bragar's face came into the light, and Chief locked onto his position. He slowly backed away more until he reached the wall and could go no farther. He looked at the line of rats in front of him. Two rats still guarded the stairway, but they were distracted and had turned to face him just as Chief wanted, so Baxter, Sikes, and Rascal could get in place.

"Speak your last words, cat," Bragar said. "You and your friends might have won for now, but we are going to kill you before we go, and that will be a message to the rest of them."

"Now!" Chief yelled out.

Baxter led and jumped over the two rats on the stairs as Rascal and Sikes followed, taking those two out. Baxter landed on the line of rats in front of Chief, coming down on top of three of them. Chief took out two that were flanking him so that he could move away from the wall and then pounced high in the air.

Surprised, Bragar moved back and swiped, but Chief was too fast and drove him to the ground. Two rats came to Bragar's aid and attacked Chief, who broke his clutch on Bragar to fend off the attackers.

"Fool cat," Bragar said. "I will remember this day, and you will pay." He shook his hand in the air. "You and your family." He turned to flee in the darkness.

Chief pounced high, clearing the two rats in front of Bragar, and landed on the white rat, tearing deep into Bragar's flesh. Bragar cried out and struggled to get away. The other rats jumped at Chief, and he dodged their teeth. After grabbing one of them in his jaws, he flung it across the room. He gave the other a right cross into the wall, keeping his left paw across Bragar, holding him down.

Bragar flung wildly about, and Chief lost his grip when another rat ran into him. He tumbled off Bragar, stood up, and threw the rat who had charged him across the room with one swipe of his claw. He looked around, but the visibility was poor, and Bragar was gone.

"They're down here," Scratch called out from the top of the stairs, and he and Dazzle joined the fight as the rats scattered and ran away.

The lights flickered on, and the basement lit up. Chief turned to see the last of the rats fleeing down a water drain nearby.

"I found the switch," Rascal said. "Are they gone?" He looked around.

Baxter and Sikes ran the perimeter of the basement while Chief stood guard at the water drain. "They chewed right through this drain guard. It will have to be replaced," Chief said. He went to the base of the stairs to meet up with the rest of the group.

"No sign of them anywhere in the basement," Baxter said, stopping at the base of the stairs. "They've all fled."

"Thanks, guys. You saved my hide," Paggs said.

"Thank Chief," Baxter said. "It was his idea."

"Wow," Sikes said as all the cats gathered at the base of the stairs. "Look at Chief! Barely a scratch on him."

"We sure showed them rats who's boss around here!" Rascal said.

"Yes," Chief said, "but we didn't get the leader." Too busy celebrating, the others didn't hear him.

"I'll check on you tomorrow, Paggs," Baxter said. "We need to get going. I want to make sure they don't try to move in on my building."

"That goes for me too," Chief said. "I need to go check the drain in my basement, make sure it isn't damaged."

"We can help Paggs clean up," Sikes said.

"I'll meet you in the alley later," Chief said. Sikes nodded back to him.

Chief headed out with Baxter. They didn't stop running until they were midway between their two buildings. "Whatever you do, don't let word of our battle get to Charlene," Chief said. "She already knows we went to check on Paggs, but I don't want her to know about all the fighting. I don't want her to worry."

"You want me to come patrol with you?" Baxter asked.

"No," Chief said. "I don't want Charlene to get suspicious. Do I look okay?"

"You look fine," Baxter said, "although I don't know how. Even I got a couple scratches."

Chief grinned. "I'll meet you in the alley later," he said and darted away.

🐾 🐾 🐾 🐾

Chief didn't stop running until he entered the hallway to his apartment, stopping short to groom his hair.

"Is Paggs okay?" Charlene asked. She popped her head out of the doorway as though she'd been waiting at its edge all day.

"You shouldn't be up," Chief scolded. "Paggs is fine, just getting a little old. How's the little one?" The two of them walked into the apartment.

"She's in there sleeping," Charlene said.

Chief looked in the doorway and spotted Mouse lying on her blanket. He turned to Charlene. "I'm worried I was too hard on her. It's just ..." He sighed and wondered how he could share his concern about Mouse. He wondered how his daughter would be able to defend herself when she was so small and fluffy.

"Is something wrong?" Charlene asked.

"No," Chief said. "We're perfectly safe. I just want you to keep a close eye on her the next couple of days. We chased some rats out of Paggs's place, nothing serious." He walked over to Mouse, who lay cuddled up in her blanket sleeping.

"What's wrong that you're not telling me?" Charlene asked, walking up beside him. She cocked her head slightly.

"You know me too well," Chief said. He walked to the front door and looked down the hall toward the basement entrance. Charlene came beside him and nudged him. He wrapped his tail around hers.

"As you know, Baxter and I went to help Paggs. I asked Sikes and his boys to go along too, thinking it would speed things up so I could get back. There were more rats than I thought there would be, and they're not Wilber's boys. Looks like a new group of them in town."

"That's all? Well, you'll just have to run them out." Charlene smiled.

"Yes, that's all. I guess it just took longer than I expected," Chief said. "Now come on; you're not going to stare down that hall all night. Let's get some rest."

Charlene walked over and lay down beside Mouse.

Chief didn't follow. He didn't know how to tell her about how vicious and violent the rats were. With what Mouse had said to him about Bragar's spies being in his building, he worried that they would retaliate now that he had helped Paggs.

"You coming to bed?" Charlene asked.

"Just give me a minute. I got to take some stuff out to Sikes and his boys."

Chief went into the pantry and grabbed two pouches of tuna. He paused and listened. "Sam's out late again."

"Ms. Sorenson keeps him busy all day," Charlene said. "Every time he comes back, the phone rings, and it's her wanting him to do something else."

"Well, at least he managed to get to the store so we have something to eat," Chief said. "I wanted him to reinforce the drain in the basement. I guess I'll have to check it myself every day until I can get his attention. I'm just going to take this out to Sikes and the boys, and I'll be right back." Chief headed out to the alley.

"I can smell that from here," Sikes said as Chief approached the four alley cats by the Dumpsters.

"Here you go, as promised," Chief said. "Is everyone okay?"

"Boys, let's eat," Sikes said. He opened up the pouches and threw one to Scratch and Dazzle. "We got a few nicks and cuts but nothing much."

"Good," Chief said. "Thanks for helping out. It was tougher than I thought. If it weren't for you guys, we'd still be over there fighting. Tomorrow night it's salmon for dinner."

"Hey, Chief, you got a mean right cross there," Sikes said. "Anytime you want to rumble, you let me know. Although we don't mind you bringing us food and all, you don't have to pay us. You and yours, well, we feel like you're all part of our family."

"Thanks, Sikes." Chief turned, noticing a dark shadow approaching in the alley. "Hey, Baxter, thanks for coming out. I know it's late."

Baxter emerged from the darkness and moved into the light. "You're sharp, Chief. No one else would have noticed me there." The two walked away from the eating alley cats. "You know, once in a while I look at other cats that are fluffier or prettier, and then I think about how people are always saying black cats are bad luck, and I wish I wasn't black. But then there're nights like tonight when it's so dark out that I can just slip into that darkness, unseen. Nothing scares your enemies more than not knowing what's in that darkness."

"Black cats are supposed to be bad luck?" Chief asked.

"That's what they say."

"I don't believe any of that nonsense," Chief said. "In fact, your coloring gives you an advantage at night. I wish I had that advantage."

"Now that we agree I have talent, I was thinking, and there's something I just can't figure out," Baxter said.

"What's that?" Chief asked. "Still trying to figure out how I moved through the building so fast? You aren't sore about me clobbering more of those rats than you?"

"Because I let you." Baxter grinned. "No, that's not it. Besides, I didn't want to work too hard."

"Yeah, right," Chief said and smacked Baxter on the side. "So what is it you're trying to figure out?"

"Well, either those rats are getting tougher, or we're getting older. Maybe a little of both. I've never seen a rat fight back the way these did. Sure, maybe when they're cornered or protecting something, but not out in the open."

"I know what you mean," Chief said. "The white ones can't be from around here. They're not normal."

"It's like somebody put it in their head that they are as tough as us," Baxter said.

"Bad idea, whoever it was," Chief said. "They should just stay in the sewers like we agreed."

"I guess the truce is off."

"Yeah. I say we play hardball with any of them we see. It's probably a good idea that we check on Paggs every day for a while, just to be safe."

Baxter nodded.

"There's something else," Chief said.

"What?"

"I didn't want the others to think I'm paranoid, but I think something big is going down. We may just be on the tip of it," Chief said. "If the rats are getting organized, they outnumber us. The only way to get rid of them is to take out the leader."

Sikes and his boys had finished eating and had faded into the background. A slight breeze blew down the alley, and the distant hum of traffic served as a backdrop to the otherwise quiet night.

"Let's go somewhere not so creepy," Chief said, and he and Baxter headed to the roof.

Moments after Chief and Baxter left, Mouse came screeching around the corner from the apartment building into the alley and ran into Dazzle. She looked up in surprise. "Sorry."

"Where are you going in such a hurry?" Dazzle asked.

"I was looking for my dad."

"He and Baxter were just here, but they took off somewhere," Dazzle said. "I don't think you should be running around trying to find them on a night like tonight."

"Oh," Mouse said and hung her head low. She started walking off slowly.

"Hey," Dazzle called out and caught up to her. "Why's that chin so low?"

"I was trying to find out what happed and make sure my dad is okay. He didn't want me along because I can't seem to do anything right," Mouse said.

"The way you came out of the shadows, well, I thought you

were your dad," Dazzle said. "You have his speed, and what do you call that move you made?"

"What?" Mouse sat down.

"That move you made," Dazzle said. "You saw it, right, Scratch?"

"I surely did," Scratch said, coming closer to Mouse. "You made some move as you came around that corner. The only reason you ran into ol' Dazzle here is because you were going twice as fast as I've seen anyone coming down the alley."

"Oh," Mouse said, "I call that my power slide."

"See?" Dazzle said. "You shouldn't worry too much about trying to be what you aren't. You're just fine being you."

"Being me?"

"Yes," Dazzle said. "You've gots your own moves. You've gots to find your own groove." Dazzle looked to Scratch, who disappeared behind the Dumpster and returned with a small guitar. "Can you play me a tune?" Dazzle asked.

Scratch started a blues riff on the guitar. Dazzle spun around in a twist in front of Mouse and came out of it dancing.

"A little bit faster," Dazzle said to Scratch. "Good. Now listen here." He sang:

> Sometimes the way you do things
> Ain't the way I do.
> Sometimes the tune you play-ay
> Is meant for only you.
>
> It's not the same to say
> Do what you want to
> When you're always being told what to do.
> Don't let life get to you.
>
> Just find your own groove.
> Badop deolada do dat doo
> Badop deolada do doo

Badap dealada do dat doo
Doo doo doo.
Just find your own groove.

You can learn my dance.
This is how it goes.
But if I show it to you,
then everybody knows.

Just add your own steps;
Make your own moves.
Don't fret that it ain't the same
Or let it worry you.

Just find your own groove.
Badop deolada do dat doo
Badop deolada do doo
Badap dealada do dat doo
Doo doo doo.
Just find your own groove.

Dazzle finished with another spin and came down right in front of Mouse.

"That was a great song!" Mouse said. "I better get back before I get in trouble. My mom doesn't know I snuck out." Mouse started running and then looked over her shoulder. "Thanks for the advice, Dazzle."

"No problem, kid," Dazzle said as Mouse headed back to the apartment building.

Whether she could find her dad tonight or not, Mouse decided she would put her best foot forward the next day and do her patrols to the best of her ability.

Up on the roof, Chief and Baxter sat looking at the night sky and the city. Suddenly, Chief stood and looked down between the buildings.

"What is it?" Baxter asked. "Are you sensing something?"

"I thought I heard some music for a moment there," Chief said, "coming up from the alley."

"That would be Scratch and Dazzle," Baxter said. "They love throwing a party. Now tell me what's really bothering you."

"We didn't get the leader," Chief said as he sat down. "He'll be back, that one. I've heard stories about the Protectors fighting vile, evil things. Up until this time, I didn't understand it. Well, this one's got it in him. He's not going down without a fight, and I think he knows what he's up against. He'll have a better plan next time."

"Let's hope he doesn't come back with more recruits," Baxter said.

"I'm glad I trusted you and kept Sikes and his boys around," Chief said.

"Maybe it's time to move out to the country," Baxter said. "I hear the people out there still appreciate animals. Farm cats lie in the barn all day eating full meals and get plenty of cream from the cows." He licked his lips.

"Really?" Chief said.

"You bet." Baxter winked his right eye and rolled over on his back, pointing his paws at the stars. "No rats out there, just little, tiny, tasty field mice." He licked his lips. "Mmm, mmm, sounds good."

"If things keep going the way they are, I just might take you up on that offer," Chief said. He got up, stretched, and headed indoors, calling over his shoulder, "See you tomorrow." He started back to his room but then remembered what Mouse had said about the rats being inside the building and remembered that he wanted to go check the drainpipe in the basement.

Chief put his ears forward and went into stealth mode. His

hair lying flat against him, he crept on the pads of his feet toward the basement. With his head barely inside the doorway at the top of the basement stairs, he listened. His heart beat rapidly at first and then settled down to a steady rhythm. He took in every smell, from the old, dusty storage bins to the damp corners. He listened to the fluttering of moth wings and the distant crawl of a beetle. He didn't sense any rats.

He went down the single flight of stairs to the water drain in the floor. *Gnawed on, and almost a complete hole.* He shook his head. Just when he was about to leave, he thought he heard a voice from the sewer pipes.

"What is it?" Charlene asked, surprising him from the top of the steps.

"Nothing," Chief said, moving up the stairs. "Why are you down here?"

"I followed you. You said you'd be right back. That was hours ago. I spotted you in the hall, and when you didn't come back to the apartment, I was worried."

"Sorry," Chief said. "Just a routine check. Let's get to bed."

The rats gathered in the large drain tunnel where they'd first met Bragar, under Chief's apartment building. Bragar stood with a group of them at a pipe entrance above the others. A small outcropping from the pipe made a perfect stage for him to speak from an elevated position overlooking the tunnel. Slim and Slouch stood at the entrance beside Bragar as he addressed the rats.

"Silence! We will get them all—Paggs, Baxter, those alley cats, and Chief," Bragar said, spitting as he said Chief's name. His hand went over the scratches on the side of his face. He winced in pain. "I promise you: we will rule those buildings."

"Uh, how are we supposed to do that?" Slouch asked. "The battle didn't go so well for us."

"Yeah, we lost those brothers of yours, and we haven't seen Darts since the fight," Slim said.

"You fool!" Bragar turned and swiped at Slim, who cringed as Bragar's claws barely missed him. "That was my plan: to test their strength. If more of you would have stood and fought instead of running like cowards, things would be different."

Slim looked toward Slouch, who shrugged his shoulders and said, "Right, those cowards." Slouch put his head down and shook it.

Bragar said, "Those cats think they are strong, but our numbers grow every day. If anything, we will make sure they are not together next time. We will take them out, one at a time."

Slim and Slouch crowded in beside him and looked at the hundreds of rats gathering below.

"See now." Bragar spread his hands out in front of him and raised his voice as he addressed them. "Oh, my brothers." The mingling stopped, and the rats looked up at Bragar. "You have come to me, and why? I will not control you or tell you what to do like Wilber. Here you can live how you want, eat what you want, do what you want. You keep what you get."

Bragar waved his hand, and two rats released a net of food to the other rats below. Cheers rang out and then died down as the swarm ate.

"Hey," Slouch said, looking down at the crowd of rats, "that was our stash."

"All I ask from you is one thing," Bragar said. Then he pointed to another opening in the tunnel. "Bring him in!"

Two large rats pulled in a cage with Darts inside. Slim and Slouch gasped.

"Darts, he's alive," Slim said, stepping to the edge and pointing.

Bragar turned and glared at Slim, who stepped back and dropped his hands to his side.

"He is a coward," Bragar said. "He ran away in the fight. I

could have been killed." Bragar turned back to the rats below. "All I ask is that you follow me. Our time is coming when we will no longer be kept in the dark. Follow me, and you will have everything you could ever imagine."

The rats cheered and chanted Bragar's name.

"But fail me," Bragar said and pointed to the two large rats holding Darts, "and you will be no more."

In the silence that overtook the tunnel, the two rats slowly lowered the hamster cage into the water and let it float away. The other rats watched as it disappeared down the tunnel into total darkness, heading toward the drop-off known as Plummeting Falls. Then all the rats turned back to Bragar.

"Go! Find food and feast!" Bragar raised his hands, and the horde of rats scurried off through every opening they could find. Bragar turned and went back into the pipe, leaving Slim and Slouch alone on the ledge.

Slim glanced down at the mess the horde of rats had left behind and said, "This used to be a quiet tunnel where we hung out."

"Yeah, right after Wilber threw us out. Wilber would never have let us leave it like this," Slouch said, gesturing toward the mess, "all the trash and scraps lying around."

"You say that like you miss him," Slim said.

Slouch didn't reply. His bottom lip trembled. "That's—that's crazy. Let's get out of here." They turned to go down the pipe and ran straight into Bragar.

"You two," Bragar said, his voice stopping Slim and Slouch in their tracks.

"Uh, us?" Slouch asked.

"I have a special plan for you two. A special mission."

"A special mission?" Slim asked, his words trembling out of his mouth.

"We lost my brothers, but don't worry," Bragar said. "I have many more. We're going to visit the rest of my family and get more to join us. Then we'll show those cats."

Chapter 11
The Rat, the Lab, and Stealth

"**Y**ou're up early. What's wrong, dear?" Charlene asked. "Did Sam forget to feed us?"

"No, Sam isn't up yet. He came back late," Chief said. "Every time he does that, he sleeps in the next day. But after a while, he'll be apologizing and giving us extra food."

"It's Ms. Sorenson," Charlene said. "She's keeping him hopping about the place."

Chief's eyes grew wider. "You seem to know a lot about what Sam has been doing."

"Oh, I keep tabs on stuff around here while you're out on patrol."

"That woman drives me crazy."

"Love is in the air," Charlene said.

"What?" Chief looked toward Sam's room. "No, that lady is cruel."

"She keeps Sam busy all the time and watches over his shoulder. I think he's caught her eye."

"Or she's trying to drive him crazy so he'll leave," Chief said.

"Why would she do that?" Charlene asked.

"Same reason I didn't want Sikes and his boys around when I first learned about them in the alley," Chief said. "You get to call all the shots when you're in charge. If you have someone challenging you, it's not so easy."

"Always skeptical of things," Charlene said.

"That's what keeps me on my toes." Chief smiled. "Besides, if Sam is thinking about having that woman around more, well, I'd have to take Baxter up on his offer to move out to the country."

Charlene shook her head. "Your ears are hanging low, as is your head, dear. I can tell when something is bothering you." She laughed.

"And that's funny?" Chief said, lowering one eyebrow as he looked at her.

"I was just thinking," Charlene said with a giggle, "about how Mouse does the same thing when she is upset. Now I know where she gets it."

Chief frowned. Then he laughed. "Well, you read us both right. I am worried. I'm worried that Sam isn't paying attention to what's going on around here. I'm worried about the rats at Paggs's place coming here, and I'm worried I was too tough on Mouse yesterday."

"You've had a lot to handle," Charlene said.

"Yes, but I had hoped to talk to her today, and she's already gone." Chief sighed. "Probably up talking to those ridiculous birds again."

"She is doing a wonderful job every day checking on Ms. Doris. She's always wanting to patrol with you so she can learn more."

"Yes, she does a good job, but she sits there and talks to those birds all morning," Chief said, gritting his teeth. "She should understand birds and cats don't mix."

"You should be proud of her," Charlene said and walked away from Chief. "Frankly, I don't blame her for making friends." She went back into the bedroom and started straightening out the pad and blankets.

Chief blinked, surprised at Charlene's words, and followed her into the room. "What's that supposed to mean?"

"She needs attention, someone to play with. She is curious and so willing to learn. You're right: you hurt her feelings."

"What?" Chief said.

"She understands you're busy, but she was just trying to help, and you yelled at her and told her she was too small," Charlene said. "How do you think she feels running around with you when you are so big and strong and she is so small? Now you've damaged her confidence, so it's natural she's looking somewhere else for acceptance. You will have to win her back."

Chief nodded. "You are absolutely right."

"Oh, honey, I'm sorry," Charlene said, nudging Chief with her head. "You're the best Protector in this city. It's a shame that you won't quit worrying and share being a Protector with her. She is so smart and eager to follow you."

"She's too small. It's dangerous out there," Chief said.

"Dangerous?" Charlene said. "I thought you said it was no big deal. Is there something you're not telling me?"

Chief quickly looked away.

"You should be teaching her. It's only natural for her to be curious," Charlene said. "She's small, but she inherited your spirit."

Chief sat down beside her and began licking her forehead. "I guess I can take her with me today. Baxter and I are going to do a patrol together, and she can come. But not in the basement."

"Thank you, dear," Charlene said.

Bragar stared out of the heating duct at the dimly lit room. It was night, and he knew there would be no one around to stop him. He squeezed out into the room and waited. A feeling overtook him, and he stopped a moment to analyze it. *Sympathy? No, that wasn't it.*

Pity? Absolutely not. Grief? Anger? None of them fit. Then he felt the proper feeling. *Disgust. Yes, that's it,* Bragar thought and nodded.

"In here," Bragar said, looking back to see Slouch pulling Slim, who barely fit, through the vent. Bragar shook his head as Slim and Slouch moved ahead of him, both shaking with fear.

"Those cages over there." Bragar pointed. "Be careful not to get too close."

The three rats climbed up an electric cord to a rectangular table. There—among boxes, bottles, electrodes, and gizmos—were five rats in a cage. Throughout the room were other tables with cages on them. The caged rats looked at them with hollow stares.

"Uh, what's wrong with them?" Slouch asked as he looked into the cage. "Their eyes—they don't look natural. What is this place?" He shivered as he looked around at the other cages. "I thought we were going to see the rest of your family."

"This used to be my home," Bragar said. "This is the rest of my family." The memories of the tests they'd performed on him flashed before his eyes, making him feel even colder.

Crunch, crunch! Slim had found a bag of cheese curls lying on the table and was helping himself. He shrugged his shoulders as Bragar shot him a disapproving look. Bragar shook his head and snapped the bag of cheese curls away from Slim.

"Watch," Bragar said as he took out one of the cheese curls and flung it into the rats' cage.

Slim and Slouch clung together as the five rats jumped and tore the cheese curl into pieces.

"Man," Slouch said, "they didn't even chew."

"Hmmm," Bragar said. "Just what I need."

He went to the cage and scraped his claw along it until the five rats faced him. Then he walked to a control and flipped a switch. The five rats went crazy as a jolt of electricity ran through the bottom of the cage. Three of the rats fell over after a few minutes. Bragar flipped the switch off. He went to the side of the cage.

"You two will follow me, understand?" Bragar said.

The two large white rats nodded. The other three remained motionless.

"Slim, Slouch, get over here," Bragar commanded. He moved up against the metal cage and pushed. Slim and Slouch followed suit, and the three of them pushed, inching the cage closer to the edge. With one last grunt, they pushed the cage off the table.

Bragar jumped to a chair and then down to the floor. Slim and Slouch followed, hitting the ground at the same time as the two large white rats emerged from the rubble of their cage.

"Come, my brothers. You are free. Back to the sewer," Bragar said.

"What about the others?" Slouch asked.

In a loud, raspy voice, Bragar replied, "They disgust me."

"No, no, no," Mouse said. "Your butt is too high." She and Little Foot were in the laundry room playing.

"Sorry," Little Foot replied. "I thought we were coming in here to check all the pockets for candy."

"We will in a minute. But if you want to help me patrol, you're going to have to learn some things."

"Oh." Little Foot went back in her stance.

"You're getting ready to pounce, not do a somersault."

"Sorry," Little Foot said, lowering her butt.

"Okay," Mouse said. She walked in front of Little Foot and lay down. "Now try to pounce on me."

Little Foot wiggled her butt, chattered the best she could, and jumped right over Mouse, landing in a pile of clothes.

Suddenly, the door opened. Mouse immediately stood up straight and marched around the room, tilting her head as she looked around the room, pretending to patrol. She stopped and looked at the lady who'd entered.

"Cute little cat, good job," the black-haired lady said and

patted Mouse on the head. Mouse peeked behind her to make sure Little Foot remained hidden. The lady piled a load of laundry into her basket and left.

"Whew." Mouse sighed and went back to where Little Foot had landed. A white tube sock started moving, and two little ears popped out of a hole in the toe followed by a nose and two eyes.

"Sorry," Little Foot said, hanging her head down.

"Let's go back to the furniture storage room; it's safer there," Mouse said. She checked to make sure the hall was clear, and then she and Little Foot ran to the storage room.

"I guess it's difficult being my friend," Little Foot said.

Mouse sat by Little Foot. "I wouldn't worry about it," she said. "After what my dad said to me, I guess we're both too small to be Protectors."

"I wish I knew my dad," Little Foot said. "I wonder if he would be proud of me."

"That's it!" Mouse said as she had a revelation. If she could prove herself to her dad, he would think she was fit to be a Protector. She stood up and stretched out her legs, which seemed longer to her, as though they'd grown. "Well," she said, "we might be small, but there are two of us."

"What?" Little Foot's ears perked up.

"We're going about this all wrong," Mouse said. "We need to quit practicing as if we're alone and start working like a team. I can handle the pouncing for now. You, you are quiet and stealthy." Mouse raised her head and nodded. "And you have good ears. No, you have *great* ears, the best for hearing important information."

"Stealthy?" Little Foot asked. "Just like you?"

"Yes, very stealthy. You could sneak up on anybody." Mouse continued nodding. Little Foot's face lit up, and she no longer frowned. "In fact," Mouse continued as she walked around Little Foot, who now stood at attention, "since I have been promoted to Junior Protector, I announce that you, Little Foot, are to be my assistant."

Little Foot smiled, causing Mouse to smile in return. "Come on," Mouse said. "Let's go see Ladie. She's always cheerful."

They were about to leave when Mouse said, *"Wait!"* She grabbed Little Foot and shoved her behind a couch at the back of the room. Then she ran to the door and peeked out. "Dad?"

"I was wondering where you were," Chief said.

"Uh, just doing my rounds," Mouse said, stepping out of the furniture storage room. Her dad's nose twitched, and he looked into the room. "Hey, Dad," she said excitedly, "I've been working on my running pounce. Watch."

Mouse ran down the hall away from the furniture room at top speed and pretended to pounce on an invisible target. She hoped it would lure her dad away from Little Foot's scent. She stopped on the other side of the laundry room.

Chief trotted down the hall after her and laughed. "Good! You look like you could have attacked, uh, something." He scratched his ear and looked at her. "I'm going over to Baxter's today to do a patrol with him. Then we're coming back here. You want to come along?"

Mouse looked past her dad at the furniture room. She wanted to go but also didn't want to leave Little Foot alone. "Not today, Dad," she said. "I think I'd rather just stick around here."

"Oh." Chief's eyes widened. "I hope it's not because of what I said last night."

Mouse didn't answer; she only hung her head.

"I'm sorry," Chief said. "I was just worried. I shouldn't have been so hasty in my words."

"Really?" Mouse said.

"Look, you are amazing, extraordinary—that's what you are." Chief cuddled up next to Mouse.

Mouse gazed at her dad. She was still hurt by his earlier words, and although she wanted to go with him, she couldn't bring herself to tell him about her new friend. She was worried about the consequences if he found out.

"You are joyful, inspiring, a bright, shining star," Chief said. "I'm sure someday you can be anything you want to be if you believe."

Mouse starting purring and rubbed her head against her dad's. She felt better, but she still wanted to prove herself by doing something brave.

"So you want to go see Uncle Baxter with me?" he asked.

"I'd rather stay around here today," Mouse said.

"Okay. But don't go running around all day. Your mom worries when you're out all day. And stay away from the basement."

Chief disappeared down the hall. "Whoa, that was close," she said with a sigh as she went back to the furniture room. "Come on, Little Foot," she called. "My dad's leaving the building. We can go see Ladie now."

Slim and Slouch tried to keep up as Bragar walked the group at a fast pace back to the sewers and to the area he'd made his den.

"This is where we live," Bragar told the two white rats.

"Hey, what should we call them?" Slim asked politely, getting closer and then backing away, scared of the emptiness in the eyes of Bragar's new recruits.

"They won't talk to you," Bragar said. "Stay here and keep watch until I get back." Bragar disappeared into a drainpipe.

"Where's he going?" Slouch asked. He tried to look down the pipe, but one of the large white rats positioned himself between Slouch and the opening. Slouch backed away to where Slim stood.

Slim whispered, "He's been collecting junk back in that pipe for weeks."

"I don't know about you, but I'm getting kind of tired of following him around everywhere," Slouch said.

"At least he doesn't make us bathe like Wilber," Slim said.

"We probably don't stink as bad as some of the others around here," Slouch said. He leaned in and whispered, "Aren't you no-ticing how Bragar's kinda starting to order us around more and more? I thought we were supposed to be independent."

The two large rats sat down by the pipe, still blocking the entrance, and waited.

"You guys some kind of tough guys?" Slouch asked. "Wilber had some tough guys. He was our leader before he kicked us out." The two rats ignored him.

"But now," Slim said, "now we're independent. We go every-where with him." He pointed to the pipe where Bragar had gone. "We saved his life. He owes us. So don't you get any funny ideas about moving in on our territory."

One of the rats sighed heavily, and Slim took a few steps back.

"Watch it!" Slouch said. He moved to stand with Slim. The bigger rats ignored him.

"Where's Bragar?" a new rat asked as he came up behind Slim, startling him. Slim turned around and looked into the red eyes of another white-haired rat.

"What's going on here?" Slouch asked. "There's starting to be more and more of you guys."

The rat offered no explanation but simply stared at Slim and Slouch.

"He's back in that pipe but said no one's to bother him," Slim said. "Who are you?"

"He told me to meet him here with these guys." The white rat pointed to a bunch of smaller white rats all lined up.

"What?" Slouch shook his head. "Man, the place is sure get-ting crowded." He backed into Slim, who shifted his weight. "You know, we were here first," Slouch said. "These sewers are ours."

The white rat looked around. "I don't like it down here. It stinks. Bragar said if we followed him he'd get us into one of those buildings where we could eat good and not have to worry about people doing tests on us."

"We'll tell him you came by," Slouch said.

"Hmm." The rat looked at Slim and then at Slouch. "I have a message for him."

"We'll tell him," Slouch said.

"Tell him what?" An old, feeble rat emerged from the drain-pipe where Bragar had been. He wobbled as he moved toward Slouch.

"Where did you come from, you old codger?" Slouch asked, looking beyond the old rat to the pipe. "Where's Bragar?"

"The cats are in the park," the white rat said. "You wanted me to tell you and bring you these lame rats."

"They'll stay exactly where I tell them?" the old rat asked.

"All they know is how to follow instructions," the white rat said. "That's what the humans programmed them for. They'll line up wherever you want."

"Good," the old rat said. "You can go."

"I hope there's better food coming like you promised," the white rat said and walked away.

"You?" Slouch said to the feeble rat standing in front of him and Slim.

Slim wondered why the white rat had spoken to the old rat as though he were in charge. He examined the old rat, his powdery white whiskers and long eyebrows. Underneath the light-gray exterior, Slim sensed something familiar but couldn't quite place it.

"Bragar?" Slouch asked.

"Yeah, what did you do with Bragar?" Slim demanded, pounding his right fist down on his left hand.

"No," Slouch said. "That's Bragar."

"What?" Slim's eyes narrowed, and he stepped close to Bragar, who laughed.

"We can't afford another frontal assault," Bragar said. "We'll have to split the cats up, use deception, and take them out one at a time. Under this disguise, they won't recognize me as your leader. I used makeup to cover my wounds."

"Makeup?" Slouch asked.

"Humans use it all the time," Bragar said.

"What's this mission?" Slouch asked.

"An important and dangerous mission," Bragar said. "Unfortunately, some of you won't make it back."

Slim tried to swallow a sudden lump in his throat. Taking a step back, he looked for an escape.

"It's time to get some sunshine," Bragar said. "We're going to get Sikes and his boys, and they won't even know what hit them. Now here's the plan."

Sikes and his boys played along a dirt footpath lined with blue flowering shrubs in the park.

"Just about ready for a raid," Dazzle said. "We'll show those pigeons. Whaddya say, Sikes?"

"Naw, let's think about it," Sikes said. "We've been charging all day and making them fly up. Then we leave, and they land. I say you guys pace around a little bit here and there, see. So that way they pay attention to you. But this is just a diversion. Meanwhile, I'll sneak around behind them there bushes and come from behind."

"They won't know what hit them," Dazzle said.

"You'll pounce right out of the bushes. Guess that's why they call it an ambush." Rascal laughed.

On the other side of the park, a large gray pigeon known as Colonel Wellington of the pigeon brigade prepped his troops.

"Look sharp, boys. Toes on the line. Those cats are sure to give us another go-around. It's up to us to protect the feeders."

"I don't know, sir," the corporal said. "Every weekend we come out here to buzz the cats that are chasing the park pigeons."

"That's right, Corporal," Colonel Wellington replied. "We're here to protect our kind."

"Yes, sir," the corporal said. "It's just …"

"What's your point corporal? Get it off your beak."

"Well, sir," the corporal said, "the cats never catch or harm anyone. They just seem to enjoy chasing the civilians around the park."

"Those civilians are pigeons just like us," Colonel Wellington said, "just lacking the common sense to defend themselves."

"Actually, sir, since the cats have been around, the park pigeons look fitter," the corporal said.

Colonel Wellington turned around and looked at the flock of pigeons around the park benches. "Hmm, yes, I see. Good point. It does keep us on our toes, and it's a good practice of strategy. If you don't feel that anyone's in real danger, then we'll call it a training mission."

"Right, sir."

"Now that that's settled, I want you all to look out there." Colonel Wellington put his right wing above his eyes and peered forward. The other pigeons followed his example. "Out there is the enemy."

"Pardon me, sir."

"What is it now, Corporal?"

"Uh, there used to be four cats. One is missing."

"An ambush!" Colonel Wellington shouted. "Scramble all fighters." He flapped his wings, and every pigeon around him took off in a matter of seconds.

"Looks like we got them on the run, boys," Dazzle shouted.

Sikes watched the spectacle of pigeons flying overhead. "Hmm, didn't even get to my spot yet, and there they go."

He spotted something walking on the path before him and

called out, "Hey, fellas, come over here." Sikes looked down at a hobbling old rat with two other rats, one on each side. "What's this we got? An old rat walking in the park."

"You wouldn't hurt an old man, son, would you?" the old rat asked, hunched over. "I just came to talk. Can you can point out the one they call Sikes."

Sikes looked around, one eyebrow raised. "I'm Sikes," he said, not knowing what else to do.

"What's going on here, Sikes?" Dazzle asked as he, Scratch, and Rascal walked up. "You're talking to a rat?" Dazzle broke out laughing, fell to the ground, and then rolled over.

"You better start thinking-a something fast," Sikes said. "Like why I shouldn't eat you right now."

The old rat said, "I represent someone who wants to send you a message, someone, you might say, who can make your life miserable, if you know what I mean."

"I can make your life miserable right now," Rascal said, showing his claws.

"Wait," Sikes said, putting his paw out to hold Rascal back. "Let's hear what he has to say. So, rat, what's that you gotta say? Say it."

"My associate is taking over this area," the rat said. "He is not at all a forgiving sort of person, but I asked him to offer you cats a chance to leave. After all, we aren't that much different."

"Waits just a minute there. What happened to the deal?" Sikes asked. "Wilber said—"

The old rat cut him off by thrusting his palm up toward Sikes. "Wilber's not in charge anymore," the rat said in an angry voice. His sunken eyes shifted suddenly. He coughed and paused. He lowered his hand. "There's someone new running things now."

"Hey, Sikes," Rascal said, "he must be talking about that new rat, Bragar. Hey, we cleaned up some-a his guys at Paggs's. Real nasty. They fought back and tried to bite us."

"Why should I listen?" Sikes asked, circling the old rat.

The rat pointed at Sikes, causing him to stop. Within claws' reach of the cats, he was showing no fear. In a raspy voice he said, "Because you and he share something in common. You're both outcasts. We don't want to fight. We're just here to change the order; that's all. You can't be bothered about that. Those cats you call your friends, they give you scraps. Make you stay outside, won't let you in, will they? It's bad enough that dogs chase you and humans throw stuff at you. However, your own kind putting you out like that? Why would you protect them?"

Sikes looked from side to side, but none of the other cats had anything to say. They seemed mesmerized by the spectacle in front of them.

The rat continued, "We're just like you. We're tired of not getting our fair share of things." He pounded his fist into his opposite hand. "Why should *we* be expected to live outside, in the cold, in the sewers scrounging for food and shelter?"

"Whoa," Rascal said. "I heard that the mind goes when you get older. Either this rat is making sense, or he's crazy."

The rat's eyes narrowed, and he hissed at Rascal, "Watch your words, *cat!*"

"We like the way we live. Free," Sikes said. "We don't answer to nobody. Now you tell your boss your message got received. Tell him our kind don't mix, not now, not ever. The alley is our home. Those cats that protect the building are our friends. He better have an army if he wants to take it from us."

The old rat hissed and bared his teeth, causing Sikes to jump back. He'd never seen a rat do that.

"He has an army, you fool." The old rat raised his hand and made a fist. "If you don't stay out of the way, he'll deal with you." The old rat moved back into the brush, still waving his fist in the air. The two other rats followed him.

"Sikes," Rascal said.

"What is it?"

"That rat didn't look so old there at the end. He was movin' too good. I think maybe, well, I think it was a disguise."

"Now what would a rat need a disguise for? C'mon, boys, let's go chase some pigeons. That'll be fun." Sikes started walking. Rascal fell in beside him, but Dazzle and Scratch remained staring at each other. "Fellas, since when do we take advice from a rat?" Sikes asked. "Besides, I've seen Chief take five of them down in one swipe."

"Even so," Rascal said, "we better stick together until we find out what they're up to."

"Right, good idea," Sikes said to Rascal. "Now go chase some-a them pigeons. That always helps them unwind."

"Where you going?" Rascal asked as Sikes headed down the alley.

"I gotta see Chief. Let him know somethin's goin' down. I'll see you back at the alley."

Rascal watched Sikes disappear and then noticed something sticking out of the bushes. "Hey, fellas," Rascal said to the others, "that rat is still here." He pointed to a white figure sticking slightly out of the bushes.

"He's too close to the footpath," Dazzle said. "Sikes says not to go out there. The ladies feeding the pigeons leave us alone, but the bikers and runners on the path, well, that's where it gets messy."

"Come on," Rascal said. "That rat is trouble. The sooner we get rid of him, the better. Sikes and Chief will thank us."

The three ran through the bushes after the white rat and straight into an animal control officer.

"Hello there, boys!" the animal control officer said. "First I keep finding all these white rats lined up like they were leading me to something, and now you cats all together. Strange day."

The surprise and the net were faster than Scratch and Dazzle. Rascal raced away, running into traffic. A car hit him, and he flew across the road. He slowly got up and stumbled off the road. "Got to warn the others," Rascal said, limping back toward the apartments.

"See you tomorrow," Chief said to Baxter as he jumped down off the fire escape into the alley. He headed over to Sikes and said, "Hey, Baxter and me just got back from Paggs's, and it looks like those rats have learned their lesson. No sign of them today." He stopped to groom a spot on his back.

"Can't say I agrees, because I got bad news," Sikes said. "We met a rat in the park, and we had words."

Chief moved closer to Sikes. "In the park?"

"Yeah. Right in the daylight as bright as ever he confronts us. He tells us Wilber is not in charge anymore and warns us that they aren't giving up. Didn't you say you got that leader with a swipe across his face?"

Chief nodded.

"I think that was him then, all dressed up messing with our heads. I gots to tell you, Chief, this group of rats, there's something just not right about 'em."

Chief knew they might have to fight the rats again. He worried about Paggs's condition, but the rest of the cats seemed to be in good shape. He looked at Sikes's gray hair and muscular neck. Other than being a bit lanky in the legs, Sikes looked like a tough cat. "I thought that same thing the other night," Chief said.

"Well, I'm not worried about me and the boys, but you, you got a family," Sikes said. "Something tells me this group ain't gonna play fair."

Chief caught movement behind Sikes and raised his hair suddenly, relaxing only when he realized it was Rascal coming down the alley. "He's limping. Come on!" Chief yelled out. He jumped over Sikes and raced down the alley, running past Rascal to protect him from whatever had harmed him. Sikes followed quickly.

Hair raised and claws out, Chief hissed as he looked around. "What is it?" he asked Rascal. "What happened to you? Did the rats attack?"

"It's okay, Chief," Rascal said, hobbling until he made it to his space behind the Dumpster. "I outran them."

"Who?" Sikes asked. "Who did this to you?"

"The rats. They're smarter than you think. They set a trap and led animal control right to us. I'm the only one that made it out. Scratch and Dazzle, they're headed downtown."

"Guess I shouldn't have left you boys," Sikes said. He lowered his head to the ground.

"No," Chief said, "then you might be with them. Now at least we know this isn't over. The rats are going to come at us where we're vulnerable. They're trying to split us up."

"What do you mean?" Rascal asked.

"They tried to come at us straight on; now they're using deception. It's that leader; I knew I should have taken him out."

"I'll take care of Rascal," Sikes said. "You better go check on your family and warn Baxter."

"Warn me of what?" Baxter asked. He looked at Rascal. "I knew those stinking rats didn't learn their lesson."

Chief looked around the alley. "It's getting late. Bring him inside. We can hide him in the furniture storage room."

"You kiddin'?" Sikes said. "With that cigarette-smoking lady in your building, no way. If she found out, she'd call animal control on us and kick you out."

"I've got a nice safe room, and no one bothers me," Baxter said. "Rascal can lay low until he feels better. I'll come and check on you later, Chief." Baxter, Sikes, and Rascal headed off to Baxter's building.

Chief watched as they disappeared into the night and then went back to his building. He jumped to the fire escape and went up to the third-floor window, where he stood and watched the alley for a second. Without Sikes and his boys, the alley was another avenue for the rats to approach his building. It was the first time he admitted to himself that he would be safer with the others around. He entered the building and went down to the first floor. He spotted Sam, hunched over, scraping gum off the floor with Ms. Sorenson standing over him.

For a moment, Chief considered getting Sam or going to Charlene. Then he turned and headed to the basement, thinking, *If those rats are planning an attack, I know where I need to look first.*

Chapter 12
Despicable Acts and Desperate Times

"**Y**ou can stop hiding. I can smell you," Chief said as he came down the stairs to the basement. He listened and waited. Nothing. He walked a few more steps into the room. The lights were on, and he had a clear view of the sinks, stacked boxes, tools, and shelves with light fixtures and stored holiday decorations. With heightened senses, he moved farther into the room and went behind one of the racks.

"Your disguise in the park didn't fool us. We know it was you. You ready for round two since you had to retreat the first time we met, coward?" Chief said, keeping his ears high. He reached out to take in every smell, every sound, every motion, and he processed the information. So far, he counted at least ten rats hiding around him. They'd made it into the basement but no farther. He knew right away that he'd underestimated their numbers and wished he'd brought Sikes or Baxter with him.

"Sikes told me about your little offer. In case he didn't tell you,

I don't take kindly to your type," Chief called out. "We know you are the leader, old rat."

"So," Bragar said, emerging from the darkness with his fake eyebrows and whiskers, "I can do away with my disguise." Two large white rats flanked him. He straightened his posture and said, "I hoped my disguise would buy us some time to talk. We didn't get a chance last time, Protector."

"I have nothing to say to you except *leave!*" Chief monitored the rats flanking Bragar. In addition to the two large white rats, the fat rat and thin rat that had been with Bragar in the storage room were off in the background to Bragar's right.

"You must have me confused with some of those rats you dealt with before," Bragar said. "Lightweights at best. I had to dispose of a few of them myself hereabouts. My group is a little tougher and more, shall we say, determined to stay."

Bragar's eyes twitched left and then right to the two rats on either side of him. Their eyes looked hollow, and Chief sensed there was something different about them. Unlike the thin one and the fat one, these two didn't flinch as he drew near.

"I don't care how many of your rats you brought," Chief said. As he stepped forward, Bragar stepped back. "I'll get you first. So you better think about what you're going to do next, because regardless of how many of them might make it out of here, you won't be among them. And you two"—he locked his eyes on the fat one and thin one, who cringed—"you two are next." Being outnumbered, Chief knew he had to play it tough. The fat rat and thin rat stepped back, and Bragar gave them a searing look.

"Look," Bragar said, "that's the problem with your kind— always wanting to dominate. You think that's the natural order. I can respect that." Bragar paced around but stayed close to his companions. "Cats eat mice and rats, and we are supposed to run in fear. Well, get this, cat." Bragar stopped pacing and bared his teeth. "We outnumber you. We aren't going to run anymore." He smiled. "But it's not you I want. You are just in the way. So I'm offering you a chance to leave."

"What?" Chief asked. He stood his ground, knowing if he backed down it would only get worse. "I can't even pretend to understand what you are talking about in your deluded world. What is it exactly that you want?"

"It's those humans you serve. They don't belong. Even in your natural order they don't fit in. They respect nothing and consider every life inferior to their own species. They can't even get along with their own kind. Why do you protect them?"

"Wow, you are one demented rat."

"They didn't experiment on you, *cat*," Bragar said as he walked closer to Chief. The fat rat and thin rat kept their distance. "They didn't rip you away from your family. They didn't flush you down the drain as if you were garbage. But you see, I survived."

"And now you're what? Going to get back at them by infesting these buildings?"

"Laugh if you will. How many cats do they slaughter every year? You've seen it, Chief. I know you're a smart cat." Bragar stood on his hind legs and pointed at Chief. The two rats at Bragar's side followed him forward while the two other rats closed in. He still had not accounted for all the rats he'd heard and started to worry. Where were the other rats?

Chief went on the defensive and leaned back instead of forward. He knew this would take him out of his stance to pounce on Bragar, but the rats weren't backing down. It was then that he heard a noise above and behind him. He realized there were rats on the shelves behind him. *There are too many to fight!* he thought.

"How long do you think you have left before your masters turn on you, decide you are disposable?" Bragar asked. "How long until you are not worth their time? You've already seen it happening, haven't you, Chief?"

"No!" Chief said, regaining his stance. He looked Bragar in

the eye. "Sam cares about me and my family. He brought me to this great place. You are a liar."

Bragar went down on all four legs. "Have it your way, *cat*!" Backing up slowly, he ordered, "Attack him!"

The two large white rats charged Chief. With his eyes focused on Bragar, Chief reacted slowly. His right claws connected with one of them, but as he dug in, the rat ignored the pain and pushed forward. The other rats jumped on Chief from the side, causing him to stumble. Chief recoiled and swiped his claws fly back and forth. Blood poured and flesh ripped, but the rats held him. The rats above him on the shelf were shoving boxes down onto him and the other rats that were around him. Tangled in battle, Chief couldn't move out of the way in time as a particularly large box fell. A loud crash rang out, and then the basement went silent.

"Chief!" Baxter called. He ran down the stairs. "Sikes, over there."

Baxter crashed through two rats at the base of the stairs, sending them flying in different directions. Sikes followed close behind and ran to the pile of boxes on Chief, where a fat rat and a thin rat were standing by Bragar.

"Impossible," Bragar said. "You were captured by animal control."

"You're gonna wish I was," Sikes said and flung himself at the three rats.

The fat rat and thin rat jumped and skidded across the floor, heading for the drainpipe. Bragar turned to fight, but all the other rats were scattering down the drain.

"We'll see how long you two last now that Chief is gone," Bragar hissed in his raspy voice and ran away.

Baxter started after Bragar, but then Sikes called him over.

"Chief, are you under there?" Sikes asked, He clawed at the boxes but couldn't lift them.

"I'll go get Sam," Baxter said. "Stay here with Chief."

Baxter guided Sam down to the basement. "Oh, my poor boy," Sam said, removing the boxes that had fallen on Chief. Two large white rats lay dead at Chief's side. "Look what has happened to you." Sam cradled Chief in his arms and headed to the apartment. Baxter followed him while Sikes returned to the alley.

"Baxter," Charlene said as they entered the apartment, "what happened?"

"Bad news," Baxter said. "Bad news all around. Come on." Baxter and Charlene followed Sam to the kitchen.

While Sam worked on Chief, Baxter told Charlene about the fight they'd had at Paggs's apartment and what had happened to the alley cats. "We chased them out good, but I can see this thing is far from over," Baxter said.

Sam grabbed his keys, wrapped Chief in a towel, and took him down the hall. Baxter and Charlene followed behind, stopping at the door to the building as Sam went outside. Baxter heard a truck start and pull away.

Baxter noticed Charlene was keeping her eyes forward as though doing so would make Sam reappear with Chief. "He's going to make it," Baxter said. "He's one tough cat." He started walking her back to the apartment.

Suddenly, Mouse came charging down the hallway from the foot of the stairs. "Mom?" Mouse said. "Hi, Uncle Baxter. Have you seen my dad?"

Charlene shook her head. "Go inside the apartment, Mouse. I've got to talk to Uncle Baxter, and I'll be there in a minute."

"Hey, kid, you sure are growing," Baxter said, bumping Mouse and rubbing her head with his paw. "I think your mom wants to talk to you in a minute, so please go ahead inside, and you do as she says, you hear?"

"Of course," Mouse said.

"I'll be back tomorrow to check on you two," Baxter said. "You should probably stay in your apartment. Those rats are running in a pack. Don't try to take them on by yourself."

Mouse watched her mom wipe a tear from her eye as she stood at the doorway where moments ago Baxter had been talking to her. She breathed in deeply and went into the apartment.

"Mouse," Charlene said, "your dad's been hurt." She told Mouse about the accident in the basement.

Mouse cried for the next three hours while she waited with her mom for Sam to return. When he did, Chief wasn't with him. Sam stopped and briefly looked at Charlene and Mouse before he went into his office and closed the door. Mouse lifted her ears and listened. Sam was crying. It was the last thing she heard before she fell asleep.

Chapter 13
The Calling

"Well," Ms. Sorenson yelled, waking Mouse, "I will have to hire an exterminator! This has gone too far."

"No," Sam protested. "That poison is dangerous. We'll have to tell the tenants if we use it, and when they find out, people will leave the building."

"Then they better not find out we have rats here," Ms. Sorenson said. "We can't live with those rats in the walls. I have no choice."

Mouse moved to the doorway of Sam's office to hear and see better. A long cigarette in a holder bounced on Ms. Sorenson's bottom lip as she spoke.

"Look," Sam said, his hands out, pleading, "there are two dead rats in the basement, which means Chief was doing his job. All buildings get rats. We were lucky to stay clean this long. That's thanks to Chief, and he has chased them out again. The building is safe."

"For how long? Now that he is gone, how long before they're back?" Ms. Sorenson asked.

"Please, just give it some time," Sam said.

"I already called someone this morning. They will be here to inspect the building this afternoon."

"Then we'll have to warn people. I've seen kids playing hide-and-seek in the basement."

"You will do no such thing!" Ms. Sorenson commanded, her cigarette and holder dropping from her mouth. Her eyebrow twitched as she looked down at the smoldering butt. She heaved her arm forward to point a crooked finger at Sam. "You will not cause a panic that will lead to people leaving this building. If I hear so much as a peep out of you," she said, crushing the cigarette with her black high-heeled shoe and picking up the holder, "I'll have your job, and you'll be out on the street." She tossed her head away from Sam and began walking away, stopping momentarily to look down at Mouse. "What are you staring at, you stupid fur ball?"

Mouse stepped back as Ms. Sorenson whizzed by her down the hall. She then peeked back in the office. Sam was sitting down on the couch, his head in his hands. She looked into the other room at her mom, who'd cried herself to sleep earlier and remained sleeping.

For a long time Mouse watched Sam, but he remained still. Suddenly, Sam stirred, and she went over to him, positioning herself in his view.

"Hello there, little girl," Sam said and smiled. He went to the refrigerator, took out a piece of fresh fish, and cut it in small bits. He put the pieces on a dish and brought it to Mouse, saying, "Your father's favorite."

Mouse ate and purred as Sam pet her.

"Time to get my act together," Sam said. "Me and your dad, we were a good team. He must've known what was going on. I should've paid attention. I'm not gonna fail him now."

Mouse purred as Sam pet her head several times. Then he grabbed his old hat; slung it across his thick, uncombed hair; and left. Mouse watched until Sam was out of sight. She sat there staring down the hall and then looked back at the apartment. It felt empty.

"I don't want to fail him either," Mouse said to herself. As she stood there, she felt a tingling sensation inside. At first, she thought she would cry, but the feeling started to change to something solid, something firm. Her hair rose up on the back of her neck just as her dad had taught her, except this time, she didn't have to concentrate—it was instinct. Her eyes narrowed, and she felt the need to do something other than sit and wait. *Somewhere out there is the answer to what happened to my dad.* Without hesitation, Mouse charged down the hall and ran up the stairs. Abandoning caution, she jumped through the third-floor window and headed down the fire escape and across the alley to Baxter's apartment building.

Once inside, Mouse had no idea where to find Baxter. Then a switch went on, and her senses came to life, picking up sounds and smells that led her onward. She followed the nearest cat scent up and down the hallways, surprising a few people in the process before she rounded a corner and found Baxter.

"Whoa there, little girl, where are you charging off to?" Baxter asked.

"Uncle Baxter, you've got to help me," Mouse said. "Sam came back and didn't bring my dad."

Baxter didn't say anything. He sat down and looked at Mouse.

"I know that means he's gone," Mouse said. "I was sad last night. My mom and Sam cried, so I know it's true. He's really gone."

"I'm sorry, kid," Baxter said. "He was the best of us. Did you come over here by yourself?"

"Yes," Mouse said. "I was so sad, but now I know what I need to do, and I need your help."

"It's dangerous for you to be out here by yourself. You need to be more careful."

"Careful? I have to learn how to fight those rats. I've got to keep our building safe."

"You got spirit, kid; I'll give you that," Baxter said, lowering his head to look Mouse in the eye. "I'm sorry about your dad. I wish there was something I could do."

Mouse looked at the floor and then looked back at Baxter.

"Come on," Baxter said. "You can help me on my patrol."

Baxter led Mouse along his route, and after a few hours he asked, "How are you feeling?"

"Better," Mouse said. "But I still need you to help me."

"Go home and eat some dinner. Then ask your mom if you can come back, and meet me here. I've got something I want to show you."

Mouse ran back to the apartment and ate dinner with her mother before heading back to Baxter's place with her mother's permission.

"Follow me," Baxter said, hurrying up the stairs. Mouse noticed his building was the same design as hers. Baxter took her out on the roof, where they could look down at the city below.

Sikes was there, looking out at the stars. "Hey, kid," he said.

"Hi, Uncle Sikes."

"Rascal's sleeping. I thought I'd come up here to clear my head," Sikes said. "If he's strong enough to make it through the night, he should be fine."

"It's nice up here," Baxter said. "I like to come up here when it's quiet and just think." He sat down on the ledge around the roof and nodded to Mouse.

Mouse sat down beside him and let out a sigh. She wasn't sure how sitting still could help.

"I got muscle, kid," Baxter said. "I'll smack anyone that treads on my turf, and you can bet they won't be getting up. But I never had the speed your dad did. You have some of that. And I'm sure you'll eventually be a great fighter, just like your dad. But you need to give things time."

"It's a big world out there full of lots of things," Sikes said. "Don't lose yourself in trying to change a bad situation."

"Sometimes, it's just best to leave things be," Baxter said.

Mouse gazed out at the city and took a deep breath. She looked down over the edge and, noticing the distance, stepped back. "I don't understand," she said. "How is this supposed to help me?"

"Rascal and I have decided to leave," Sikes said. "Baxter, you can come with us. You were talking about the country and how nice it'd be. Time to find out, I guess. Day after tomorrow. I'm tired of the city. Times are changing, and people don't want us around like they used to. I figure it's time to get out while I'm still young enough to get around and before something else goes wrong."

"What about Scratch and Dazzle?" Mouse asked.

"They're gone, kid," Sikes said. "Animal control got 'em."

"Uncle Baxter." Mouse looked at him. She'd never stood in front of him by herself. Her dad had always been with her. He towered over her. She noticed his thick neck was full of scars, and his left ear had tears on the end that she imagined were from fights he'd been in.

"What is it, kid?"

"You can't go," Mouse said. "Now that my father is gone, I need someone to teach me how to be a Protector like him."

Baxter smiled. "Look, kid, you ain't exactly—" He stopped. "I'm not going anywhere just yet. I'll come by tomorrow and do the rounds with you, make sure your father's territory is still safe. But understand that times are tough. I have to keep on top of things at my place and help Paggs. The rat that started all of this is still out there."

"I know," Mouse said. "I can sense him."

"What?" Baxter asked, lowering his head to her level. "Did you say you could sense him? How?"

Mouse jumped down from the ledge, her eyes narrowed, and she tiptoed across the roof, smelling and stopping to listen. Patrolling just as Chief and Baxter did, she stayed in the shadows. Baxter leaped down and caught up with her.

"I can sense him," Mouse said. "There's a quiver on the back of my neck and a foul feeling in my stomach. He's not around now, but I know he hasn't gone away." She stopped. They had done a full circle of the roof and all the vents.

"Come on, kid," Baxter said. "It's about time you were told who you are."

Baxter took off across the roof. He raced along the fire escape, down through his building, and into the alley. Mouse stayed on his tail. He glanced back at her and then turned up the speed, needlessly weaving in and out of obstacles. She thought he must be trying to test her. He jumped through an open window and headed down the hall. They were in her building now. Mouse kept up with him stride for stride. He seemed surprised she was keeping up.

Baxter ran up the stairs, out the ninth-floor window, and up the fire escape to the roof, where he stopped. He walked around for a moment. "Here," he said, jumping up on the ledge. "This is where your dad meditated."

Breathing heavily, Mouse stopped beside him. She looked down. "I don't see anything."

"You have your father's speed," Baxter said. "For a minute there when we were running, it felt like he was behind me."

"What am I supposed to be looking for?" Mouse asked.

"Don't look," Baxter said. "Feel."

Baxter gazed at the stars as he sat down. Mouse followed his gaze and sat down beside him on the ledge.

"Those stars are sure beautiful," Baxter said.

Mouse turned her head, and Baxter looked directly at her. His eyes glistened in the starlight.

"The stars are ancient. They have been up there longer than the world has existed. If you listen, you can hear the distant voices of the past," Baxter said.

Mouse listened to the sound of the night as she gazed at the endless stars. After a time, the stars seemed to move, and she could see pictures in them.

"The Protectors," Baxter said, "existed before humans. They were the protectors of the spirit. When humans came, their spirit was among the most fragile, as it was younger than the other animals'. Cats and humans walked beside each other as companions, as hunters. In ancient times, cats were revered as gods. We guarded their temples, their homes, and their families from carriers of death like the snake, the hyena, and the rat."

The starlight burst into shapes and outlines, showing statues of cats and ancient households with cats curled up by the beds and by the doors. She rubbed her eyes, but it had no effect; the vision continued.

"As times changed, humans lost sight of their spiritual heritage and turned more to things they could touch: hard things, material things. Their spirits grew weak, and wars raged. The Protectors became just animals to them. Some were discarded. Some became pets. The larger of our species rebelled and went into the wild, never to serve again. The spirit of the cat was broken. Only a few remained to serve as Protectors to keep the humans safe against the countless dangers.

"Thousands of years have passed, and the light of the Protectors has dimmed, but the spirit has remained in a few cats throughout the generations. Your father is one of those chosen to carry this light. He's one of the greatest Protectors."

The figures in the sky disappeared, and the stars went back to their places. Mouse opened and closed her eyes, but the stars remained still.

"There is a calling that comes at night when darkness approaches and the enemies of the spirit are about," Baxter said. "It is the calling of the Protectors. More ancient than any of us, this spirit has lived on. It tells us to protect the weak, gives us courage to stand against all odds, and reminds us that we are not alone."

"Oh," Mouse said. "Were the Protectors the first hunters for humans?"

"No," Baxter said. "Being a Protector is more than hunting.

Hunting is for food or because of one's nature. Being a Protector is a calling to defend those you serve, even against impossible odds."

"What about dogs?" Mouse asked. "I thought they guarded humans."

Baxter shook his head. "Dogs are hunters and companions for the humans. However, they are loyal regardless of how they are treated and allow the humans to indulge in their weaknesses and fall from the grace of creation. They will attack even the weak if their masters command it. The Protectors are nobler than this. They do not bow to every command of the humans and are unafraid to stand alone in the purpose of a higher cause."

"A higher cause?"

"A just and true spirit that is free of temptation and that understands service," Baxter said. "That is what our human friends have lost but so much desire, and that is why the world is what it is today."

Mouse again looked at the stars and listened to the night around her. She remembered how she felt with Little Foot and how she'd felt with Slim and Slouch. Her instincts told her that Little Foot posed no danger and was not harmful, but she felt that Slim and Slouch were bad news and that she couldn't trust them. When she thought of Bragar, whom she'd never met, she sensed a cold darkness in him.

"When you learn how to use the sense that only Protectors have—the ability to see patterns and sense good and evil—then you will be guided by a force that has existed since the dawn of time."

"I feel it," Mouse said. "I'm not afraid." A warm familiar feeling overtook her, and she sensed a presence. "Dad?" She stood and turned around, but Chief wasn't there.

Baxter looked at her and smiled. "That is the spirit of the Protectors, an energy that is left behind from every Protector that has come before you. Let it guide you."

Mouse's sorrow and worry for her father began to disappear

and turn into something different. If her father was a Protector, then she needed to honor his memory. *Crying and moping won't accomplish anything,* she thought. *I must be strong. I must protect like my father did.*

"I was older than you when my father taught me," Baxter said. "I serve and protect the people in my building, but I've never felt the calling."

Mouse closed her eyes for what seemed like only a moment but opened them to find Baxter gone. She spotted the silhouette of a cat on the fire escape and took off after it. For the next hour she ran. She ran down the fire escape, through the building down to the alley, and back to her building. She ran up and down the hallways patrolling and listening. Twice she looked behind her and spotted the dark figure of a cat following her. She thought it was Baxter. She decided to give him a surprise and stopped around a corner. She crouched against the wall and held her breath, readying herself to pounce. But he didn't follow her around the corner. Mouse waited. She noticed light coming in from the window and realized that the night had passed. Her mom was alone and probably was worried about her. She would head back soon, right after getting Baxter. *Okay, you won't come to me,* she thought. She readied herself for an attack, sure that Baxter had spotted her and was waiting for her. Mouse pounced around the corner, but the shape didn't jump. The shadowy figure stood at the end of the hall right under a window. She could tell by the outline that whoever it was was facing her. "Uncle Baxter?" Mouse called out. The figure didn't respond and instead rose impossibly up the wall and exited out a high window.

"A shadow?" Mouse said. She went to the wall and sniffed, but no scent was present. She remembered Baxter talking about the spirit of the Protectors. The tingling sensation finally left her, and she felt tired. She turned and ran back home to her apartment.

🐾 🐾 🐾 🐾

"Dad?" Mouse called out, rising from her bed. She shook her head, freeing herself from the heavy sleep. Her memories of the previous day came rushing back. She looked over to where her mom had been sleeping, but her mom wasn't there. Mouse walked over to the water dish and drank. Her body felt heavy, sleepy.

Suddenly, Mouse's attention went to the doorway, where something moved. She jumped to the door and out into the hall, immediately tackling the creature that had peeked in the room.

"Help!" a squeaky little voice rang out.

"Little Foot?" Mouse said. "What are you doing here?"

Little Foot looked at Mouse with frightened little eyes as she stood. She shook her body and gained her balance. She grabbed her tail and wrapped it around her. "I was worried about you."

"You shouldn't be down here." Mouse frowned. Then she smiled. "But I'm glad you came. We better get out of here before my mom comes back." Mouse took off down the hallway.

"Where are we going?" Little Foot asked, running as fast as she could to keep up with Mouse.

"Hold on," Mouse said, zipping behind Little Foot. She gently picked Little Foot up with her mouth and flipped her on her shoulders. "We can get there much faster if you ride on my back." Mouse ran down the hall, timing each turn with her power slide and running up the stairs in leaps until she was at her destination: Ms. Doris's apartment.

"Wow, that was fast!" Little Foot said as she jumped down. She licked her paws to fix her hair.

Mouse looked in through the doorway to Ms. Doris's apartment. "Coast is clear," she said and went inside. Little Foot followed.

"Hello, Mouse," Ladie said. "We've been wondering when you'd come by."

"Sorry, Ladie," Mouse said. "I couldn't make it over. We need to talk." Mouse looked around the apartment to make sure it was clear.

"Don't worry. Ms. Doris is out for a while. Carl and I were just visiting. Oh, hi, Little Foot. It's good to see you again."

"We heard about your dad," Carl said, perched on the stool. "Awful shame it is. If there's anything we can do ..."

"Yes, Mouse," Ladie said. "If there's anything we can do, let us know."

"Thanks, Carl," Mouse said. "There is something I need help with."

"At your service," Carl said, saluting with his right wing.

"You can help me find Bragar."

Carl stumbled off the stool and flapped his wings enough to lightly touch down.

Ladie cleared her throat. "Honey, don't let this whole thing get you so upset you do something rash. We all loved your dad, but you need to think things through."

"There's no thinking to be done," Mouse said, pacing in front of Carl. "I need to act. I need to set things right again."

"Well, I'll be," Carl said. He walked closer to Mouse, who stopped pacing. He turned his head sideways to look her in the eyes with his right eye and then turned his head to look with his left eye. "There's a fire in those eyes. I think we should do as she says," Carl said. He turned toward the stool, took two steps, and flew back up to it.

"But a frontal assault may be dangerous," Carl said, "unless you know what it is you are up against. You might consider an alternative strategy. If you were to find Wilber, he might be able to tell you why the truce was broken and who this Bragar character is. If anyone's going to have information on a rat, it's another rat. Find a long-nosed rat named Streets, and he will help you find Wilber. That is, if he's still around."

"Where do I find Streets?" Mouse asked.

"He hangs out two blocks south of here in an old abandoned

warehouse," Carl said. "If Streets takes you to Wilber's hideout, make sure you tell him you're Chief's daughter, or it might be your first and last trip to those sewers."

Mouse turned, head and tail high in the air, and marched toward the door. Little Foot ran alongside her, stumbling to keep up along the way.

"Mouse," Ladie called out, "please don't do anything hasty. Come see us when you get back."

Carl watched Mouse and Little Foot leave. His feathers fluffed up in front, he looked at Ladie, who glared at him. "What?" he asked.

"You encouraged her. She's already stubborn enough, and you've put her on a dangerous path."

"Come now, Ladie, with all the intuition you have, you didn't see it?"

Ladie shook her head.

"Well, I'll be," Carl said, raising the orange feathers of his crest. "I thought you were the more observant one of us and able to read emotions. You didn't see the change in Mouse? The only reason I helped that cat is she is not the little fluff ball that used to come up here. There's a fire in those eyes. She's had the calling. She's becoming a Protector, just like her father. It may be his spirit that is in her."

"We don't know without a doubt if Chief has passed," Ladie said. "Be careful not to start a rumor."

"The pigeons have not seen him return from the veterinarian's office," Carl said. "It may not matter anyway. If he's hurt bad, he can't protect us anymore."

"And you think Mouse can?"

"That may be the choice fate has given us," Carl said.

"She did seem more determined," Ladie said.

"If those rats take over this building, it won't be safe for any of us," Carl said.

"I guess then," Ladie said, "we better think of a way to help the little dear. Lord knows what will happen to Ms. Doris and me."

"I'll contact Colonel Wellington and the pigeon brigade. See if they know anything," Carl said and flew out the window.

Carl's flight took him high over the buildings, and he headed inward to the city. He flew fast and took a low-altitude dive down among the traffic, finally coming to rest on an old theater building. He looked around to make sure no one was paying attention to him and then dove down into a hole in the wall.

In the ruins of the theater twenty pigeons stood on the stage in formation. A large gray-and-white pigeon was at the front. He marched back and forth while the others stood in line at attention.

"And that's why it's important for us to evacuate the lower Main Street Bridge. The city workers have started construction, and it's no longer a safe haven for our kind," Colonel Wellington said.

"Yes, sir," the rest of the pigeons said in unison.

Carl landed away from the formation and was immediately flanked by two guard pigeons. "I need to speak to the colonel," Carl said to the guards.

"Wait right here," one of the guards said. He went out to the formation and spoke to the commander.

"Right," Colonel Wellington said and looked over to Carl. "Flight formation to the bridge for evacuation. Be back here for drills at oh nine hundred hours. Dismissed." He walked over to Carl. "Sergeant Major, what seems to be the distress?"

Carl relayed the story of Mouse, her dad, and the rats trying to take over the building.

"Let me get this straight, Sergeant Major Carl," Colonel Wellington said. "You are asking me to send the brigade into action to help a cat?"

"This cat is different," Carl said. "She realizes the strategic advantage of allies. Already she has taken me, a canary, and a mouse into her confidence. But I realize the brigade has more important things to do than to help out a Protector." Carl turned and feigned that he was leaving.

"Wait," Colonel Wellington said.

"Yes?" Carl turned partially around.

"Did you say this cat, Mouse, is a Protector?"

"Certain of it," Carl said. "Her father was one of the best. And I can see it in her. She's going to be a great one."

Colonel Wellington stared off into the unoccupied seats. "I had no idea Chief's daughter was a Protector too. How did you know?"

Carl cleared his throat. "Let's just say the cats and I share a superior sense of these things."

I'll have to check with our intelligence department and see why I wasn't notified. Imagine the chance to serve side by side with the Protectors."

"Yes," Carl said, jumping at the chance to use the colonel's ego. "I'm sure any great commander would love to tell the story of how they fought alongside a Protector. I can hear the oohs and aahs." Carl held his wing up to his ear and pointed to the empty seats as though they were occupied. "A great commander. A bold bird. That's what they will say about you."

"Yes, of course you are right," Colonel Wellington said. "But I'm not sure how we can help, Sergeant Major. We cannot fight in the sewers."

Carl tapped the end of his wing to the bottom of his beak. "There may be a way."

"You have a plan?"

"I do." Carl started singing:

When I find myself in a bad situation,
I just call upon my imagination
To think outside the box,
To find a better way.

It's a simple mathematical equation,
$S = IP^2$, the calculation.

It's the key to overcome, so make this notation.
You will find it useful in many situations.

"$S = IP^2$?" Colonel Wellington asked.

"Yes," Carl said. "Success is the product of imagination and perseverance squared."

"Perseverance squared?"

"Yes. It means you must keep trying to find a better way. You just have to learn the proper words to say." He started singing again:

If you find yourself in a losing proposition,
You just have to find a better disposition.
If you think the door is shut
And you say you're in a rut,
Consider a brand-new relation
With your own imagination.
Let your creative side do the talking;
your ideas will be up and walking—
The outcome of a spending combination.

It's a simple mathematical equation,
A magical statistical relation.
Use it in any situation.
$S = IP^2$ ... the calculation.

"$S = IP^2$. I'll remember that," Colonel Wellington said.

"So you're in?" Carl asked.

"Colonel Wellington and the pigeon brigade would be honored to assist you and the Protector on a mission. But our skills are no good in the sewers and limited inside of the buildings. If you can draw them out in the open ..."

"Leave that to me," Carl said. "I'll send word when it's time to mount an assault and let you know the plan." With that, Carl left.

"There." Mouse pointed to a rat as it scurried down the alley and then hid behind some cardboard boxes. She and Little Foot sat perched upon a fire escape watching the alley. "We went two blocks south just as Carl said. That must be a rat. Look at its tail."

"Too big for a mouse," Little Foot said, examining her own tail in comparison.

"Come on," Mouse said, jumping down. "We're going to see where it goes."

With Little Foot hanging on to her neck, Mouse darted in and out of the alley, following the rat closely until it entered an abandoned building.

"That must be the warehouse Carl mentioned," Mouse said. She followed the rat down the stairs into the basement. Keeping her claws retracted, she walked silently and followed until the rat went down a sewer pipe.

"What a creepy place," Little Foot said, jumping off Mouse's back. She went over to the hole the rat had crawled down. "Whew!" Little Foot turned her head and held her nose. "They must live down there because nothing else will."

"I'm going down there," Mouse said, moving forward. She stretched out her claws. She looked at Little Foot, who shivered. "There's no need for you to go down there. Stay here. If I don't come back, you can tell Ladie and Carl."

Little Foot stopped shivering. Grabbing the fur on Mouse's chest with her little paws, she pulled Mouse's face close and looked her in the eyes.

"Ouch," Mouse said. "Not so tight."

"You said you were a Junior Protector and I was your assistant." Her nose touched to Mouse's nose. "What do you mean I'm not going? I'm not afraid. I'm going to see this through."

"Okay, okay," Mouse said, backing up. She licked her paw and combed her fur back where Little Foot had grabbed it. "Stay close behind me."

The two companions entered the dark tunnels and went down

wet, dirty pipes for what seemed like hours. "Cockroaches, bugs, spiders, bad smells. Please tell me after this we'll never come back here," Little Foot said.

"Quiet," Mouse said, coming to a stop. "There he is."

The rat they had followed was directly in front of them eating something. It looked in their direction. As Mouse approached, the rat didn't move. It had beady black eyes; a gray face on top of a lank, scruffy body; and, the most distinctive feature, a long nose. She didn't know if the rat could see her.

"Why isn't it running?" Little Foot asked. "Surely it can see you by now."

The rat stopped eating, looked directly at Mouse, and twitched its nose. "Why are you following me?" the rat asked in a clearly male voice.

"I'm here to find Wilber," Mouse said. "If you're Streets, you can help me."

The rat stood on his hind legs and sniffed the air. "There is only one of you?"

"Yes," Mouse said.

"You got some nerve, kid, coming down here," the rat said. "What makes you think I'm going to help you?"

"Are you Streets?" Mouse asked.

"Who wants to know?"

"We have a common friend, Carl, the cockatoo," Mouse said.

"The sergeant major? Hmm, interesting. Yes, he and I have been on some missions together."

"My father is Chief. He and Wilber had a treaty," Mouse said.

"Hmm," Streets said, scratching his head. "I don't suppose you could harm anything down here, and it'll be fun to see what Wilber decides to do with you. I suppose he'd want to know what's going on. Follow me." Streets scurried along the wall.

"How did you get your name?" Little Foot asked politely.

The rat turned around, his eyes narrowed. He looked at Mouse and then back to Little Foot. "Streets, you know, I know what's going on in the streets. I'm the one everyone comes to for information."

They went down deeper into tunnels and through pipes. Mouse stepped lightly across the wet floor and let Little Foot ride on her back. Light barely filtered in from the streets above. Mouse spotted a dozen rats up ahead and thought they'd finally reached their destination when Streets came to a sudden stop.

"What is it?" Mouse asked.

"Hush, be quiet," Streets said, motioning them against the wall.

The group of rats passed in front of them and into a side tunnel.

"But those were rats," Mouse said. "Why would you be worried about other rats?"

"Silly cat, you think all rats are the same," Street said. "Those are hooligans. They fight your kind and their own kind. They respect nothing. Writing on the walls, taking without respect. Dirty, filthy. That's who's causing your problems."

Mouse glanced at Little Foot, who shrugged her shoulders.

"See, that's what you don't understand. Wilber's boys have class. They'd never be caught looking and smelling like those hoodlums. Well, come on if you ever want to get there," Streets said and moved along the wall.

They entered and exited many of the sewer tunnels, staying to the sides away from the water that flowed down the middle. At each intersection, Streets waited and listened before proceeding. It seemed to Mouse that they were going through an endless maze—down and down in darkness until they came to a large opening. The tunnel was lighter at this part, and Streets stopped on the ledge and looked across to the other side.

"The current's too strong. We'll never make it across," Mouse said, following Street's gaze.

Streets picked up a stone and tapped on the wall. The tapping echoed down the tunnel. Then an answer came in the form of three taps. Little Foot quivered and backed under Mouse's front legs as a rounded door opened to reveal a pipe on the opposite side. Five sets of beady eyes emerged.

"It's me, Streets. I got someone here to see Wilber."

The rats stared across the water at Mouse and then huddled and discussed. Finally, one of them nodded, and the others went to work pulling two ropes. A piece of wood rose across the water, making a bridge.

"Follow me," Streets said. "And be careful. It's much deeper than it looks."

Mouse and Little Foot crossed the bridge and entered the pipe, which was large enough for Mouse to remain standing. The rats lowered the secret bridge under the water.

At the end of the pipe, they came to a large room lit by candles. In the middle of the room were multiple tables and chairs of an assorted variety, dollhouse furniture, cans, and pieces of wood. Scraps of material served as tablecloths. Rats sat around each table eating. At the front of it all was a large rectangular table. Two husky rats stood on each side of an older rat who sat down facing the rest of the group, a plate of noodles in front of him.

"It smells like spaghetti," Little Foot said, causing the group of rats to notice her. The room went silent as the eating stopped, and Streets led Mouse and Little Foot out into the open.

"Mr. Wilber, sir," Streets said, "my apologies for disturbing you while you're eating. I've got someone here who you might be interested in talking to."

Wilber looked at the plate in front of him and then at Streets. "Streets, I know you've been playing both sides and giving information to that hooligan rat. Tell me why I shouldn't have one of my boy's whack you right now." Wilber clenched one paw in a fist and slapped it against his other paw.

Streets stopped walking toward Wilber, curled his hands around each other, and glanced back toward the exit. Mouse thought he might make a run for it, but he turned back to the front table.

"I thought you worked alone, Streets," Wilber said and looked at Little Foot.

"The mouse is not with me. She's with the cat," Streets said.

Wilber raised his eyebrows.

"This cat is Chief's kid," Streets said. "She wants to know what went wrong with the truce."

Wilber looked at Mouse for a moment and then nodded. "Come closer so I can hear you better."

Little Foot shivered and backed into Mouse. Mouse kept a close watch on the two large rats beside Wilber and the rats flanking her as she approached. Hopelessly outnumbered, she knew her only chance was to remain calm. Her senses told her there was no danger, but what she saw worried her. The rats could easily surround her and cut off her escape.

Her thoughts were interrupted as Wilber said, "You? You are the son of Chief?"

Yes, that's why I'm here, because of my father, Mouse thought. "Daughter," Mouse said, finding her voice. "I am Chief's daughter."

The room erupted in laughter, but Wilber put up his hand, and immediately the room went silent. "Need I remind the rest of you what Chief did to earn our respect? He took out five of our best. Since then, he respected our truce," Wilber said.

"That's right," one of the rats said.

"Kept his end of the deal, he did," a rat in the back of the room said.

"Now what can I do for you?" Wilber asked.

"I want Bragar," Mouse said. The room filled with mumblings. Even Wilber cringed as Mouse said the name.

"Do not speak that name here," Wilber said. Standing from the table, he pushed his plate forward.

"Can I get you something else, boss?" a rat to Wilber's right asked.

"No, Quido, clear the room," Wilber commanded.

Wilber used a stick as a cane as he walked around the table and stood in front of Mouse. One of the husky brown rats picked up a chair and hauled it around the table so Wilber could sit down. Aside from Wilber, all but three rats left the room. The two large rats stayed at the table, and Streets stayed by Mouse and Little Foot.

"That rat has brought shame on all of us," Wilber said, shaking the stick out in front of him. "Everywhere he goes there has been death and destruction."

"He doesn't work for you?" Mouse said.

Wilber raised his eyebrows and slowly shook his head. "No. We don't know where he came from, but he is not one of us. The youngsters flock to him. He tells them they can do what they want and gives them anything they want. They don't see the greed, the selfishness. Many of them die because of it." Wilber shook his head and looked down.

"The family has existed for thousands of years. We have survived plagues, human persecution, cats, and being poisoned, experimented on, and preyed upon by our own kind. At one time I believed without a doubt that we would outlive all of these persecutions and be here long after the cats and their owners. But now"—Wilber bowed his head and shook it—"the biggest threat to us is one of our own."

"Then, we have a common enemy." Mouse narrowed her eyes and said, "Bragar killed my dad. I'm going to find him, and when I'm done with him, he won't be a problem for you anymore."

"Ah, yes, your father," Wilber said. "He was an honorable cat, maybe the only one I've ever known. I heard rumors that he was injured but didn't know he was, well, departed. You have my condolences ... You have his fire; I can tell that. Come to my table."

Wilber walked back to the other side of the table. One of the husky rats accompanied him, picked up the chair, and set it down so he could sit. Wilber snapped his fingers, and two rats emerged from the back of the room, one carrying a napkin and the other a plate. They took the old plate of noodles away and sat the new one down on the table in front of Wilber. Then another rat emerged and set a plate in front of Mouse, eyeing her nervously until he was out of her reach.

"Thank you, Quido," Wilber said.

The two large rats that flanked Wilber looked alarmed as they glanced at each other wide-eyed and then back to Mouse. Mouse approached the table carefully. Little Foot and Streets stayed back.

"The hooligans, they have no respect," Wilber said. "Quido, some music."

Within seconds, two rats brought in a small toy piano and a matchstick violin with whiskers for the strings. They began playing slow, soft music.

"Now," Wilber said. Taking a deep breath, he exhaled slowly. "Let me tell you something. You see, my family came here to the new world to live a better life. In that life, there was order, respect. We knew where we stood, and we took the scraps that no one else wanted." Wilber gestured with his arms as he spoke.

Mouse looked back toward Little Foot, who motioned with her hands to her mouth, encouraging Mouse to eat. Mouse slowly lowered her mouth down and slurped up a few noodles.

"Irresistible," she said. Wilber smiled.

"Now as I was saying," Wilber continued, "when my family first arrived here, it wasn't about who was strongest. It was about being organized and surviving. Everyone had a part. Some foraged, some led, and some served. This new generation, though"—he shook his head—"they want everything. They want it all without working for it, without earning it, without respecting where it comes from. If that hooligan had his way, he would do away with the humans. But then, who would be around to make the buildings? Who would be around to fill the trash cans?"

Wilber sipped up a long noodle, getting sauce on his lips,

which he promptly licked clean. He looked at Mouse. Mouse put her lips to the plate and sipped up another noodle. It snapped at the end, and she winced as it hit her nose.

Wilber gave her an amused smiled. "Who would make the spaghetti?" He gestured and kept eating.

Mouse didn't know what to say. She wanted to sound intelligent, so she said something her father had told her. "My dad said the world is changing, and he didn't seem to like the way things are going. Everybody is rushing around all the time. No respect, he said."

Wilber put his paws down on the table. He leaned toward Mouse. "If you do what you say you're going to do, then maybe things will change. I don't know. That hooligan seems to be so busy with you right now that he hasn't been bothering us. But in my gut, I know that will not last for long. His kind, they are never satisfied with just a piece. They always want more."

"Do you know where I can find"—Mouse paused and decided to use Wilber's term—"the hooligan?"

Wilber nodded to Quido, who nodded back and left the room. "I like you, kid. You got spirit, and I can tell by your little friend there," he said, gesturing toward Little Foot, "that you can distinguish between threats. You seem confident, but face it: you don't have a chance by yourself."

"I'm not by myself," Mouse said. "Like my friend Carl, I believe in allies."

"Carl?" Wilber said.

"He's a cockatoo."

"In the event you did succeed, what would keep you from coming back here to finish me off, now that you know where my hideout is?" Wilber glanced to Streets as he said the last part, and Streets let out a nervous laugh.

Mouse remembered what Carl had said about the importance of alliances. "You had an agreement with my dad, unlike our enemy. I would honor that agreement," Mouse said. "You could stay here free from harm. Isn't that what you want?"

"You learn quickly, kid," Wilber said.

Quido returned to the room and whispered in Wilber's ear. Wilber nodded, and Quido stepped away. "My intelligence tells me that the hooligan is coming to find you. With your dad gone, he may feel he has nothing to fear. So you keep your eyes out. *Capisce?* Streets will show you the way back. Don't come down here anymore. It won't be safe for you. Those hooligans are pushing us out. We're going to be moving to the suburbs soon. I might suggest you do the same."

Mouse wiped her face with her paw. "From what you've told me about how long your family has existed, I thought you'd be one willing to go against the odds," Mouse said. "With no one to stand up to him, what's going to keep Bragar from pushing more? It's time for someone to push back." As she stood, she felt no fear of Wilber. The two husky rats that flanked Wilber flinched when she looked at them, filling her with more confidence.

"Go if you must. I'll stay and fight." Mouse headed for the exit. She turned back just before going. "Pleasure to meet you."

Wilber put his arm out across his body and rotated it forward as he bowed his head to her.

"I wasn't prepared for all of that," Mouse said as they stepped out of the pipe and crossed to the other side.

"Not what you'd hoped for?" Little Foot said.

"It's too early to tell," Mouse said. "I was hoping that if I stood up to Bragar I might encourage others to do the same."

"At least you found what you were looking for." Streets chuckled. "Or rather, it's coming to find you. How do you expect to beat Bragar when your father couldn't? I mean, at least he had some muscle."

Little Foot frowned at Streets. The three watched Wilber's rats lower the bridge and disappear into the darkness.

"Well, I'm just stating the facts," Streets said as they resumed walking. "I mean, you might as well pack it in and go to the suburbs with them. At least you'll have some friends there."

"Friends?" Mouse said.

"I think Wilber kind of likes you, kid. I've never seen him warm up to anyone that way," Streets said.

"That's it!" Mouse said in a loud voice, causing Little Foot and Streets to stop.

"What's it?" Streets asked.

"I need to see Ladie as soon as possible. Streets, speed it up and get us topside. I promise I'll get you some good scraps."

Streets sped through the tunnels, and they came out a different tunnel from where they'd entered. "We're in the park," Streets said. "Your building is right down that way."

"Thanks, Streets," Mouse said. She grabbed Little Foot and flung the mouse on her shoulders and ran all the way back to her building.

Back in the sewer tunnels, Wilber pushed his plate forward. He'd been picking at it since Mouse had left.

"What's wrong, boss?" Quido asked. "Food not good enough? We can go get some fresh noodles. The restaurant's right above us. You sure picked a good spot to hide, boss. Too bad we're gonna move again." Wilber glared at him, and Quido looked down at his feet. "You want me to get you some fresh noodles, boss?"

"No," Wilber said in a soft tone. He patted his gut. "There are too many noodles down there already." He tapped his fingers across the table. "You're right. I picked a good place to hide."

Wilber pushed his chair back. Immediately Quido was by his side to help him stand.

"No." Wilber pushed him away. "I got it." Slowly, with great effort, he stood. "That kid had guts. Reminds me of myself when I was young," he said, staring in the direction where Mouse had exited. Wilber clasped his paws, bent them out, and cracked his knuckles. "Bring in the boys."

Quido left the room and returned with ten rats, who lined up in front of Wilber. The rats looked nervously around the room, at each other, and then back to Wilber.

"The boys are here, sir," Quido said.

"Thank you, Quido; I can see that," Wilber said.

Wilber walked behind the rats, patting each one on the shoulder. "Good, keeping in shape I see," he said to one. "Ah, a little soft there." He faked a punch to one who immediately countered. "Reflexes are still there I see." Wilber was now in front of the group.

"My sons," Wilber said, "it has occurred to me that we've been pushed around long enough. There's no respect in that. I haven't wanted to fight our own kind, but times are changing. We're going to help that kid." He pointed to the exit where Mouse had left. "We're going to take back what is ours."

Chapter 14
A Tale of Tails

"**Y**ou sure about this, kid?" Sikes whispered in the darkness of the alley.

After leaving the sewers, Mouse and Little Foot had stopped in the alley to talk to Sikes. Mouse had just filled him in on her plan.

"Yes, I want you and Rascal to stay clear while I set a trap for Bragar. It will take me a few days, and then we will lure him in."

"How are you going to lure him in?" Sikes asked.

"That's about to happen now," Mouse said. "Just say what I told you." She winked at Sikes and looked back. She spotted a rat's shadowy figure against the wall and knew Streets had finally caught up with her. She didn't know whom he spied for, Bragar or Wilber, but she was counting on him hearing the conversation. She hoped he would take the information to both of them.

"Rascal," Mouse said, "it's good to see you're doing better."

"I'm fine, kid," Rascal said. "Who's your friend?"

"This is Little Foot," Mouse said.

Little Foot positioned herself under Mouse's chest.

"Well," Sikes said, "doesn't that just look cute. You two match colors, and she blends right in."

"What are you going to do now?" Mouse asked.

"Well—" Sikes started talking, but Mouse motioned with her paw to cut him off.

"Louder," Mouse whispered.

"*Well*," Sikes said, "we're going, kid. We've had enough, and we're going. No more worrying about rats or that Ms. Sorenson. We'll be *faaaar* away from here." He winked, and Mouse winked back.

Mouse looked to where Streets had been standing. The shadow disappeared down the alley.

"Who was that?" Rascal asked.

"A rat," Mouse said. "And let's hope he lives up to his reputation."

"Do you think he heard us?" Sikes asked.

"Yes." Mouse nodded. "Now I'll only need you if plan A doesn't work."

"What's plan A?" Rascal asked.

"You don't wanna know," Mouse said. "If it fails, I'll need your help."

"Yous best be careful with that plan," Sikes said. "That Bragar, he's a trickster. You'll think he's coming one way and then … *bam!* He's got you by the tail."

"I'll send word in two days," Mouse said.

"We'll be waiting in the park," Sikes said as he and Rascal headed down the alley to the park.

"*Mouse*, where have you been?" Charlene tapped her paw against the floor as Mouse approached the apartment.

Mouse didn't want her mom to know what she was doing, so she said, "Still sad, I guess. I like to go see Ms. Doris and her bird. They help cheer me up."

Her excuse worked. Charlene's face lightened, and she stopped tapping the floor. "That's fine, dear, but stay out of the basement and closets. Ms. Sorenson has someone putting poison out to kill the rats."

Right away Mouse thought about Little Foot. The poison would put her in danger as well as the rats. She'd have to warn Little Foot as soon as possible, but her mom wouldn't like it if she tried to leave too soon. Mouse went into the apartment, ate some food, and drank some water.

"You smell awful," Charlene said, curling her nose as she came close to Mouse.

"I was in the laundry room," Mouse said. "I guess some of those people have stinky clothes."

"Hmm," Charlene said.

Mouse knew her mom was suspicious and worked up the best sad face she could.

"I'm going to go check around the building. Do you want to come along?" Charlene asked.

"No, but I can take care of the fifth floor and look in on Ms. Doris again."

"Just don't stay out too late."

"Okay, Mom," Mouse called as she left the apartment and ran down the hall.

She went to the laundry room. Little Foot was there shaking.

"What's wrong?" Mouse asked.

Startled, Little Foot jumped and then ran to Mouse. "There was a man in here, and he's poisoned the place. I don't know what it looks like. I'm a goner for sure." She held her tail in her hands and shivered so hard she fell over.

Mouse poked at the scared mouse with her paw.

"Ouch!" Little Foot yelled and sat up. "That hurt."

"Serves you right," Mouse said. "All doom and gloom. Now get up. We've got work to do."

"Work?"

"Yes. I've got a plan," Mouse said. "I need to tell Ladie and Carl. We've got lots of work to do."

"Not so fast," Little Foot said. She crawled to the service sink, threw down the plug, and jumped down to stop up the sink. Then she turned the water on and added some soap. She looked at Mouse. "I'm not going up there smelling like this."

"What if some people come in?" Mouse asked.

Little Foot pointed to the machines. "I've learned when those dials are on and to the one side, we're safe. It's when they get to the other side and buzz that the people come." She waited until the sudsy water in the sink was at the halfway mark. "Cannonball!" She jumped in.

Mouse laughed and jumped in as well. Suds flew about the room as the two cleaned themselves. They used some folded towels to dry off.

"That was fun," Little Foot said.

"But now it's time to get back to work," Mouse said.

"What about me?" Little Foot asked. "It's not safe around here!"

Mouse tossed Little Foot on her back. She ran down the hallway and took the stairs.

Little Foot shivered. "Oh my. I don't know what I would do if I got poisoned. Where do you think it would be safe?"

Mouse stopped running for a moment. Her ears went forward, and her hair stood on end.

"What is it?" Little Foot asked.

"Nothing," Mouse said. "I thought I heard something. It's a good thing most of these people take the elevators." She turned her head back and looked at Little Foot. "The baby's room. That's where we'll put you."

"The baby's room?"

"Yes. It's a mess with the baby. There's plenty of stuff around the floor and in the closet for you to hide behind, and the baby constantly drops food on the floor."

"Yes, and it's full of slobber," Little Foot said.

"Well, at least not poison," Mouse said. "They wouldn't put poison around the baby because he crawls around on the floor just like you."

"I hope he drops some of those little cheddar crackers," Little Foot said and rubbed her tummy. "You think it's safe?"

Mouse nodded. "I'll bring you back here after we go see Carl and Ladie. Now hold on tight."

Mouse raced to the fourteenth floor with Little Foot on her back. A multitude of ideas formed in her head as she got closer to Ms. Doris's apartment.

"Is Ms. Doris here?" Mouse asked, zooming into the front room with Little Foot on her back.

"No, she's out playing bingo," Ladie said. "Hi, Little Foot."

Little Foot jumped down as Carl flew in.

"Sorry, sorry," Carl said. "Sorry to stop by so late, but I have important business." He landed on the stool across from Ladie. "Those two alley cats went through the park just a little bit ago. I think they left the alley. Now there are some rats roaming around in the trash down there."

"Good," Mouse said.

Carl's eyes widened. "What?"

"It's part of the plan," Mouse said. "Sikes and Rascal are only pretending to leave. They'll be back when the time is right. The fact that the rats are there means they believe that they've left for good. Now what's the story on our help?"

Carl puffed his chest out. "The pigeon brigade and Sergeant Major Carl are ready and willing to assist. But we're no good in the sewers or in the basement."

"Of course," Mouse said, pacing back and forth. "Well, hopefully plan A will work. Now this is what we're going to do."

For the next twenty minutes, Mouse outlined her plan to Carl and Ladie.

"Ah, a deception," Carl said in a confident tone. "A useful strategy when one is outmatched."

Ladie opened the door and stepped out of her cage. "If those rats are getting closer, this is getting serious."

"And so we have a plan," Carl said. "I didn't expect someone as young as Mouse to understand warriors' terms. But she has a splendid idea, pulling her resources together, using a bluffing technique."

"I don't know," Ladie said. "It still sounds risky."

"Look," Mouse said, pacing back and forth across the carpet, "you've all stated it clearly. Ladie, you are correct; the truth is, I'm not my father. I don't have his strength or his size. I can't stand up to those rats. There are too many. But I can outwit them."

"That's the *spirit*!" Carl cheered and raised his wings. The orange feathers on his head went forward and stood erect.

"I'll be right behind you," Mouse said. "If they get too close, I'll hold them off. Look, it's better than my other plan."

"What's that?" Carl asked.

"You don't want to know," Mouse said. "So are you in?"

Little Foot and Carl nodded. They looked at Ladie.

"Oh …" Ladie hesitated. "Okay." She flew across the room and into the kitchen. Mouse heard her fluttering about. She returned with a small blue-and-white packet with two round tablets in it. "You're going to need these."

Mouse smelled the danger. In the middle of the night, long after all the people in the apartments had gone to bed and her mom lay sleeping, she snuck out. There, at the top of the steps, she looked down to the basement. She'd been told repeatedly not to go down into the basement, but she needed to draw Bragar out, and that was where she sensed him. She spotted the shadow against the wall. Ears forward, she listened. When it appeared there was only one, she moved down the steps slowly until she reached the bottom.

Her nose picked up the scent immediately, and she followed

it to the rear wall. There by a floor drain, an elderly-looking rat hobbled into view.

"You better run if you know what's good for you," Mouse said. She puffed her fur and bared her claws.

"Run? From you? Why, I'm here to talk to you. I heard you were friends with many animals. Mice, birds. Why not a rat?"

"We don't like rats. They destroy things. People don't like them."

"Ahh, people. Are they your masters?"

"I think you should be going now," Mouse said. "I'm looking for the leader of the hooligans. Clearly, that's not you."

"Nonsense. We are on the same side." The rat curled his lips and lifted his chin. "The people are the problem. They want to control everything, take everything. Then they get mad at creatures like us. Why? Because we aren't cute and cuddly. What do we want from them? Nothing, I tell you. Nothing. We have a right to live, kid."

"I don't care if the rats live, but they can't be in the buildings."

"Oh, and you think you're free up here because you live in the buildings? You are only as free as they let you be. That's why they hate us. We're free. Even now, they're pumping poison into the place to kill us. They disguise it in food to trick us into eating it. You Protectors think we're evil, but how evil is that? You think that'll just hurt us. No, that'll kill you too, kid ... Join us."

"You sound like one of those hooligan rats. There's a reason the people hate you: you're disgusting," Mouse said. "This is my dad's building. You leave before I ..."

"Before what, kid?" The rat raised his arms, and six more rats emerged from among the boxes. "I am this leader you are seeking; Bragar is my name," he said. "I'm giving you one chance to join us. You have one day to think about it."

Mouse hissed, baring her teeth and extending her claws. She moved forward one step by instinct, not sure what was driving her.

Bragar blinked quickly, as though surprised she was

challenging him. He stepped back, and the other rats disappeared back into the shadows. "I gave you a chance, kid." He turned and ran down the drainpipe.

It took Mouse several minutes to calm down enough to retract her claws. Even then, her hair still felt different, as though it was permanently stiff.

She started walking up the stairs but heard a voice from the drainpipe. She went over to the pipe, staying where the rats couldn't see her but where she could listen. She smiled as Bragar gave his commands.

"You will take my brother here," Bragar said, "and take a look around. We need to explore the fifth floor and find out what this trap is that she is setting up."

"Uh," another rat said, "what about the other cat that's in the building?" Mouse recognized the voice as belonging to one of the rats she and Little Foot had overheard from the broom closet—Slouch.

"The pet cat?" Bragar said. "Don't worry about her. Without Chief, she's nothing. But that little one, Chief's daughter, she's a planner. We need to take care of her. I don't want any surprises tomorrow when we move in to the upper floors. Take my brother, and take care of the little cat tonight."

"Right, boss," a third rat said. It was the other mouse she and Little Foot had overheard from the broom closet—Slim. "Let's go."

Mouse walked down the hall and up the stairs, taking her time so that her pursuers could keep up with her. She kept her ears turned back enough to make sure she heard the footsteps behind her. When she reached the fifth floor, she stopped and said loudly, "That rat has made me so angry. I'm ready to *kill* anything in sight." She charged down the hall.

"Places, everyone," Mouse said as she came through the door to the furniture storage room. "They're right behind me."

Slim and Slouch emerged from the stairwell and hesitated at the end of the dark hallway.

"She went this way," Slim said.

"You go first," Slouch said, pushing Slim out into the hall. "You're the one always saying, 'Yes, boss, whatever you say, boss.'" The two tugged at each other as they slowly went down the hallway together.

"Why don't we let him go first?" Slim asked, pointing to the rat Bragar had called his brother.

"Good idea," Slouch said. "Go tell him." He pushed Slim forward.

"Hey, buddy," Slim said to the white rat, "whaddya eating there? You don't look so good. Maybe you should lighten up on that peanut butter cracker. It looks old anyway with that white powder on it. Could be mold."

"I'm not sure he can even hear us," Slouch said. "But as long as he follows, we can use him as bait."

"Bait?"

"Yes," Slouch said. "If that cat comes after us, we just have to outrun him. You know, we'll tell him we're running to get reinforcements or something."

"Bragar told us to take care of that little cat," Slim said.

"He's getting good at ordering us around all the time," Slouch said. "I say we look around a little bit and tell him we couldn't find her."

"Do you hear that?" Slim asked. "A lot of noise at the end of the hall."

"What's going on in there?"

"Sounds like a party or something going on it that room up ahead. We better go have a look. Hey," he said, looking back to the white rat, "keep up."

"You first," Slouch said, pushing Slim forward.

"You afraid of that li'l cat?" Slim asked, scowling at Slouch.

"No," Slouch said. "I was just thinking maybe we should let

him go first." He pointed to the white rat, who ignored him. As they walked down the hall and approached the furniture storage room, the white rat remained two steps behind Slim and Slouch. Slim was horrified at what he saw. In front of them were two pigeons lying dead on the floor.

"My goodness, their necks look broken," Slouch said.

Overheard, a cockatoo flew out of the room and crashed to the ground in the hallway behind Slim and Slouch and right in front of the white rat. Slowly, the bird raised his head. "She's gone mad! Rabid! We're all *doomed.*" His head fell to the ground, and he closed his eyes.

Slim and Slouch shivered and looked at each other.

Mouse peeked from behind a couch. "Okay, now," she whispered.

Little Foot broke off a piece of the white tablet as Ladie had instructed and put it in Mouse's mouth. The tablet started fizzing. Then Mouse picked up Little Foot in her mouth, and Little Foot went limp.

"Hold on," Mouse said in a muffled voice. She sliced a ketchup pack with her claws and dunked Little Foot in it before she jumped out from behind the couch.

Slim and Slouch were still standing on their hind legs looking at Carl when Mouse jumped behind them. They whizzed their heads around and stared at her as she moved toward them slowly.

Mouse couldn't hold in all the fizz from the tablet anymore. She dropped Little Foot to the ground and spat out some of the white foam. Little Foot remained limp and played dead. Mouse made an awful hissing sound and stepped toward Slim and Slouch. The two rats shivered, and Slouch jumped into Slim's arms. The white rat went stiff. He started mumbling, but nothing made sense.

"I need more, more to kill!" Mouse said. She drooled, the fizzy liquid running out of her mouth. "Birds, mice, *rats*, kill, kill, kill," she said, getting closer to Slim and Slouch. She bared her claws and rolled her eyes before locking onto the rats.

"Run, run for your lives! Oh, the *petmanity*," Carl said, picking up his head long enough to mutter the words and then flopping it back down.

"Come on, dude," Slim said, still holding Slouch, "let's get out of here."

The white rat turned to Slim, closed his eyes, and fell over.

"She scared him to death!" Slouch said. He jumped out of Slim's arms.

"Run, run for your lives," Carl said.

"Me first," Slouch said. He pushed Slim and took off down the hall. Slim followed.

"Meeerooow!" Mouse let out an unnatural howl after the two. She followed them all the way to the basement and stood at the head of the drainpipe. The basement remained silent. Mouse breathed a sigh of relief and went back to the furniture storage room.

"We did it," Mouse said. "They're gone!"

Carl stood up, followed by Little Foot, who immediately licked the ketchup off her body.

"Good show!" Carl said, clapping his wings together. He looked back at the furniture storage room. "Guys, you can get up now. Show's over." The two pigeons slowly stood.

"Thanks," Mouse said to the pigeons. "I'll keep my word. As long as I'm in charge of this building, no cat living here will kill any pigeons."

The two pigeons saluted Mouse with their wings as they passed her and flew down the hall.

"We sure did put the fright in them," Carl said. "That's the best time I've had in a while."

"Bragar wasn't with them," Mouse said. "I was hoping to scare him."

"Those other two will give him the message," Carl said. "Why do you think this other one died?" he asked, poking at the rat.

"I don't know," Mouse said. "But it worked in our favor. I'll have to get rid of him."

"Well, best tell Ladie we're all still alive." Carl flapped his wings and took off down the hall.

"My mom's going to kill me if she finds out," Mouse said. She looked at Little Foot, who was still grooming and wiping. "Sorry about all that drool. That tablet was terrible."

"It sure did the job," Little Foot said. "You looked rabid."

"Hey, time to get you to a safe place," Mouse said. She picked up Little Foot and took her to the apartment with the baby in it. "I'll wait here by the door for a minute in case there's something wrong. If you don't come right back, I'll head home for the night."

"Okay," Little Food said and squeezed in under the door.

"Be careful," Mouse whispered.

Little Foot didn't come back out, so she ran back to the furniture storage room. She carried the dead rat out to the Dumpsters and went back to her apartment.

"What?" Bragar's voice thundered over Slim and Slouch as they gave a report on what had happened on the fifth floor. They mentioned how the white rat, the one Bragar had called his brother, had been scared to death.

Other rats overheard the conversation. Like Slim and Slouch, they were not looking as confident as before.

"Those were mice and birds. She couldn't take on all of us," Bragar said, stretching his hand out over the other rats, "not if we stick together."

Slim and Slouch backed away, drawing a sharp look from Bragar.

"Cowards," Bragar said.

"That's not our only problem," another rat said. He pointed to a rat who had fallen to the ground twitching.

Bragar, Slim, and Slouch all went up to the rat that had now stopped twitching.

"Is he…?" Slim asked.

"Dead," Bragar said. Bragar sniffed the body. "Poison." He looked at the line of rats. "None of the food from the apartments is safe anymore. Only what we gathered before."

"We're almost out of that food," a rat called out.

"Yeah, and there's so many of us now. We're going to starve," another rat said.

"*Quiet!*" Bragar yelled. "I'll have to take care of this, alone."

"What are you going to do?" Slouch asked.

"They think they can poison us out. We struck back at the cats. Now we are going to strike back at the people." With an evil grin upon his face, he stormed off.

Bragar went up the pipe to the basement of the building. "Where are you, little cat?" he said to himself. The whiskers on his nose twitched as he sniffed the air. "You won't be expecting me to return so soon." He headed up the stairs slowly, stopping and listening.

"I'll break your spirit, kid. I'll get you and the people all at once. Then we'll see who rules around here."

Bragar snuck along the rooms and into dark places. He knew exactly where he wanted to go and made it to the baby's room. There, he crawled along the crib until he spotted the little baby asleep inside.

"All snug and asleep," he said as he jumped down and moved about the apartment.

He went to the pantry. The door was cracked open. Bragar used his body to push the door open ever so slightly so that he could squeeze in. Once in, he looked around. "There." An evil grin crossed his face. He carefully grabbed the box of powder labeled "poison," making sure he touched only the cardboard and not the powder. Then he jumped to the cabinet and searched until he found a box of small cheddar crackers that had been opened already. "Perfect," he said as he pushed the small crackers off the shelf.

Bragar remembered his days back in the lab, how some of the scientists had put white powder on food and fed it to some of the rats. They had died. He dunked some of the crackers in the powder, being careful not to get any on his paws. Then he pulled a napkin out and wrapped the crackers inside. He picked up the napkin in his mouth and walked slowly across the room, scanning about for any sign of movement.

Without Chief here, these people have no one to protect them, he thought. He went into the baby's room and scampered across to the crib. "Here's a little breakfast for you when you wake up tomorrow," he said, dropping the crackers in the crib. All but one had fallen out of the napkin when he heard a sound.

"Stop, you!"

Bragar turned to see a mouse at the foot of the crib. He jumped down.

"Who, me?" Bragar played innocent.

"Yes, what are you doing up there?" the mouse asked.

"Me? I was just curious to see what one of these little people looked like."

"Don't you know there's a cat in this building?" the mouse asked. "A mean, rabid cat that kills rats?"

"It doesn't kill mice?" Bragar asked.

"Uh … that's why I'm hiding in here. I'm trapped. I'm sure if that cat found us, she'd kill us both. Now what are you doing in here? You better not be with those bad rats."

"What rats?" Bragar asked. "I don't know anything about other rats. Here." He took the last cracker stuck in the napkin and offered it with the poisoned side to the mouse. "Maybe we could be friends."

"I guess it wouldn't be polite of me to refuse." The mouse took the cracker. "Well, thank you," she said and nibbled it. "I guess you could be nice. But you better watch out. There are some rats running around, and their leader is crazy."

Bragar's smile turned from pleasant to evil as his eyebrows sank. "I am their leader. And you're right. I am dangerous." He hit the mouse so hard she tumbled over.

She stood, but something was wrong. She rubbed her stomach.

"You just ate poison, friend to that cat. You'll be dead soon, and so will that baby." Bragar started to leave and grabbed the small box of rat poison to take with him. When he looked back, the mouse, in distress from the poison, was struggling to make her way back to the closet. "Your cat friend will be next."

Chapter 15
Bravery

Mouse woke to the sounds of commotion in the hall. She ran to the door. "What is it?" she asked her mother, who stood looking down the hall.

"Something's happened on the fifth floor. The baby is sick," Charlene said. "Mouse, be careful," she called out as Mouse charged down the hall.

Mouse was worried about the baby but also about Little Foot. She reached the apartment and spotted firemen on the floor in the kitchen with the baby. A tube or something ran down the baby's mouth, and the baby was vomiting. She scrambled through some feet to get into the apartment, trying to stay out of the way as she watched.

"Here, I've found something," one of the firemen said. "Powder on the floor." Kneeling on one knee, he put his finger to the powder, lifted it to his nose, and sniffed, pulling it away quickly. "It's rat poison, and there's more on the floor in the pantry. Looks white just like what's on the crackers in the baby's room."

"Rat poison?" the baby's father said. "How did that get in there? The apartment has cats to keep the rats out. There aren't supposed to be any poisons in the building. Hey, the building manager is right there! Let's ask her."

All eyes turned to Ms. Sorenson, who immediately tugged on her skirt and flicked a strand of hair away from her eyes. "Oh, you can bet I'll have a talk with our maintenance man about this!"

Mouse hid under a chair as feet went wild and everyone started leaving the apartment. A fireman carried the baby out of the apartment. The parents hastily put their shoes on and grabbed coats to follow. Only Ms. Sorenson remained.

"What have I done?" Ms. Sorenson asked. Her hands trembled as she tried to draw a cigarette from her pouch only to drop it on the floor. She picked it up and looked at it a moment. "That poison could be anywhere," she said and threw the cigarette in the trash before exiting the apartment.

"Little Foot?" Mouse called out as she entered the baby's room. Mouse spotted a partially eaten cracker between the baby's crib and the closet door. The cracker had the white powder the firemen had been speaking about on it. She noticed the closet door was cracked open.

She put her paw in and pulled back on the door. The light crept in slowly, revealing Little Foot's body lying on the floor.

"Nooo!" Mouse yelled, jumping forward.

She grabbed Little Foot in her mouth and ran down the hall. She raced down the stairs to her room and set Little Foot down.

"Mom! Mom!" she called, but her mother wasn't in the apartment. She nudged Little Foot, but there was no response. She picked her up again and took the stairs to Ms. Doris's apartment.

"I see," she heard Carl say as she ran around the corner to the living room. "Thank you for the information."

Mouse spotted a pigeon flying out as she ran in. Carl and Ladie sat across from each other. Mouse put Little Foot down. "Help. Little Foot's been poisoned. Rat poison."

Carl flew down immediately and put his head to Little Foot's chest. "She's still got a heartbeat. It's weak." He flew across the room, grabbed a spool of thread from Ms. Doris's sewing chair, and dropped it in front of Mouse. "Quick," Carl said. "Put her across this, belly down." He leaned against her. "We'll need to keep her from choking."

Mouse picked up Little Foot and did as instructed. Little Foot's body curved around the spool of thread.

"Now press on her back, not too hard," Carl said. "That's too soft. Massage it, like this." Carl rolled his foot back and forth.

Mouse tried rolling Little Foot back and forth on the spool, but nothing happened.

"Quick," Ladie said. "Ms. Doris is coming."

"Harder!" Carl yelled.

In a panic, Mouse hit Little Foot on the back hard. Little Foot belched and threw up. Mouse curled her nose at the smell. Then Little Foot opened one eye.

"Little Foot, can you hear me?" Mouse asked.

"Bragar did this," Little Foot whispered before she passed out.

"Good job, kid," Carl said, patting Mouse with his wing. "The poison's out. Now keep her warm and try to get her to drink some water." Carl flew back up to the stool.

The door to the apartment opened, and Ms. Doris entered. Carl and Mouse froze as she crossed the living room and went into the bathroom. Both breathed a sigh of relief that they weren't noticed.

"Watch your back, kid," Carl said. "If Bragar came in the building to get her, it's sure he'll be back. This isn't over." He looked at Little Foot. "You've done all you can. Get her out of here. Ms. Doris won't be happy seeing a mouse in here. I'll see you later." He flew out the window.

"Sorry, Ladie," Mouse said and picked up Little Foot. "That's fine, honey. You just take care of yourself."

Mouse carried Little Foot to the furniture storage room. There, she set her in a corner. Little Foot shivered, and Mouse curled up around her. "I'll keep you warm. You just need some rest. That's all." She curled as close as she could. "Oh, what have I done?" Tears formed as Mouse tried to keep Little Foot warm.

House later, Mouse woke to feel someone grooming her. "Mom?"

"I guess I'm just going to have to give up on you coming home on time," Charlene said. "Just like your father."

Mouse stood and shook her head. "Sorry. We just lost Dad, and I couldn't stand to lose her too." Mouse looked down at Little Foot, who remained motionless.

"I understand," Charlene said. She sniffed Little Foot and then rubbed her with her chin. "She's still warm but barely breathing. What happened?"

"She got into rat poison," Mouse said. Her stomach grumbled.

"I'll stay with her," Charlene said. "Why don't you go back to the apartment and get some food and water? Something big is going on. My owner, Mrs. Ryan, is back with her husband, who owns the building. He's in talking with Sam and Ms. Sorenson right now."

"You're not mad at me for having a mouse as a friend?"

"This particular mouse looks like the pet that boy lost. I don't think she's dangerous. But you shouldn't be afraid to tell me things."

"Thanks, Mom," Mouse said. "Sorry about being out all night."

Mouse started to go downstairs to eat but decided to go up and check on Ms. Doris and Ladie. She felt tired and sad. By the time she walked in the door, she felt like crying.

"Oh, my little sweetie, what is troubling you so much that your head is almost touching the ground?" Ladie asked. "Come up here, child."

Mouse hopped onto the stool, plopped down, and hung her head. A tear came out of her eye. Ladie reached out one little wing with soft feathers as far as she could stretch. It was enough, and Mouse picked up her chin and looked into the canary's blue eyes.

"I thought I could change things," Mouse said. "I thought I could help get things back to the way my dad would have wanted. I tried to make things right. But Bragar's too strong. My plan failed, and now Little Foot is dying, and the baby is hurt, and Sam is going to be fired."

"Well." Ladie turned around in her cage and pulled out one of her mirrors. "No wonder your head is hanging so low with all that you're carrying on your shoulders. Child, you've learned a great lesson here. The world is a big place full of many things—some good, some not so good. One thing is for sure: it's not out there to just give you what you want."

"What?" Mouse said, surprised at Ladie's response.

"You've got to try."

"I did," Mouse said. "My dad was right. I'm just too small. Even you thought my plan was too dangerous. I should have listened."

"Yes, I did think your plan was dangerous, but I was wrong to tell you not to do it."

"I don't understand, Ladie. It didn't work. I tried to beat Bragar, but I'm not as strong as my father is. I'm just a failure. A cute, fluffy failure. He would be ashamed of me." Mouse plopped her chin onto her front paws.

"Mouse …" Ladie hummed a short melody. "Your father would be proud of you." She turned and picked up one of her mirrors with her teeth and put it against her cage so that Mouse could see herself.

Mouse looked into the mirror. It changed colors, and the picture started to blur and change as Ladie's soft singing hypnotized her into relaxing.

Oh, where does the time go?
Weren't you just a child?
You looked at your father and shared a smile.
He showed you all the joy that life can bring.
You laughed and shared such wonderful things.

It seemed it would never end,
But times change as we grow older.
It's not the same, you say,
But the memories will always stay.
It's time for you to know;
He would want you to grow
And be bold and strong and true.
He would be proud of you.
So lift your head up high,
And let your spirit fly.
He would be proud of you,

Mouse saw visions of her and her father running and patrolling. She remembered when he took her to the roof and taught her how to pounce as Ladie continued singing:

Brave little one,
You were born to run free.
Give it all you've got
So the world will see.
You can have everything if you hold on to your dream.
Everyone has a choice
When they have a fall.
Do you stay down or stand up strong and tall?
Just let your spirit soar,
And let them hear you roar.
There's strength inside of you,
And we will see this through.
He would be proud of you.

Ladie stopped singing. Mouse looked at her reflection as it came back into focus.

"A cute, fluffy failure?" Ladie said. "Your father was strong, Mouse. But that's not all he had. He had a strong heart and a determined will. I see that in you. I know it's in your heart. And no one can overcome that or take that away."

In the mirror Mouse could see her face lighten. She raised her ears confidently. She turned and noticed Carl had flown in and was sitting on the windowsill.

"You don't have your father's size," Ladie said, "but you have something else."

"What's that?" Mouse asked.

"You have friends," Ladie said and held out her wing. Carl stepped beside her.

"That's right," Carl said. "Your first plan put fear into some of those rats, even if we didn't get Bragar. You can't give in now. It's time we take a stand."

"Carl is right," Ladie said.

"You think so?" Mouse said, surprised Ladie wasn't telling her to be more cautious.

Instead, Ladie whistled another tune and started to sing again:

> When you are young and small,
> The world is so big and tall,
> Full of wonderful things.
> Every day is a surprise,
> much more than meets the eye.
> But not all of it is good.
> You'd change it if you could.

Carl took over on the next part:

> And that's when I say,
> Round up your courage.
> Think up a plan.
> It's time to make a stand.
> We won't allow it,
> Not one more day.
> The bullies won't get their way.
> It's time to take a stand.
> It's time to make a stand.

Mouse clapped her paws together for Carl, and then Ladie continued the song:

> When things are going rough,

You think you've had enough.
Every day you get by,
Don't worry how or why.
We'll give it one more try.
It's time to set things right.
Carl joined in, and the two sang together:
Round up your courage.
Let's make a plan.
It's time to make a stand.
What are you waiting for?
I'll meet you at the door.
We'll find our wings and soar.
It's time to make a stand.
It's time to take a stand.

"That's a wonderful song," Mouse said. "You have a great voice too, Carl."

"Well, of course," Carl said. "Have to live up to the reputation of my species."

"Do you feel better now?" Ladie asked.

"A little. But I'm worried."

"You have your father's courage and spirit," Ladie said. "Not knowing what to do is not your problem. You can't stand not doing something about it. It's not in your nature to stand by."

"Ladie's right," Carl said. "You have your father's speed and grit."

"Grit?" Mouse asked.

"Yes, toughness right down to the bone. Chief had the courage to stand his ground, and he earned respect that way. He wasn't the biggest cat around. He was the boldest. You've earned respect with the deeds you've done, and you have a friend in every corner."

Several pigeons flew in behind Carl, landed on the stool, and looked at Mouse.

"This is Colonel Wellington," Carl said pointing to one of the pigeons.

"Colonel Wellington and the pigeon brigade are at your

service," Colonel Wellington said as he saluted. "It's a pleasure to meet a Protector."

"Nice to meet you," Mouse said and nodded.

"Honey, we will help you," Ladie said. "Yesterday, I saw a small cat that had grown. Carl saw it too." Carl nodded. "Are you going to so easily accept failure, or are you going to be a Protector? Only you can decide."

"That's right," Carl said. "What we did took guts. It's just that we're dealing with one mean rat. If you are going to stand up against a bully, you need a plan."

"I have a plan," Mouse said. "But it will take all of us, and it's much more dangerous than the last one." She raised her ears, narrowed her eyes, and fluffed her tail. Carl backed away from her as she jumped off the stool and headed for the door. "I'll be back to give you the details as soon as I check on a few things."

Mouse headed to her apartment to quickly get some food and water. As she rounded the corner, she spotted Sam standing outside Ms. Sorenson's office and apartment. His eyes lit up as Mouse approached.

"Hi there, little one," Sam said. "Doing the rounds like your father taught you? That's a good girl." Sam held out his hand, and Mouse rose up on her back legs and bumped her head against his hand as she'd seen her dad do.

"Sam, we're ready for you," a deep voice called from inside the apartment.

"That was Bill Ryan," Sam said. "He's the owner of these buildings and my boss. Guess I better see what he wants and find out if we still have a place to live."

Mouse remained just outside the door of the manager's apartment, where she could see in and hear.

Sam went into the office inside the apartment and shook hands with Bill Ryan, who was sitting at Ms. Sorenson's desk. Ms. Sorenson sat in one of the two chairs across the desk, her hands twisted and turned together, searching for the cigarette that wasn't there.

"Please sit down, Sam. We have some things to talk about," Mr. Ryan said.

Sam sat down in the chair adjacent to Ms. Sorenson and across from Bill Ryan. He glanced at Ms. Sorenson, but she kept her eyes to the floor as if she didn't know he was in the room.

Mr. Ryan started the conversation. "We all know the Joneses' baby got hurt yesterday, and now the parents are threatening to sue us. The tenants are asking questions."

"Well …" Ms. Sorenson reached for her cigarette case, but Mr. Ryan shook his head. She put it back and bit hard on her right middle fingernail. "We can't be responsible for what our tenants bring into their apartments."

Sam's eyes went to Ms. Sorenson and then back to Mr. Ryan. When Mr. Ryan looked at him, Sam looked to the floor, not in shame, but in anger.

"Mrs. Jones said she didn't buy the rat poison and doesn't know how it got into her apartment," Mr. Ryan said.

Sam shifted left in his seat and then right. He met Mr. Ryan's eyes for a moment and then found a familiar spot on the floor to look at.

"Sam," Mr. Ryan said, looking at him, "do you have something to say?"

Afraid for his job, Sam shook his head. He didn't know what to say, and he didn't know how much or how little Mr. Ryan knew about what was going on.

"Well," Ms. Sorenson said, "it's obvious that Sam's cat couldn't handle the task of such a large building. He did tell you that it got hurt, right?"

Sam shifted in his seat.

"Is there something you want to say, Sam?" Mr. Ryan asked. Sam again remained quiet.

"Apparently the residents feel threatened," Ms. Sorenson said. "So some of them have gone out and bought rat poison. Sir, I'm not so sure Mrs. Jones didn't buy it herself. I don't blame her." She rolled her eyes in Sam's direction. "It's obvious we need to make some changes around here if our tenants don't feel safe."

"Enough!" Sam stood from his chair. He was surprised when he realized the protest had come from his own mouth. He pointed his right finger at Ms. Sorenson and then tapped the desk as he said, "Mr. Ryan, I am the facilities manager around here. I am responsible for the situation."

"You should be," Ms. Sorenson spat.

"Ms. Sorenson," Sam said, pointing his finger at her, "has kept my cats from doing their patrols by forbidding them to ride the elevator and trying to get me to only let them out after the tenants are asleep. Maybe if she wouldn't have interfered, the problem wouldn't exist. Every building gets a few rats in it from time to time; that's the nature of the job. Chief did get hurt defending your building. No kids got hurt. Chief did his job. Scared because Chief got hurt, Ms. Sorenson brought in the exterminator and put rat poison in the building without telling the residents. She waited until they were out and used the master keys to get into their apartments."

Mr. Ryan's jaw dropped, and Ms. Sorenson slouched in her chair.

"If she would have stayed out of my way and let me do my job, there would be no dangerous chemicals in the building. All I hear anymore is about going back to safer, more environmentally friendly things." Sam crossed his hands in front of him, making a cutting motion. "Well, Mr. Ryan, you can fire me, but I'm taking the poison out of this place and letting my cats do their job. Moreover, if Ms. Sorenson doesn't like it, maybe she should have my job. But I doubt she's going to be able to fix the elevator if it breaks."

"Okay, okay," Mr. Ryan said. "Let's all calm down here. First thing we've got to do is get rid of any poison on the premises. We can't afford another injury. I will offer to pay the medical bill for the Joneses and give them free rent for the next couple of months. Sam"—Mr. Ryan looked at Sam, his eyes narrow and his voice loud—"you have one week to let me know how you plan to take care of this rat problem. And you"—he looked at Ms. Sorenson—"I don't care if you are my wife's sister, another mistake and you're out."

Shaking his head at Ms. Sorenson, Mr. Ryan stood, grabbed his hat, and walked out of the room.

Without as much as a look to Ms. Sorenson, Sam went over to the door and, with one hand on the doorknob and the other extended outward, said, "If you don't mind, I've got a lot of work to do."

"*Hmmph!*" Ms. Sorenson said as she put a cigarette in her holder and lit it.

Sam went back to where Ms. Sorenson sat and grabbed the cigarette out of the holder in her mouth. "One more thing," he said, dropping it to the ground and smashing it under his boot. "This is a *no smoking* building—read the signs."

Ms. Sorenson flashed her eyes, but Sam stood his ground. "Hmmph," she managed to say again before standing and stomping out of the room. She looked down at Mouse, who stood at the entrance to the office. "Stupid fur ball."

Mouse raised the hair on her back a bit, and Sam thought she was going to hiss, but instead she rubbed right against Ms. Sorenson's velvet skirt, leaving a good deal of hair behind.

Sam laughed. "Looks like you have a new friend," he said.

"Ahh!" Ms. Sorenson gasped and stomped down the hall. Halfway down, she broke a heel and had to limp the rest of the way.

Sam chuckled and smiled at Mouse. "Come on, girl," he said and walked back to their apartment. He took some fresh fish out of the refrigerator and sliced it up for Mouse, who ate heartedly. Then Sam opened a cabinet and reached back far under the sink, slowly pulling out a jar. He opened the jar and took out a wad of money held together by a rubber band.

Several minutes passed while Sam counted the money. He patted Mouse on the head. "Hmm. Your dad used to look at me just like that when he was ready to go out on a patrol." He reached the amount he needed, secured the rest with the rubber band, and returned it to the jar. He placed the jar back under the counter.

"I promised to change things." He petted Mouse again. "Look, I've got some important business to tend to. You keep an eye on the place until I get back." He grabbed his jacket and headed out the door.

After Sam left, Mouse headed back to her food dish. She drank some water first and then went to eat some more fish. Then she stopped and thought about her next move; her plan was more dangerous than anything she'd ever attempted, and she was scared. She wished her dad was there to help her and give her confidence. Instead, she found comfort in her reflection as she looked into her water dish. She started singing to it.

I am so scared,
Not alone,
But on my own.
My friends are close,
For them I fear
The darkness coming ever near.

How can I stand against the tide?
Should I just run and hide?
I remember what my father said to me:

Amazing, extraordinary,
That's what you are.
Joyful, inspiring,
A bright shining star.
One day you'll be
Anything you want to be.
This I believe.

The time has come for me to rise,
Find the courage that's inside.
The words he said
I still hear
In my heart,
Driving out the fear.
I must believe there's strength inside of me

Amazing, extraordinary,
that's what you are.
Joyful, inspiring,
a bright shining star.
One day you'll be
everything you want to be.
This I believe.

Amazing, extraordinary,
All that I am.
Joyful, inspiring,
Do what I can.
Today I'll be
Everything that I can be.
Now I believe.

By the time Mouse was done singing, she was no longer at
her food dish but in the middle of the living room. It was quiet,
and no one else was there. Still slightly hungry, she looked

toward her food dish but didn't go there. Instead, she headed for the door.

"Good, hungry and ready! Time for plan B." Mouse started toward the stairs but hesitated and stopped in front of the elevator. "No time to waste." She jumped and hit the up button.

With a *bing* the elevator arrived and opened. The elevator attendant looked down at Mouse as she entered.

"Whoa, little cat. I might have let your father ride, but this is going to stop. Ms. Sorenson doesn't want pets on the elevator." He reached down to pick up Mouse.

Mouse hissed and growled. She stood her hair on end and fluffed her tail while slashing her right claw out twice.

The attendant immediately jumped to the back of the elevator. "It must run in your family."

Mouse hit the button for the fourteenth floor. She was heading to tell Ladie and Carl her plan.

Chapter 16
Yes, Sergeant Major Carl

"**O**h, c'mon, Sikes, let's make some of these pigeons fly," Rascal said. "They've had it too easy without us around. Looks like they've been eating too much popcorn and stuff—they're all fat."

Sikes didn't respond. He watched the pigeons, and then he hung his head low.

"We've been hanging out in this park for two days," Rascal said. "What is it? Why don't we get out of here and head for the country?"

"It's not the same without the boys," Sikes said. "We're to wait. I promised Mouse I'd help. You ain't gotta go back if you don't want."

"Are you crazy?" Rascal asked wide-eyed. "You want to go back and tangle with that psycho rat? He'll get us both caught."

"Look, Rascal, we been hangin' together a long time. But it's time for me to tell you, I ain't gonna do this. I ain't gonna let that freaked-out rat get the best of me. Those were my boys, my family. That Bragar, he's gonna pay. Mouse has a plan. She's got her Dad's smarts, all right, and I told her we'd wait. I told her we'd help, so that's what we're doing—we're waiting."

"Okay, okay," Rascal said. "How do we know when it's time to go back?"

"I told her we'd wait in the park." Sikes scratched the back of his neck. "She wants Bragar to think we've gone. That's why we can't chase no pigeons. We gotta be incon … incosp … make it look like we ain't here. I didn't think to ask her how we'd know what time to go back."

"It's time," a strange-looking bird said from the branch above them. He swooped down and landed a few feet away.

"Sikes, I think that bird just talked to us," Rascal said.

"Yo, bird, you say something?" Sikes asked.

"Yes, I said it's time." The bird stepped closer and spread his wings out.

"Hey, funny-lookin' pigeon, you want us to eat you or what?" Sikes asked.

"My heavens no," the bird said. "Although I'd probably taste better than those wretched birds you chase. I'm a cockatoo, not a pigeon. Carl's the name."

"Well," Sikes said, leaning in and lowering his voice, "truth is that we don't eat them. We just like to chase them around for sport. Keeps us lean, and it's fun."

"That's good that you don't eat birds," Carl said, "because part of the deal is that we work together."

"So what's your biz?" Sikes asked.

"Gentlemen," Carl said, and Rascal and Sikes looked around to make sure he was addressing them, "I have come to call you to action."

"He called us *gentlemen*," Rascal said. "We couldn't eat him now after he did that. So, bird, what are you talking about?"

"I am a friend of Mouse. She needs our help."

Sikes walked closer. "Mouse sent you?"

"Yes," Carl said. "You'd like to get back at Bragar, right?"

Sikes smiled, baring his teeth and standing the hair up on his back. "You just show me where to find that dirty rat."

"Good," Carl said. "Then I can count on you?"

They nodded.

"Then listen up."

"Sorry, Little Foot," Mouse said, getting up from where she had been cuddling with the mouse. She put her nose against her tiny friend. "Oh, I wish you would just wake up." She shook Little Foot with her paw and then pulled a blanket over the mouse with her claws. "This will keep you warm. I've got to go. Today's the big day. I'm going to make that Bragar pay."

Mouse stretched out her neck, back, and legs. She looked at Little Foot one more time and headed out into the hallway. She ran down the hallway, up the stairs, and out to the fire escape. She went through the alley to Baxter's building.

"Uncle Baxter?" Mouse yelled out.

She went through his building searching from floor to floor. She was about to give up when she saw him running down the hall. "For a minute there, I thought you'd gone to the country just like you said," she said.

Baxter smiled. "Just checking on Paggs. You know I wouldn't leave without saying good-bye to my favorite little cat. Although, you're not so little anymore."

"So you're still leaving?" Mouse asked.

"C'mon, race you to the roof."

The two cats ran down the hall, raced up the stairs, leaped through an open window, and headed up the fire escape. As Baxter cleared the last step and prepared to jump to the roof, he had to duck as Mouse jumped over him.

"Ha, I win," Mouse said. Her chin and tail high, she winked at Baxter.

"My, but you have grown. Your dad would be proud of you," Baxter said, lying down flat.

"I think he'd be proud if I got rid of the rats and took back his building," Mouse said.

Baxter didn't respond and kept looking forward across the cityscape.

Mouse looked out at the city and then back the way she'd come. She turned to Baxter. He wasn't moving but kept staring forward. *I'm going to have to work hard to convince him*, she thought.

"Do you have a plan?" Baxter asked.

"Of course," Mouse said, her ears perked up. "Plan B. This one will work."

"We'll be outnumbered," Baxter said. "Those rats gave your dad and me a tough fight, and we had Sikes and his boys helping us. They're gone now. How do you plan to pull this off?"

"They're not gone as far as you think," Mouse said. "Sikes and Rascal are close by. Carl's giving them instructions as we speak. They'll be here tonight."

"Carl?" Baxter said.

"The cockatoo, from Ms. Doris's apartment."

"What else does this plan of yours entail?"

"Pigeons, cats, rats, and a canary," Mouse said. "Like you said, we're outnumbered. So I've brought in a few allies to even the odds."

Baxter stood and walked around Mouse, settling in front of her. Still much smaller than him, she had to look up to see his eyes.

"I hope you know what you're getting us into," Baxter said.

Mouse smiled. "Does that mean you're in?"

"Of course, kid. Just tell me the details."

"First, we've got to draw them out into the open, into the alley, and then ..." For the next hour, Mouse briefed Baxter on the plan. When she'd finished, she said, "Well, I've got to go talk to Carl and Ladie." She headed to the fire escape and then looked back. "Oh, I promised the others you wouldn't eat any of them."

Baxter laughed and nodded. "Very well."

Mouse stood in the middle of the silent apartment. Her eyes tightly closed, she tried to recall the things that had once made her happy: Sam calling out that it was time to eat; her mother and father standing over her, licking her head; long naps by her mother's side.

She opened her eyes. "Mom?" she called out. Her mom wasn't there. Neither was Sam or her dad. The place was all but empty. Mouse sighed and turned to the door. She picked up speed as she ran down the hallway. She stopped at the entrance to the basement.

"No going back now," she said to herself. The scent of rats was strong even before entering the basement. She couldn't smell Bragar, but others were close by. Slowly she crept down the stairs. She remembered her father telling her how dangerous the basement was even for him. Words of encouragement rang out in her head from Ladie, Carl, and Baxter. Her muscles went rigid, and she lifted up her front right paw, extending her claws. They still weren't as big as her dad's, but they weren't as small as they had been six months ago. They seemed to say to her, "Ready!"

Mouse descended, keeping her eyes and her ears forward. She stepped off the bottom step, immediately noticing movement across the room by a large sink. She moved closer.

"Streets?" Mouse said.

"Good eyes," Streets said. "Hey, you remember I helped you and all, right?"

"I'm not here to kill you," Mouse said. "But I don't want you in my building."

"Your building?"

"That's right," Mouse said, marching a little to the right and then snapping back left. She looked at Streets, who trembled as she approached. "But I'm going to let you off this time because I need you to do something for me." She got closer. Streets seemed smaller to her than before, and she noticed he wasn't as confident as when they'd met in the sewers. He took a few steps back.

"S-s-sure," he said, shifting his eyes left and right, "anything you say."

Mouse heard two other rats come up from the pipe by the sink. They remained in the shadows.

"I need you to take a message to Bragar," Mouse said. "You tell him I'm going to kill him. You tell him if he thinks he's so tough, he can meet me out in the alley tonight at midnight. Just me. Just him. If he's not a coward, that is."

"What makes you think he'll come?" Streets asked.

"I don't think he'll come," Mouse bluffed. "Because he's a coward. And when all the other rats see he can't even take on one small, fluffy cat, then they'll leave. So you tell him, Streets. You go right now and tell him. I might not be as big as my dad," she said, extending her claws in full view of Streets, "but I can take care of one crazy, fat rat if I need to. And you use those words exactly."

"I'll tell him, kid," Streets said. "But he ain't the one that should be worried." Streets turned and scurried down into the drainpipe.

Mouse breathed out heavily and tried to slow her rapid heartbeat. *Dad was right. This basement is creepy!* she thought. She turned and ran up the steps.

Slim and Slouch were waiting in the drainpipe for Streets.

"What are you two bums doing?" Streets asked as he ran into them.

"We heard that conversation you had with the cat," Slouch said. "How do you know her?"

"I know everybody," Streets said, examining his paw with importance.

"Yes, you do!" a voice rang out.

The three rats jumped at the familiar voice.

"Wilber?" Slouch said, stumbling backward. He grabbed onto Slim to regain his footing. "What are you doing back in these parts?"

Quido emerged carrying Wilber's chair and sat it down in front of Slim and Slouch. Streets took a step back but stayed close enough to hear.

"Is that any way to greet the rat who raised you?" Wilber scolded, coming out of the shadows. He looked at the chair but passed by it and walked around to the other side. "I came to talk to you because I too have a message, but it's for you and the other rats that follow that hooligan.

"Now you, Streets, I understand you're in the business of selling information, so I guess I forgive you some in working for both sides. I'm not here to get rough with you boys. Look around you. Rats are being killed every day. By the cats, by poison, and now we're fighting each other. How many rats has this hooligan Bragar lost since he took charge?"

"Poor Darts," Slim said. "Ugh," he said as Slouch elbowed him in the gut.

Wilber smiled. "I may have treated you boys harshly, but we ate good, we lived together in safety, and we respected our own. Without that respect, well," Wilber said, walking around to the back of his chair and putting his hands on it, "we're just a bunch of rats."

Wilber picked up the chair and slammed it down on the ground, shattering it into pieces. Slouch quivered and backed away as Wilber grabbed one of the wood legs and, holding it tightly with his right paw, tapped it on his left.

"I'm done sitting down, and I'm done retreating. You tell all those boys who follow that hooligan that Wilber's back. I'm not as old and feeble as they think I am. That cat," he said, pointing up to the basement where Mouse and Streets had spoken, "is not the enemy that threatens us this time. It's one of our own. The rats that follow him, you included, better decide quickly which side they're on because next time I come this way, I'll be cracking skulls." Wilber cracked his knuckles, causing Slim to shiver.

Wilber turned to leave, and Quido bent down to pick up what remained of Wilber's chair.

"Leave it," Wilber said and walked away with Quido following.

"Wow, did you see how he broke that chair?" Slouch said, moving forward to pick up a piece. He admired it like a collectible item and handed it to Slim, who did the same. "He looked pretty tough."

"Since you heard the conversation I had with the cat," Streets said, "do me a favor and take the message to that rat you work for?"

"Hey," Slouch said, "we're independent. We don't work for no one."

"Whatever you say," Streets said. "Just deliver the message for me."

"What?" Slim said. "You don't want to give him the information yourself and take all the credit like you usually do? I thought that's how you made your living—in the information business and all that."

Streets started walking away and looked back. "The information business is getting too dangerous around here. I'm leaving."

"He's got a point, you know," Slouch said as he and Slim watched Streets disappear down the sewer pipe.

"What point?" Slim asked.

"About how dangerous it's getting around here," Slouch said. "I don't like the way Bragar is running things—running us … running you."

"What else we gonna do?" Slim shrugged his shoulders. "Come on. We better tell him what's going on."

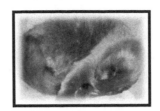

Chapter 17
Fabulous Little Friend

"**W**here are you going, Mouse?" Charlene asked as Mouse walked to the door.

"I'm going to check on Little Foot," Mouse said.

Charlene smiled. "I guess it won't do any good to tell you not to stay out all night, will it?"

"I'm sorry ..."

"Don't be." Charlene licked her on the head. "You seem to have matured a full year in only a week."

Mouse purred and sat still.

"You get more like your father every day. I'm proud to have a daughter that's had the calling of the Protectors."

"You know?"

"I can tell that it happened," Charlene said. "There were too many changes in you to explain. So do what you must, but be careful."

Her heart pounding, Mouse smiled at her mom. Then she turned and ran out of the apartment at full speed. She did a power slide at the end and, without breaking her stride, ran up the stairs and to the furniture room. There, behind one of the couches, she had hidden Little Foot in a small blanket. Again her heart pounded as she approached the blanket, dreading the moment she'd check and her friend's body would be cold.

"I'm sorry I haven't been around much today," Mouse said, moving the blanket up to cover Little Foot. A tear formed in her eye. She lay down, surrounding Little Foot with her body. "I can't stay long. I've got some important stuff to do. I wish you'd wake up, Little Foot."

Mouse was startled when she felt some motion from under the blanket, and she stood.

"M-Mouse," Little Foot said in a tiny voice. She wiped her eyes with her paws.

"Little Foot!" Mouse jumped around. "You're alive! You're alive!" She licked Little Foot's face.

Little Foot smiled and sat up, stumbling as Mouse licked her. "What's going on?"

"You were poisoned. I thought you were going to die," Mouse said.

"What?" Little Foot looked around the room. "Well, I'm fine, but a little hungry."

"I'll be right back." Mouse raced toward the door and then right back. "Don't go anywhere," she said and then ran down the hall.

She went all the way to the first floor and snuck into the kitchen. On one of the tables, she spotted her prize and took a napkin to wrap up some food. She headed back to Little Foot.

"Here you go," Mouse said. Opening the napkin, she revealed several crackers, a slice of cheddar cheese, and an olive.

"Thanks," Little Foot said and started eating. Mouse waited patiently until Little Foot stopped.

"How long have I been out?" Little Foot asked.

"Two days," Mouse said. "I was worried about you."

The two friends talked as Little Foot ate. Hours passed, and Mouse seemed to lose track of time, happy that her friend was feeling better. Then something inside of Mouse called out to her, *It's time.*

Mouse's eyes flashed, and she ran to the doorway and looked down the hall. The footsteps in the hours before had all stopped, and the place was quiet. "It's getting late. I've got to go. I'll bring you some more food when I get back."

"Where are you going?" Little Foot asked.

"You've been out for a couple of days. Bragar didn't leave. It's time for plan B."

"You're getting him into the alley?"

"Yes."

"Why can't I come along?"

"It's going to be dangerous."

Little Foot went over to the half-eaten olive, took the tooth-pick out of it, and held it across her front like a sword. "I'm going."

"No, you're not," Mouse said.

Little Foot walked over to Mouse and pulled her face down to her level. "I just survived rat poison. I think I'll be okay."

"How do we tell the good rats from the bad ones again?" Sikes asked as he and Rascal entered the alley. It was fifteen minutes before midnight.

"The good ones will be wearing bow ties," Rascal said. "That's what Mouse told Carl. We're not supposed to hurt those ones."

"Right, we don't hurt the rats in bow ties," Sikes said. "This sounds crazy."

"Let's just hope Mouse knows what she's doing. Look, Baxter and Paggs are coming. At least we can count on them for sure."

"It's, like, good to see yous all," Sikes said as Baxter and Paggs came closer. "I thought we were gonna have to do this all on our own. I sure hope this kid knows what she's doin'."

"She has the blood of a Protector running through her," Baxter said. "Besides, if she fails, we fail."

"What do you mean?" Sikes asked.

The four cats walked down the alley toward the Dumpsters.

"That kid is betting on us. And let's face it, without Chief, we're just a bunch of broken-down cats who aren't getting any younger."

"Right, old friend," Paggs said. "If we're going to go out, let's go out in style and take this hoodlum with us."

"You sure you can disguise us?" Baxter asked.

Sikes cocked his head. "Been hiding in these alleys for years, and nobody ever knew. Trust me, those rats will walk right by us. And when we spring the trap, *wham!* They won't know what hit 'em. This time, no prisoners."

"For Scratch and Dazzle," Rascal said and held his paw up.

"For Chief and Mouse," Baxter said, and the four patted paws and went to their positions hiding among the Dumpsters.

🐾 🐾 🐾 🐾

Perched on the fire escape three floors up, Mouse scanned the alley below her. The shadows seemed to move in an unnatural way. She flexed her ears forward. The street grew silent, as though even the people knew a showdown loomed in the darkness below.

Little Foot gulped and said, "We're going down there." Her hand trembled as she pointed.

"No," Mouse said. "I'm going down there. You are staying up here where it's safe."

"I will not. I am a Junior Protector," Little Foot said. "And you're not my father." She stomped her foot.

Mouse stared into the night. "Father?" She looked down at the tiny mouse in front of her. "I'm sorry, Little Foot. I do sound like my father." Mouse lowered her shoulder, and Little Foot climbed up. "Hold *on!*" Mouse said. Then she jumped down the fire escape so fast it was more like flying.

"You two," Bragar scolded Slim and Slouch, "stay by me."

He walked into the alley, heading toward Mouse's building. Other rats passed by Slim and Slouch and headed into the alley.

"You know," Slim whispered, "it wasn't all that bad seeing Wilber."

"Nope," Slouch said. "He never treated us bad. He was right—we were lazy. At least he didn't pretend he was our friend and then boss us around."

"You know," Slim said, "I've been thinking the old days weren't so bad after all. It'd kind of be nice to go back to the way it used to be."

"Come on, you two," Bragar called, pointing to Slim and Slouch.

Slim and Slouch caught up to Bragar. "I thought you were supposed to go alone," Slim said. He crouched as Bragar's red eyes flashed his way.

"No. That's what the stupid cat might think. She's young and small, and I'm going to teach her a lesson. Tonight we make a final statement." Bragar brought his right fist down on his left hand. "After tonight, there'll be no more trouble from these cats. We're going to take them down one by one. First, our smallest challenge of the night."

Mouse jumped down the last step of the fire escape and landed at the end of the alley closest to Baxter's building. *There!* her senses screamed. The hair on her back went up as her tail flickered back and forth.

"I can sense them," Mouse said.

"I can hear them," Little Foot said. She jumped down from

Mouse's back. "One, two, twelve, *twenty*? More than twenty I'm afraid."

Mouse looked down the alley, which was lit by only a few lights from the side of the building. Dozens of beady eyes moved toward her. Most of them kept to the sides of the alley—all but five. In the middle, Bragar stood flanked by two large rats. Mouse noticed Slim and Slouch close behind him. The two shuddered as she narrowed her eyes and glanced their way.

Bragar put up his right hand a few steps away from Mouse, and the rest of the rats stopped. The rats in the shadows remained close to the walls.

"I should've known you wouldn't come alone," Mouse said through clenched teeth. "I guess I was right; you are a coward." She raised her tail, feeling a streak of courage.

"Distrust has kept me alive this long, *cat*. Your bird friends won't fool us this time, no matter how many of them you have playing dead. This time we're going to settle things. You still don't understand what you're dealing with. You see, that baby wasn't poisoned by accident. I did it. I'm not afraid of those people anymore. And if I'm not afraid of them, I'm certainly not afraid of a fluffy little *cat*."

"You scum," Little Foot said, coming out from behind Mouse. She gripped the toothpick and pointed it forward.

Bragar's eyes widened. "You? You're still alive?"

"Guess you're so incompetent you couldn't even take care of a little mouse," Mouse said. "The baby you tried to poison is recovering. Your plans are failing."

"We'll see about that," Bragar said. He motioned to the two larger rats that stood by him, and they started moving forward.

Hissing, Mouse bared her teeth and flexed her claws for the rats to see, causing them to stop. "I've got to hand it to you," Mouse said, pacing in a line in front of the rats. "You did teach me a lesson about trust. You see, I knew you wouldn't come alone. And I don't fear you, you demented, deranged, deceitful, despicable, dirty creature."

"Ohh, she got you good," Slim said, laughing.

Bragar raised his eyebrows and folded his arms. "You are outnumbered, just like your dad." He signaled, and more rats came out into the open. Some went along the wall and took up positions behind Mouse.

"I asked myself," Mouse said, stopping and looking at him, "why go after just you? Why not get all your friends out here too?"

Bragar looked at his rat followers, who had stopped moving forward and were looking back and forth at one another.

"You see, friends are good to have," Mouse said.

"Friends who'll stand by you when you need them," Carl called as he emerged from the darkness and flew down by Mouse.

"Friends who don't care that you're different," Little Foot said, jumping up on Mouse's back with the toothpick still in her hand.

"Friends who are loyal and have respect," Wilber said as he walked up behind Mouse with a dozen husky brown rats. He cracked his knuckles, and the rat next to him handed him his chair leg, which he wielded as a club.

Slouch fainted, and Slim helped him back to his feet.

"The more the merrier," Ladie said, flying down the alley leading a group of pigeons. Some landed on top of the Dumpsters, and others lined the window ledges and fire escapes. Colonel Wellington led another group in from the back of the alley.

Bragar whipped his head around when Baxter, Paggs, Sikes, and Rascal emerged from the Dumpsters behind him and his rats.

"Friends who are there to watch your back," Baxter said as he and Paggs took up positions on the left side of the alley behind the rats.

"Or back you up," Sikes said, extending his claws. He and Rascal took up the right side of the alley. The four cats now blocked the rats' escape. "You're gonna pay for what you did to Scratch and Dazzle."

"You two—impossible," Bragar said.

"Yeah, we remember you too," Rascal said, extending his claws toward Slim and Slouch, who huddled together beside Bragar.

"You see?" Mouse said. "No one likes you around here, coward." She started moving forward with Wilber's rats flanking her. "You want to take what's not yours and boss everyone around. We think it's time for you to leave."

"Yeah," Slim said, "you're nothing but a bully." He grabbed Slouch and moved toward Wilber's rats. "We never liked him anyway." He stuck his tongue out at Bragar as they passed him and walked to stand by Mouse.

Slim looked up at Mouse and flipped around to face Bragar. Slouch grinned at Mouse and then promptly passed out again when he made eye contact with Wilber.

Bragar hissed and bared his teeth. "You two are going to pay for this," he said, pointing to Slim and Slouch.

Mouse sat back on her legs and prepared to pounce. She knew she needed to come down on Bragar with the full weight of her body.

Bragar moved forward.

"Now!" Mouse called out.

Rascal and Sikes sprang from the back with Baxter and Paggs close behind. Carl took off flying, and he and Colonel Wellington led a group of pigeons down the alley. The birds swooped down, grabbed several rats, and dropped them in the Dumpsters.

Mouse pounced and landed on Bragar's back. The two rolled, and Mouse dug her claws in while turning her head to avoid his teeth. Bragar pulled away and came at her, snapping his teeth as he snarled. In a move that surprised even her with its quickness, Mouse flung her right paw across her body and laid Bragar out. He skidded across the concrete and didn't get up right away.

"Wow," Baxter said, making it to Mouse, "just like your father. Guess you won't need my help." He turned and chased two other rats.

"You still on?" Mouse asked, waiting for Little Foot to adjust her position.

"Barely, but I can't get close enough to fight anyone," Little Foot said and jumped down. "Look out," she said.

Mouse turned to see a rat coming up behind her. Little Foot poked the rat with her toothpick. "Eeek!" the rat yelled in pain and ran.

Mouse turned her attention back to Bragar. Bleeding from fresh cuts on his face, Bragar scrambled to his feet and pushed another rat in front of him before he fled down the alley toward Paggs's building.

"If he gets down the drain, we'll never get him," Baxter said. "We've got things here, kid; go finish him. For your father."

Mouse took off after Bragar. He was moving faster than she had expected, but she was gaining on him. *Got to catch him before he goes into hiding,* Mouse thought. Bragar reached the corner of the alley and turned out of her view. Instead of slowing, Mouse sped up and executed a power slide around the corner. Her feet gripped just in time to give her a boost and catch Bragar.

Bragar yelled out as Mouse's claws pulled him from going down the drain and flung him across the street. He shook his head and pushed himself up to face Mouse.

"Nowhere to run now," Mouse said.

Bragar stood panting and spit blood. "You shouldn't have come after me alone, kid." Bragar smiled, and Mouse noticed he was looking at something other than her.

Oh, no, they're behind me, she thought. At that moment a figure emerged from behind Bragar and leaped over Mouse. She ducked and watched as the form tackled the two large rats who had been sneaking up behind her.

"Mom? What are you doing out here?" Mouse asked.

Charlene slammed the two rats to the ground. "Get him, Mouse!" she said, looking toward Bragar, who stood frozen.

Mouse approached, breathing heavily. The hair on her neck stood up. Bragar's eyes widened as he made one last effort to run. Mouse pounced, landing directly on him. The two rolled, and she clawed him again.

Bragar tumbled away and didn't get up. Trembling, he rolled

over on his knees and pleaded, "Stop, please." He tried to stand but was too weak and fell down.

"You're pathetic," Mouse said. "I don't even know if I have the heart to kill you."

"You did good, kid," Wilber said from behind Mouse.

Mouse turned to see all her friends coming around the corner to where she had caught Bragar.

"We got 'em on the run," Little Foot said, holding up the toothpick.

"The truce is back on." Wilber moved forward with Quido. He spat on his paw and held it out for Mouse to shake. Mouse spat on her paw and shook Wilber's paw.

"What do you want to do with him?" Wilber asked, pointing to Bragar.

Mouse looked down at Bragar, who was breathing heavily and looked ready to pass out. "I'm just a cute, fluffy little cat." She licked her paw and smoothed her fur back. "I have a reputation to protect. I can't be seen with this garbage."

"Yes, ma'am," Wilber said. "If you don't mind, we'll take care of this trash. It's what we do." He walked up to Bragar and leaned over him. "I hear you're familiar with Plummeting Falls." Wilber nodded, and two rats flanked Bragar and drug him off by his arms.

"You got spirit, kid," Wilber said.

"Thanks," Mouse replied.

Wilber disappeared with his rats, including Slim and Slouch, down the alley.

Baxter, Ladie, and Little Foot accompanied Mouse as she walked with her mother back to the alley, setting off cheers from all sides of the alley. Pigeons and cats stood together, and Little Foot jumped on Mouse's back.

"You did it, honey," Ladie said, flying down by Mouse. "You found your voice and your courage."

"Yes, I did, didn't I?" Mouse smiled. "I had a lot of friends to help me."

"Your fans await you," Ladie said. "Your dad would be proud of you."

Mouse stopped and looked at all the faces smiling at her. She was glad that the battle was over but found a different feeling welling up inside of her. She no longer had the distractions of her mission to keep her from dwelling on the fact that her dad was gone. She took a deep breath.

"We have beaten the bully, Bragar," Mouse said. The alley went quiet as she spoke. "As we go back to being what we are—pigeons, cats, rats, a mouse, a cockatoo, and a canary—let us not forget this night when we stood together as one. It's because we worked together that we now can take with us something greater, this moment we shared."

"Well spoken," Carl said. He put his wing to his head and saluted.

Mouse was going to continue her speech but was interrupted by Sam's truck entering the alley by the side door. The pigeons flew away, and Sikes and Rascal disappeared. Mouse and Charlene ran to the end of the alley and watched as Sam exited carrying something wrapped in a towel.

"You better come with me," Ladie said to Little Foot. Little Foot nodded, and the two traveled together away from the parking lot.

"Chief?" Baxter said. "You better go see what's going on," he told Mouse and Charlene.

"Dad!" Mouse yelled out and ran to Sam.

"What's going on here?" Sam asked as Charlene and Mouse approached him from the alley. "What are you two doing out here?" Mouse bumped Sam's leg. "Yep, I got your dad here. He's a little groggy, just got out of treatment, but he's going to be fine. Let's take him inside so he can get some rest."

Mouse and Charlene followed Sam to the apartment, where he lay Chief on the floor in one of the cat beds. Then Sam went into the kitchen. Mouse walked up to her dad. He had stitches on his chest and a cast around his leg where he'd been hurt. Charlene licked Chief's head.

"I'm sorry," Chief said. "I should have paid more attention."

"Let's not worry about that now," Charlene said. "Let's just get you better."

"Mouse?" Chief said.

"Yes, Dad?"

"I need you to go get Baxter for me. He'll need to help us with our rat problem until I get better."

Mouse looked at her mom and then back to Chief. She wasn't sure how to tell him what had been going on. She was worried he wouldn't approve and would scold her.

"There's no more rat problem," Charlene said. "Your daughter, your brave daughter, took care of the problem. So get some rest. Come on, Mouse; let's get something to eat." Charlene headed toward the kitchen, but Mouse stayed behind.

Chief raised his head. "Just what has been going on since I was away?"

"Lots, Dad," Mouse said. "Bragar is no more, and the truce with Wilber is back in place. The apartments are safe."

"I'm sorry I doubted you," Chief said. "I guess …" He didn't finish.

Mouse thought she spotted tears forming in Chief's eyes. "It's okay, Dad," she said. "If I saw me coming, all fluffy and small, I would have doubts about my toughness too. But it's kind of like my camouflage; you see, I'm tougher than I look. I've also learned that I'm stronger with my allies than by myself."

"I see." Chief smiled. "I guess we all better watch out." He tapped Mouse on the forehead with his paw. "Now go get something to eat, and then come lie down by me."

After Mouse ate, she joined her mom and dad on the cat bad and slept through the night.

Chapter 18
A Protector is Born

It was early morning, and Chief stood in the alley at the head
of a group consisting of cats, pigeons, a mouse, and Wilber
and some of his rats. Mouse and Little Foot stood still, chests
out and chins up in front of Baxter, Charlene, Sikes, and Rascal.
Ladie and Carl landed just in time to hear Chief say, "We are here
to say good-bye to our dear friend Paggs, who has decided to retire
out to the country with his owner. We wish him well and thank
him for his dedicated service."

The group applauded as Paggs bowed to them.

"On that note," Chief said, "I will be taking care of the duties
in what was Paggs's building, leaving my apartment building in
need of a new Protector. As you know, our complex is now safe
again because of the bravery of two small friends and their allies.
It is therefore my honor to promote my daughter to the rank of
Protector and turn the security of this building over to her."

The group shouted and clapped.

"One more thing," Chief continued. "Since she will be need-
ing help in this, I will also promote her assistant, Little Foot, to
Junior Protector."

"Thank you, sir." Little Foot smiled and saluted.

Chief saluted back. Then he and Charlene headed back inside. "Mouse, are you coming?"

"In a minute, Dad," Mouse said. She turned around and ran up to Sikes and Rascal, stopping in front of them. "What's up?" she asked.

Sikes smiled at the greeting. "What's happening?" He put out his paw, and Mouse pawed him back like Dazzle had shown her. "You're getting the groove. Dazzle would be proud."

"That's why I wanted to talk to you," Mouse said.

"What's this about?" Sikes said.

"Wait a minute," Mouse said. She looked back down the alley and called out, "Carl!"

Carl flew down the alley holding a piece of paper. He landed in front of the cats, eyeing Sikes suspiciously. "Here you are, Mouse." He spread the paper out in front of them. "Colonel Wellington and the pigeon brigade are ready to provide air support for this operation."

"Operation?" Sikes said, wide-eyed. "Are there some bad rats out there or something?"

"No," Mouse said. "This operation is for you." She looked down at the paper. "This is a map of the city, and there," she said, pointing, "is animal control. We're going to get Scratch and Dazzle. We have confirmation that this is where they are being held."

Carl, Rascal, and Sikes looked at one another. No one protested the bold idea, so Mouse said, "Here's the plan." She started to explain but was interrupted by a tug on her fur. She turned around to see Little Foot, who pulled Mouse's face down so she could look her in the eyes.

"You didn't forget me in your plan?" Little Foot said.

"Of course not; you have a major role," Mouse said, pawing Little Foot closer to the group, who all leaned in as Mouse spoke with courage and purpose—no longer a small, fluffy cat but a bold, courageous leader.

Coming Soon …

*The Calling of the Protectors: The Mighty
Adventures of Mouse, the Cat*

CPSIA information can be obtained
at www.ICGtesting.com
Printed in the USA
LVHW091451230220
647916LV00003B/4/J